T0086544

FLEEING
AFGHANISTAN,
STRANDING IN
AMERICA

The Life of an Interpreter's Family

HAJI RAZMI

authorHOUSE

AuthorHouse™
1663 Liberty Drive
Bloomington, IN 47403
www.authorhouse.com
Phone: 833-262-8899

This is a work of fiction. All of the characters, names, incidents,
organizations, and dialogue in this novel are either the products
of the author's imagination or are used fictitiously.

Published by AuthorHouse   07/15/2021

ISBN: 978-1-6655-3160-3 (sc)
ISBN: 978-1-6655-3159-7 (e)

Print information available on the last page.

Any people depicted in stock imagery provided by Getty Images are models,
and such images are being used for illustrative purposes only.
Certain stock imagery © Getty Images.

This book is printed on acid-free paper.

Chapter I

Grandpa, go for the fight—not only for me but for all humanity.

He was listening, in his imagination, to the voice of his late granddaughter as he packed his personal items and cleared his desk.

"Friends," he addressed his coworkers at the county social services office when he was ready to say farewell to them. "It has been a pleasure working with wonderful people like you for so many years. I am going to miss each and every one of you. Please pray for me, as I have a noble cause to pursue."

"Of course, buddy," said Bryan, his long-time friend and coworker. "Stay strong, don't give up."

"Yes, it's a noble cause, we wish you all the best," Ramona, his supervisor echoed his wish.

"We still feel for you," she added in a consoling tone. "Your granddaughter was so cute, I can still remember her beautiful smile from the day you brought her here."

On his way home, he made a brief stop in front of the elementary school that was located halfway to his residence and whispered to the one-story building.

"Dear Sheila, I will fulfill your wishes. I promise I will avenge your blood."

Once home, he leaned back in his armchair, took a deep breath, and thought: *I have just started the second phase of my life; it must be productive."*

The six-month wait was painful. His work

responsibilities had not allowed him to pursue his dream as he had wished. Now, he was excited to finally be able to function according to his own schedule. Even more so, his thirst to keep his word to his little girl further inspired him to go ahead and fulfill his long overdue goal. To this end, he needed to solve the mystery of the incident that had broken his heart and had astounded the entire neighborhood as well as the law enforcement community alike.

To him, the significance of this task was enormous. He needed to get to the bottom of it-- to find the motive of the man who created this mess. By doing so, he was proud to have taken on the fight against a monstrous power that had been threatening the safety and peace of mind of millions of Americans. His retirement at the age of 62 was motivated by this goal. Although still quite energetic and able to work, he decided to retire from his job because he could no longer afford to put off marching to the frontline of the battle. Even the anxiety he felt at the possibility that, after retiring, he might feel lonely and become depressed, didn't stop him from doing what he had to do.

On the first morning of the second phase of his life, he woke up early as always. He went straight to his bookshelf, grabbing a bunch of books that he had purchased and read a while back. He placed them on his desk for a second review. It was 7:00 a.m. As part of his new daily schedule, he turned on his TV and started checking the newscasts and commentaries on several national and local channels—taking notes on the points of his focus. *Again, of course,* he thought to himself. There were at least two bloody stories that happened that morning in California alone: A man killed his wife and their three children, and a teenager murdered his parents. He took notes of the dates and times of the events, their circumstances, the perpetrators' identity information, possible motives, and other related aspects revealed throughout the newscast. Then, he turned his computer on and googled some of the nation's major newspapers, such as The Washington Post, The New York Times, and the Los Angeles Times. He checked the online versions of several analytical articles published by the papers that covered the most recent such events.

Around noontime, he finished the first task of the day. Then he called the *Meal on Wheels Company* and ordered lunch because he knew he wouldn't have time to cook for himself—at least not for a few days. Before his lunch arrived, he took a long walk in the neighborhood park, purposely circling the corner from which he could have a clear view of the elementary school building. Afterward, he hurriedly returned home. Once he finished his lunch, he wasted no time—he grabbed his notebook and reviewed what he had documented about Sheila's school shooting. He was preparing for a war against the destructive forces and the systemic plague that had taken the life of his granddaughter and the lives of millions of other innocent humans. His first step was to equip himself with the pertaining knowledge and information in order to effectively fight this ruthless public enemy.

It was 8:30 a.m. Hekmat was supposed to be at work, but the street leading to his office was blocked by police cars, fire trucks, and ambulances. With their engines running, the vehicles were surrounding the elementary school that he walked by every day when going to work. Police had blocked the street in front of the school with yellow ribbons and were directing pedestrians to an alternate route.

He was in shock. Standing on the sidewalk across from the school, he watched with disbelief as several paramedics carried bloody bodies of schoolchildren to their ambulances. In a few minutes, the two ambulances, loaded with injured kids, moved. With their sirens wailing, they opened a path among the crowd of mothers and fathers, who were anxiously looking for their children. Police cameras were flashing and taking pictures of a man who was covered with a white cloth and lying on the ground.

After the crime squad allowed the parents to get their children, they rushed from the other side of the road, and he too ran toward a police officer.

"Officer, where is my granddaughter, I don't see her?" he cried.

"What's her name?"

"Sheila."

"Did you bring her to school today?" the officer asked.

"No, sir. Her parents did," he said, his voice shaking.

"Are you sure they didn't take her home already?"

"Yes, I am sure. Her parents traveled out of town after they dropped her off at school and asked me to pick her up."

"I don't know the children by their names," the officer said.

"Sir, "a female school teacher who was there assisting the

parents in getting their children, knew him and shouted from a distance. "Your granddaughter was transported to the hospital."

"How was she? Was she injured badly?" he cried.

"I hope not. You can go to the hospital and find out."

The road in front of the school was a scene of chaos and desperation. Some children were crying loudly, looking for their parents and shouting "dad!" and "ma'am!" while some parents, who couldn't see their children were screaming, "Ah, my son!" or "Ah, my daughter!"

Hekmat was one of them. "Oh, God, the Almighty, save my lovely Sheila!" he repeatedly prayed, while figuring out what to do and where to go next.

He needed help. He felt too weak to run back home and take his car. He was shivering, nervous, and faint. He ran to his office, which was half a mile away and closer than his home, to ask one of his coworkers to give him a ride to the hospital.

Everyone at his workplace was talking about the incident. He impatiently listened to them, hoping to hear someone say something like, "There was a shooting at the elementary school nearby but, according to the police, there were no casualties."

That was not the case.

The friend he was looking for wasn't there.

"Lue's grandson got shot," one lady shouted emphatically.

Another employee, who had just learned that his daughter was also shot was crying while running toward his car. Hekmat rode with that employee to the hospital, with his eyes full of tears.

This tragedy took place six months ago. That day, he realized that his worst fear had come true—he had finally experienced the terrifying reality, the reality that he had been worried about since the first day he came to the United States thirty years ago. When he had arrived in New York, it was near the end of June. Some friends had told him that the sounds of gunshots he heard at night were fireworks for the 4th of July celebration. However, after Independence Day had passed, bullets continued to fly in the air almost every other night. Even though he was used to the terrifying sounds of machine guns, rockets, and artillery in his native country, he couldn't believe that bullets were being fired here, in America without the existence of a civil war that was going on in his homeland. In a few months, he realized that guns and gun violence were an inseparable part of his new home's social fabric. *But why, why in America?* He asked himself repeatedly.

Sheila was a third-grader. Together with five other students and a female teacher, she died in the shooting. Her two classmates, Amanda and Kathy, whose names she would always mention at home because they were her friends, were also among the dead. Besides being devastated by the loss of his granddaughter, Hekmat was stunned to learn that the man who had so ruthlessly taken the lives of these innocent children was none other than Amanda's father. After killing his own daughter and six others, this young man then shot himself in the head with his revolver.

The murder of his granddaughter rekindled Hekmat's resentment toward gun violence, which he had been carrying within him for decades. Today, sitting alone in his living room and thinking of little Sheila —of her straight and tall stature, happy face, hazel eyes, long shiny hair, and sweet smile—he tried to cope with his anguish. Nothing in the world could console him, except to fulfill his promise to her. While thinking of that, he repeatedly asked himself, *why would a man take the life of his beautiful daughter? Why would he kill my Sheila, other innocent kids, and a teacher?*

Finding answers to these questions was essential for him. The truth about the motive of the crime was going to help him get his hands on the missing piece of the puzzle. He was searching for the role of gun- possession in the equation of any criminal act as he has been suspecting it all along. Therefore, he devotedly mandated himself to discover the reason behind the brutal act of a father murdering his own little daughter. Likewise, as a strongly anti-gun person, he wants to make a clear-cut case against gun ownership. His wishes to do so, further enforced his zeal to discover the reasons that propelled the murderer.

In the months before his retirement, he gathered police reports and additional information published by the media related to the massacre. The police investigation indicated that the murderer was a 32-year-old Italian man who had immigrated to the US with his parents when he was a child. He earned a bachelor's degree in computer science and worked for Microsoft for over ten years. His wife, originally from Los Angeles, worked for a prestigious department store. Together, they parented only this one daughter and had a healthy family life. The police had interviewed his wife and several other family members and neighbors, all of whom reported that he was a calm, courteous, and family-oriented gentleman. The family did not have a history of domestic disturbance or violence. At his workplace, he was regarded as an honest, well-mannered, and hardworking employee. Besides, he was a healthy man with no history of physical or mental illness whatsoever. These facts further intensified the mysterious nature of the crime. To solve this mystery, Hekmat plans to conduct case studies related to other school shootings and to seek help from science in the field of criminology and criminal psychology to learn about the criminal mind and its psychological elements.

Going through numerous articles on the Internet related to the topic, he came across suggestions that, in addition to the many underlining reasons for gun violence, the possession of a gun by itself might potentially contribute to causing a criminal ferocity, regardless of the gun owner's intention. He was excited because this was what was looking for; Since there have been countless instances where law-abiding individuals committed violence in cases such as accidental shooting, road rage, anger due to domestic disputes, and so on. This notion struck him because he had always thought that carrying firearms makes committing a crime easy.

His search also recommended several works by known criminologists, sociologists, anthropologists, and other scholars. Hence, he went ahead and ordered the following books from Amazon: 1. The Gun Debate by Philip J. Cook and Kristin A. Goss, 2. The Politics of Gun Control by Robert J. Spizer, 3- More Guns Less Crime by John R. Lott, Jr, 4. Guns in American Society by Gregg Lee Carter, 5. Second Amendment by Michael Waldman, and 6. Hunting Humans: Inside the Minds of the Mass Murderers, by Elliott Leyton.

Reading these works opened for him a gateway to an unknown world—the world full of information on crimes so heinous that he could never have imagined. Over the years, he had heard the news reports of these crimes but never realized the magnitude of their scope. He studied the history of a wide range of criminal acts and the life stories of several mass murderers, serial killers, and snipers. Similarly, he came across the shocking facts and countless instances of mass shootings in various public places, such as schools, hospitals, buses, markets, movie theaters, bars, clubs, churches, and highways, during which hundreds of thousands of innocent human lives fell victim to gun ferocity. The number of those who lost their lives to suicide and in individual armed conflicts by the use of firearms was also staggering. The more he learned about the atrocities committed by guns, the further convinced he became that there must be a relationship between the ownership of a firearm and the commitment of crimes in general. *I am certain that the possession of a murder weapon stimulates criminal intention and thus, has a place in the criminality of gun violence equation*, he reconfirmed his own belief.

The death of Sheila had broken his heart. The

image of her lovely smile, long hair, and pretty face—now covered with blood—never left his mind. She was there all the time, calling on him, *Grandpa, go for the fight—not only for me but for all humanity.* Subsequently, as a father and grandfather, as well as a proud citizen of this great country, he considered himself to be obligated for doing something in the face of the gun violence threat. Now, by learning about the enormity of the problem, he became deeply uncomfortable with the immeasurably destructive gun culture that existed in the nation. So he felt the need to tell the world about how the monster of the gun market has been taking innocent lives for so long, to spread awareness about the true nature of this so-called "freedom," and, finally, to begin a revolt against the empire of the gun lobby by writing a book based on the true story of his granddaughter's murder.

As a child, I wondered what it would feel like to be a father. As a father, I wondered what it would feel like to be a grandfather. As a grandfather, I found the meaning of true love—to love unconditionally and to be loved the same way in return. Maybe this is a common feeling that every grandpa shares. But to lose such unconditional love is beyond anyone's imagination; it's a world empty of all the good things.

After composing this paragraph, he felt a bit accomplished. *It's like the best medication for my emotional trauma.* He cheered silently. From now on, he documented every detail of his research for the motive and every bit of information about the ongoing gun violence with utmost precision. Thus, his longing for getting to the bottom of that mystery, and writing about the ugly face of the gun lobby got further and further reinforced.

It has been said that if you want to fight someone, first you have to make an enemy; and to make an enemy, you first need to find an excuse. Still, in his case, he didn't need an excuse—his enemy itself gave him plenty of them. Guns were destroying lives, the gun lobby was spreading death, it was manipulating civilians to arm themselves on false pretexts and cause them to kill one another. Thus, he had more than enough reasons to pursue his cause and fight this destructive force.

With all his zealous intent, however, even three months after his retirement, he wasn't making enough progress in his endeavors. Mass shootings, serial killings, armed robberies, burglaries, suicides, and numerous other crimes committed at gunpoint were so abundant that they constituted news stories almost every other day. This situation engrossed his mind so much that he couldn't concentrate on searching for the motive behind the elementary school shooting.

Tonight, again, like during so many days and nights in the past few months, he tried to alleviate his stress and frustration by focusing on his project. Again, he excruciatingly visualized Sheila's lovely smile, splattered with blood. He closed his eyes and abruptly, a memory invaded his mind: His little girl sitting next to him on the sofa, asking him in her sweet childish language.

"Grandpa! How much do you love me?"

"I love you from here to the sky," he had replied as

he pulled her closer to his chest and kissed her on the forehead.

"I love you from here to the sun. My teacher says the sun is farther than the sky," she said pompously.

It was past midnight. He went to bed, feeling sleepy, frustrated, and tired. His mind was still clinging to the pleasurable memory of conversing with his Sheila and at the moment he closed his eyes around 1 a.m., the sound of a gunshot on the street switched his mind back to the real world. In a matter of seconds, another bullet smashed through the window by his bed. He rolled down off the bed and remained to lie flat on the floor for a few minutes until the red and blue police emergency lights illuminated the street. He crawled out of his bedroom and sneaked out through the peephole of his house door. He saw no one, but the presence of three or four police cars on the street encouraged him to open the door and walk over to where a group of police officers stood.

"Sir, go back inside your home, we have a fatality!" a police officer ordered him loudly.

"What? Did a bullet hit anybody?" he asked vehemently.

"Yes, give us a minute, we might have some questions for you, too!"

"My window got smashed by a bullet," he told the officer while shivering in panic.

"Really?" the officers yelled. "Ok, we'll be with you in a moment, go back to your home, please!"

"Show me which window got smashed?" asked a

police officer a few minutes later, walking over to his house and standing by the door. "Which one?"

He directed the officer to the shattered window, which was facing the street.

"This one."

The officer examined the window and asked Hekmat if he could go inside his house to see where the bullet had gone.

"Yes, sir. I was terrified," he responded and walked the officer inside his one-story house and up to his bedroom.

The police officer found the bullet stuck in the wall opposite the window and pointed to the full-sized bed by the window.

"Were you sleeping on this bed?"

"Yes sir," he affirmed, his voice shaking as he realized how close he had been to being hit by that bullet.

"You were lucky. I think the bullet missed you just by an inch or so."

"What happened outside, who got killed?" he asked the officer.

"Your neighbor."

The officer pointed to the house of his next-door neighbor on the left.

"Oh, God, who would want to kill him, he was such a nice man?"

"Your other neighbor," replied the officer, pointing to the house across the street from Hekmat's house as he left the bedroom.

"Oh, no! But—they were friends. I can't believe it," he shouted in disbelief, following the officer to the ambulance on the street while a paramedic was loading the dead body.

"I know," stated the police officer, looking at Hekmat and implying to him to stay where he was.

The police officer handed him a paper and said, "Here is the report of the incident concerning your window. We might call you sometime in the future if needed."

"Sure, thank you."

It was a sad day for the neighborhood because a good man and neighbor had died, while another good man and neighbor went to jail for killing him. The dead neighbor left behind a disabled wife and four kids between 13 and 20 years of age. Hekmat particularly mourned the death of his next-door neighbor because the 49-year-old man—who was originally from India—had been friendly toward him, paying him a visit on some Saturday evenings and playing chess with him.

The following evening, after everyone in the neighborhood, returned home from work, they held a candlelight vigil in front of the deceased man's house. They prayed and offered their condolences to his family. Then, they visited the family of the shooter. They offered their support and sympathy to his wife, whose husband was now in police custody. The lady was deeply sorry for what had happened the night before. She hugged every visitor.

"You all know that my husband is a good man; he is not a criminal. And you are all aware of his reputation and his good behavior both at school as a teacher and around the neighborhood," she said while weeping.

"Of course, we do," agreed all twelve men and women from the neighborhood who had gathered at her house.

"I am glad that the burglar didn't do any harm to you and your husband. Do you have any idea whether he was armed?" Hekmat asked the lady, sympathetically.

"Honestly, I don't know if he was armed or not. But when we heard that someone was trying to smash the sliding door of our family room at the back of our house, my husband ran downstairs and met the guy face-to-face. The guy tried to run but my husband followed him." The lady paused, trying to find the proper words to describe the rest of the situation. "My husband said that it seemed that the guy was pulling out a gun from his pocket while he backed off toward the side gate. He shot at him...unfortunately, our Indian neighbor was in his driveway at that very moment and was hit by the bullet instead."

"I wish your husband didn't follow the thief when he saw him running," one relatively older neighbor said.

"I agree. There was no point in chasing an armed burglar," said the older man's wife.

"So our Indian neighbor was in the wrong place at the wrong time," another neighbor, who looked to be in his mid-thirties, added.

"No, my friend," Hekmat disputed his younger neighbor's assertion. "He wasn't in the wrong place, he was in his own driveway. According to his wife, he had just arrived home from a job-related seminar in Los Angles. So he wasn't there at the wrong time either. Actually, the unnecessary use of the gun created a mess."

"Right," another couple, who also lived next door to the Indian neighbor, nodded approvingly. "Shooting and following a running burglar—armed or not—is wrong."

"I wish the burglar got what he deserved," said a lady who was a good friend of the shooter's wife. "If it were me, I would have blown his head off."

"That's the point," Hekmat argued. "In such a subtle situation, you can never be a hundred percent sure that you will hit your intended target. It's also possible that you might get hit by the invader instead."

"Well," the lady murmured disagreeably, "I will be smarter than anyone who breaks into my house."

The lady of the house gazed at her friend but said nothing.

That night, Hekmat's next-door neighbors, on the right of his house, invited him for dinner as a gesture of sympathy. This American couple was Kathy's parents. Kathy was Sheila's friend and classmate. Hekmat accepted the invitation and had a lengthy conversation with the middle-aged, highly educated couple that night.

"We are glad that you weren't hurt last night," Kathy's mother said kindly.

"Thank you. But I was scared to death, to be honest," Hekmat replied.

"No doubt about it," said the man of the house. "I apologize for not offering you to stay at our house last night, I completely forgot. We have an extra room and you are welcome to use it at night and to sleep here until you get back to normal."

"That's very kind of you. I think that, from now on, I should change my perception—of always feeling safe in my own house. But now, it's only common sense to say that there is no safe place—not even inside your own home— as long as the gun market is open for everyone." Hekmat paused but, to clarify his point, he quickly added: I really missed the time they were playing and have a good time in my front yard. I always watched them from my living room."

"Have you sought counseling?" the host lady asked their guest.

"No, ma'am. I think I should. But I also believe that I need a break and get away from here for a while."

"What do you mean, where do you want to go?"

"I'm thinking about traveling to my home country, Afghanistan, for a few weeks."

"Do you have family there?" Kathy's mother inquired.

"Well," Hekmat paused while thinking about his answer. "Yes," he stated firmly, "I have a cousin who is also my best friend and I have another friend who is like my brother—we've been friends for over half a century, very close friends, and I miss them very much."

"But it's not safe there either. We regularly follow the situation in that country because my nephew is in the navy, stationed in Kandahar. There are a lot of news reports about suicidal attacks, roadside bombs, and individual acts of terrorism," she said confidently.

"Yes, that's true. One of my best friend's son was killed by a suicide attack very recently," Hekmat said with a deep sigh and added: "But still, my nostalgia drags me there. I'll try to stay in a safer place, maybe with my cousin who lives in Kabul."

"Make sure, you look after yourself wherever you go in Kabul." Kathy's father said.

"Yes, I sure will," Hekmat said, and looking at Kathy's mother, he addressed her:

"Recently, I have got an idea of writing a book about the story of our children's murder."

"Oh, ok, good luck," The lady said excitedly. But suddenly, the signs of sadness appeared on her face. After a short silence, she continued, "Kathy would have been nine next week."

"Yes, so would my Sheila," the guest said sorrowfully. "But "I am sorry for mentioning that sad event," Hekmat said remorsefully. "I will never forget the two girls. I miss the times when they were playing and had a good time in my front yard. I always watched them from my living room."

Hekmat sipped tea from his cup and continued, "But one problem that I'm having is that the shooter's motive remains a mystery. I'm still conducting a thorough investigation to figure out why that man killed his only child and then take his own life."

"I think, in this case, the reason for killing is obvious," Kathy's father intervened. "Like in other mass killings, where almost all perpetrators are mentally ill people, this man must have been a psycho as well."

"No, he was not," Hekmat responded politely. "In this particular case, the shooter was not a mentally ill person."

"How do you know?" The host asked enthusiastically.

"The police report says it clearly. I've been following all related police reports and media information, including interviews with his family, friends, and coworkers. They all confirmed that he had no mental problems whatsoever.

His medical record also didn't indicate any." Hekmat paused a bit and then added, "Unfortunately, this is a false perception—that all mass shooters and serial killers are psychos. I don't agree with this belief," Hekmat stated confidently and went on to say: "Let's suppose mental illness is to be blamed for all criminal murders, especially mass murders, then we should ask ourselves the question that why the mentally ill individuals have access to guns and machineguns to be able to commit such horrible crimes?"

"Yes, if you are questioning why mentally ill people can obtain firearms, I would agree with you. They shouldn't be able to obtain firearms. There should be stricter regulations and stronger background checks to prevent them from acquiring guns," Kathy's mother said.

"Right, but my point is something else," Hekmat said impatiently because he thought he had a more compelling point of view to offer. He pulled a paper out of his jacket's pocket. "I've always had a gut feeling that the gun itself—I mean the mere possession of a firearm—contributes to the criminality of actions that result in violence." He opened the paper and said, "The other day, I was doing online research and came across an interesting article." He unfolded the single-page paper and then asked the couple, "Do you mind if I read it to you, it's not too long?"

"Not at all, go ahead!" both the wife and husband replied in unison.

"The article is titled *The Psychology of Guns* and it was posted on October 4, 2015. The author of the article is Dr. Joe Pierre. He says, in one part of his article, that "Shooting guns is fun. If you want to understand the appeal of guns, you need to hold one in your hand and shoot it. The bottom line is, it's fun..." Hekmat looked up at his hosts and then continued reading the paper. "Just what is that makes shooting fun? There's an undeniable sense of power that comes from shooting a gun..." Hekmat folded the paper, held it in his hand, and said, "I think if you have a gun on you, even if you are not mentally ill and have no criminal intentions at all, in some situations—such as becoming involved in a road rage or trying to defend yourself when facing a likely assault, for example—makes it easy for you to commit a violent act."

"No way," Kathy's father said irritably and set back in the armchair. "You sound like being antigun. I don't agree with such a notion."

"I would say, he is right. That's exactly what happened to our neighbor. He was such a good man, but the fact that he owned a gun caused this tragedy." The lady of the house contradicted her husband who frowned without looking at her.

"Precisely," Hekmat exclaimed. "Even though Dr. Pierre is absolutely right about gun psychology, I don't think, however, that the elementary school shooter took seven lives, including his own, just for fun? It doesn't look like a reasonable conclusion because the guy was neither a crazy thug nor a child. Apparently, he was a normal human being. I am sure he had a reason which was reinforced by the power that emanated from the position of a gun. That's why I agree with Dr. Pierre about the notion that gun possession does contribute to committing a violent act."

"Well, knowing that guy's motive wouldn't give me my Kathy back," the host lady said mournfully. "But still, it would be better to find out about it, at least for the purpose of your research and your book."

"Absolutely. As I said I would like to get to the bottom of it. I want to find out why a normal man would commit such an inexplicable act of mass murder. I would like to find out if he owned the firearm long before the murder or he just acquired it for this purpose. That's why I am planning to go and talk to Amanda's mother, as well as the elementary school's staff to obtain further knowledge about the private life of this family when I come back. It might help me get a clue regarding the underlying causes of the tragedy."

"You have the same opinion as one of our friends," Kathy's mother said. She grabbed a bunch of paperwork from under his coffee table and explained, "Here are a lot of factual statistics concerning your point of view, which confirm what you just said."

"Really, what is it?" Hekmat asked with great interest.

"It's an article published on the Internet—a friend of mine gave it to me. He works for a non-partisan and non-profit organization that has a website, namely ProCan.Org, which presents the most reliable research about highly controversial issues, such as the issue of gun violence."

Hekmat attentively reviewed parts of the 20-page paperwork that reflected on the gravity of gun violence and contained statistical information that he found interesting. He thanked his neighbor for informing him about the article and handed the papers back to him.

"Here," Kathy's mother turned a few pages of the printout, pointed to page 13, and gave it back to Hekmat. "Please read this part, all of it. It speaks exactly about what you just discussed." The host lady sat back on his sofa and looked at her guest. "It doesn't mean that I agree with the entire article, but I do think it's interesting."

"You don't agree with it?" Hekmat asked, smiling.

"No, because it's too liberal."

Hekmat was further excited by his host's disagreement with the article.

"Let me read it to see what it says."

He read the title, typed in bold letters, "**Armed civilians are unlikely to stop crimes and are more likely to make dangerous situations, including mass shootings, more deadly.**"

"This is exactly what just happened here on our street," Hekmat said and read an excerpt from the papers. "None of the 62 mass shootings between 1982 and 2012 was stopped by an armed civilian."

"It's very true," Hekmat said. "Do you have a copier at home, I would like to have a copy of this?" he asked the couple,

"You can keep it; we don't need it," Kathy's father said waving his hand twice.

"Thank you, of course."

During the few days that followed the shooting and death of his next-door neighbor, Hekmat's mind kept evoking the terrifying sound of the bullet that shattered his bedroom's window, the memory that served to continually remind him of the bitter reality—even living in the most developed and the wealthiest country in the history of mankind was not without fear and insecurity. He has such thoughts almost every night before falling asleep.

To kill his time and cope with his constant anxiety, he resumes reading a book titled, *Hunting Humans—Inside the Minds of Mass Murderers*, written by Elliott Leyton. The information provided by this book was remarkable. It was, however, incredibly depressing to him as well. It took him inside a strange world—inside the minds of several odd people, including a mass killer who confessed that he had murdered more than a hundred human beings, a serial killer who terrorized Queens New York for several months, and another serial killer who terrorized people across Nebraska. On page 201of the book, he astonishingly noticed that one mass murderer, Charles Starkweather, was quoted as having said, "Shooting people was, I guess, a kind of thrill. It brought out something."

Exactly, shooting is entertaining. The shooter himself had said so. Gun is potentially provoking violence, he murmured to himself. After finishing the book, he took a deep breath and thought, *I can't believe how dark, how vicious, and how cruel human nature can be.*

From now on he feared even walking in the park near his home or going shopping. He would look behind him very often whenever he had to go leave his house. He was suspicious of any man walking behind him or coming face-to-face with him while holding a paper bag in his hand. This is how a serial killer would carry his gun, in a paper bag, and would pull it out whenever he was ready to attack his targets. Hekmat would watch all such pedestrians from the corner of his eyes. When inside a supermarket, department store, post office, or in a clinic to which he went for his medical appointments, he would look for an exit he could use in case there was a mass shooting. Such fear cost him his sleep for many nights.

I really need a getaway. He thought

He decided to take his trip to his native country sooner rather than later. That night he made an international phone call. When his best friend answered the phone, he spoke with utmost enthusiasm, "*Salaam*, brother Majid!"

"*Salaam*, Hekmat, how are you?" unexpectedly, his friend replied in a low and gloomy voice instead.

He paused and tried to make sense of the unusually cold manner in which his friend greeted him.

"I am fine. What about you, are you okay?" he asked.

"I am better now."

"What happened?"

"You don't know?" Majid asked in surprise.

"No, what's going on?"

"My son, Aman, was killed," his friend said in a low voice.

Hekmat overheard him sobbing.

"Oh, no! When, why?"

"A couple of weeks ago, by a suicide attack."

"Oh, God! I am sorry to hear that. How did it happen?"

"We were together, going to the mosque for Friday prayer," Majid moaned.

"Were you hurt too?"

"Yes, but I didn't die. I wish I had died instead of my son."

"I am heartbroken, Majid, I feel for you. May God console your soul. Did Aman Jan have any children?"

"No. He just got married a few months ago. Remember, I told you on the phone back then?"

"Right, but I am very sorry for your loss. Thank God that you are alive."

"Listen, brother Hekmat," Majid spoke loudly. "I was going to call you and ask you for a big favor. Now that you called, I'm going to ask you that favor now."

"Of course, brother Majid, tell me, what is it? I will do anything that is in my power."

Majid suppressed his wheezing through a light cough and said, "My other son, Zahir, is working with Americans in Kabul as an interpreter. Both my sons took this job with the hope that, after two years, they would give them and their families visas to go and live in America." Majid sighed heavily and continued, "Aman lost his life but may God save Zahir. He has three kids, whom I love very much. When they go to America, I want you to promise me, as my childhood friend and as my brother, that you will help them and care for them as if they were your own children."

"Without a doubt, brother Majid, I will care for them like they are my own children, don't worry."

"Promise?" Majid emphasized this word.

"A hundred percent, brother! You and I have been like brothers for over half a century. I owe this to you."

"Now I feel good. Thank you," Majid said.

"Sure. And listen, Majid Jan, I am thinking about coming over."

"Really? That would be great. I'll be so happy to see you here after such a long time."

"Me too."

"But Hekmat Jan," Majid uttered firmly, "you don't have to come to Kandahar to visit me and then go back to Kabul to see Sultan. I will travel to Kabul to see you and to also see my grandchildren for the last time because they will be in Kabul for only a few more weeks."

"That's wonderful. I'm going to let Sultan know, too."

The next night, which was daytime in Kabul, Hekmat phoned his cousin and friend, Sultan, to inform him about his intention to travel to Afghanistan.

"Really? Thank you for the good news. When are you planning to come?" Sultan asked happily.

"I feel like flying over there right now, but first I have to prepare and buy a ticket."

"Have you talked to Majid lately?" Sultan asked.

"Yes, I just talked to him last night. I'm so sad because of his son's death. Why didn't you call me to let me know what happened?"

"Actually, he told me not to. He said he didn't want to bother you with the sad news."

"I still think you should have called me. Anyway, I'm glad he is alive. Did you go to Kandahar to attend *fateha* (the service)?"

"I sure did. It was a distressing atmosphere in his family," Sultan said. "May God give them peace. It's good timing for your trip because your visit will alleviate Majid's suffering a bit."

"I'll talk to you again soon and give you the day and time of my arrival."

"Sounds good. I'll have a separate room ready for you at my apartment."

Talking to his childhood friends, Majid and Sultan, and making a decision to visit them, greatly revived his spirit. It also took him back to all the good memories and happy days that they had spent together. Fifty-five years of dedicated friendship is something that he had treasured dearly all along. Sultan was his first cousin; their fathers had been very close to each other. Hekmat and Sultan had been friends from very early childhood. Majid was their mutual friend. The three of them grew up in the same neighborhood, went to the same elementary school, and remained classmates until they finished high school. They continued to be good friends all these years.

A good friend is a gift that one gives to himself, he recited the quotation. He congratulated himself for not losing these two friends despite being away from them for thirty years and living in America.

He stayed in his bed with his eyes open for several long hours. He wasn't able to overcome the excitement. He got up unusually early and jumped on the treadmill that he had just bought for his daily exercise, instead of walking in the park. He then immediately started preparing for his long journey, beginning with an online search for a plane ticket to Kabul. After making a reservation, he took his luggage out of the closet. The books that he had recently read, as well as a notebook containing the notes that he had taken related to the elementary school shooting, were among the first things he put in his suitcase. One day before his trip, he said farewell to Kathy's parents. He gave them his house keys to take care of the few roses he had in his backyard.

"Have a nice trip, stay safe," Kathy's mother said when her husband moved his vehicle to take their neighbor to SFO.

He couldn't nap on the airplane. Neither could he socialize with strangers unless other people initiated a chat with him. Even though flying on a Lufthansa aircraft was nice, he was a bit uncomfortable with himself while sitting between two strangers. The guy on his left went to sleep as soon as the craft reached the ultimate altitude and the "Fasten seat belt" sign went off. The person on his right was enjoying looking at the blue sky from his window seat. Trying to cope with this unfavorable condition, Hekmat opened his laptop but didn't turn it on for a while as he didn't feel like doing anything. He noticed his brain, thus far predominantly occupied by the puzzle of Sheila's killer's motive, slowly swapped over to thinking about his motherland, his best friends, as well as Majid's son and his children moving to America. His mind went back and forth between America and Afghanistan for a long while until he felt mentally tired. And finally, as in the past, he took refuge in playing chess on his computer.

He lost two games. He tried hard to concentrate and played the third game more carefully. He won.

"Bravo, you won!" said the person on his right, a silver-haired American man.

"Hi, I am Allen, what's your name?" The man extended his hand toward Hekmat for a handshake.

"Hi, my name is Hekmat," he said shaking hands with his neighbor.

"I saw you won the game; you must be a good chess player," Allen said.

"Not really. It was just a coincidence."

Hekmat's nicely trimmed salt and pepper mustache, half-bald, bright eyes, penetrating looks, and erected nose made it easy for the Caucasian - American guy to correctly identify his nationality: "You look Afghan, a typical Kandahari Afghan, am I right?"

"What makes you think so?" He asked.

"I can tell by your face and unique accent," Allen replied confidently.

"You are right, I am an Afghan, living in America," Hekmat said humbly.

"Have you been to Afghanistan or you have Afghan friends?"

"Both," Allen replied with a smile.

Despite his long silver hair, Allen seemed to be a few years younger than Hekmat but had less white hair in his nicely groomed mustache and a goatee beard. He had a professional look and his massive and robust shoulder and arms visibly gave him the appearance of a sportsman.

"I sometimes play chess, too," Allen said and continued after a brief pause. "Whenever I get tired of my work. I play chess with my computer because it's a good mental exercise."

"Yes, it is," Hekmat agreed. "Where do you come from?"

"I am from San Francisco, but currently working in Afghanistan. And you?" Allen asked.

"I am also from the San Francisco Bay Area," Hekmat answered with a slight smile. "What are you doing in Afghanistan?"

"I own a security company."

"Hmm," Hekmat said with a smirk. "I have heard that the security business in Afghanistan is a lucrative one, isn't it?"

"Well," Allen reciprocated Hekmat's smirk. "Any business in Afghanistan makes good money." Allen then looked through the window and, to change the subject, he asked Hekmat,

"When did come to America?"

"Over 30 years ago."

"Wow, that's a long time. How do you like it?"

"Well," Hekmat said sounding pretty sure about his answer. "There are a lot of good things In America, it's a free country but I think, in some areas, it's too free a country."

"What do you mean, it's too free a country?" Allen asked irritably.

"I mean in this country anyone can acquire any number and any types of weapons and then kill any small or large number of people they want." Hekmat sounded a bit emotional.

"Pardon me, what did you say?" Allen asked with astonishment as signs of annoyance appeared on his face. "I believe that having a weapon is vital to the peace of mind and security of everyone."

"Do you really think so?" Hekmat asked humorously.

"Of course. You know, the world would be like a jungle without weapon ownership because thieves and thugs would take people's lives and property."

"Look, Mr. Allen!" Hekmat said in an unruffled tone. "If thieves and thugs can plunder people's lives and property, they can do so only because they have guns—without guns, nobody can loot property or take lives easily."

"Huh," Allen said as his voice became heftier. "Mr. Hekmat, with all due respect, I think you are out of touch with the reality of today's life. I am saying this because the world is full of bad individuals—good people need protection. Every good and law-abiding person cannot afford to hire a bodyguard to get that peace of mind.

"You are absolutely right, my friend. However, I think, in this case, every law-abiding person should carry a gun for their protection, right?"

"Well, they should, if they can."

"What if some folks don't like to have a gun or cannot afford to have one, what then?"

"Then…" Allen paused briefly, unsure about his answer. "Then it is up to them to find the means if they want to have a gun—they can get one, it's a free country. Actually, there are plenty of cheap weapons available out there, so all people have every right to either own or not own a gun."

"But my question is," Hekmat said resolutely, "you know that there are still millions of Americans who don't own a gun for whatever reason and, as you just said, there are a lot of bad people who are a threat to other people's lives and properties—so what do you think would be the best way for those unarmed citizens to protect themselves from the danger posed by the wrongdoers?"

"The answer is simple," Allen replied, throwing his hand upward implying that Hekmat should have known this common-sense fact. "The police and other law enforcement forces are doing their best to maintain law and order and provide protection against crime to everyone. Still, the criminals will try to infringe on the people's right to live a normal life and to conduct their business peacefully. That's why the law entitles them to own guns and defend themselves.

Hekmat was listening to Allen attentively and then replied calmly.

"I don't want to dispute the fact that our police and other security forces are doing whatever they can to prevent crimes, but the question remains," Hekmat stopped talking abruptly and then continued speaking to Allen in a softer tone. "If you don't mind I will outline my point more clearly after asking you a simple question, to clarify some facts, so here it is: Despite having such strong and powerful police and security forces and intelligence agencies, which are—without a doubt—the most trained and equipped in the world, how do you explain that we still have the highest crime rate in the whole industrialized world?"

"What's your point?" Allen sounded irritated.

"Well, my point is my question."

Allen waited for Hekmat's explanation, but he remained silent and stared at Allen instead.

"So, you think that there should be more police

patrols, and cameras and that kind of thing?" Allen asked in a harsh tone as if ridiculing Hekmat's point.

"No, not at all!" Hekmat answered.

"So, what's your point? What is your answer to your own question?

"The point is that gun freedom is not the solution," Hekmat replied decisively. "Increasing the number of police forces isn't the right answer either. The problem lies in the system, in the gun market, in the fact that guns are so easily available to everyone—to law-abiding people and criminals alike. As you are aware, so many of our police officers are targeted by criminals. This is unfortunate because everyone has access to the most advanced and deadly assault rifles available in the market. Just look at the number of mass shootings committed with the use of such weapons."

Allen turned to Hekmat and questioned him, "What's the relevance of mass shootings to our discussion? I'm strongly concerned about the scale of mass killings and believe that they must be prevented."

"Really? How can you prevent mass shootings if there are thousands of semi-automatic machine guns in the hands of bad people?"

"Well," Allen softened his tone, "the reality is, as you know, that the people who commit mass shootings are mentally ill persons—normal human beings would never commit such crimes."

"First of all," Hekmat reacted confidently, "there should be laws and regulations to prevent mentally ill persons from acquiring such weapons. Why aren't they fingerprinted and why isn't their background thoroughly checked? Second, there are thousands and thousands of guns available on the street, which the government has no control over them, and any person, mentally ill or otherwise, can easily obtain one."

"Of course, there is a background check and fingerprinting, especially in California. Weren't you fingerprinted when you purchased your gun?"

"Mr. Allen," Hekmat said with a heavy sigh. "You know more than I do that background checks are not enforced in gun shops everywhere in the country. Neither are they enforced when one is buying a gun from private individuals, even in California. Let alone for the firearms that can be purchased illegally on the streets from criminals."

Hekmat paused, but before Allen could say anything, he raised his hand to indicate that he was not finished yet. "By the way, I've never purchased a gun and never even touched one in my entire life."

Allen turned to Hekmat as if he didn't understand the language he was speaking at all.

"What? Did you say, you've never even touched a gun?"

"Yes, sir, never!"

"How strange! How long have you lived in the United States?"

"Around thirty years, as I said before."

"Hmm," Allen sneered while looking Hekmat in the eyes. "I can't believe it. You come from a country where civil war has been going on since the Soviet invasion— almost decades ago. A considerable portion of the population is armed with pistols and even Kalashnikovs.

I am wondering how you were able to defend yourself, especially in the face of the ongoing individual terrorism, which has also existed in the country for a long time?"

"Well, I'm glad that you brought up this issue," Hekmat responded calmly. "Actually, the personal security condition changed after the 1978 upheaval. Before that, Afghanistan was a country where the sound of a gunshot was a rare phenomenon. No civilians were allowed to carry firearms; even regular police soldiers didn't carry guns. The stories of mass murders were unheard of. Whenever there was an incident of armed violence, entire neighborhoods—even entire towns—would speak about it as if an extremely unusual thing had taken place." Hekmat sighed and continued, "This was not because the country had a stronger police force or because bad guys didn't exist there—no, it was because gun ownership was not allowed for civilians at all. There was no free gun market available and, most importantly, no gun lobby existed there!" Hekmat sighed again, looking at Allen and touching his hand. "As for the current situation in the country, I agree with you, it's in some respects, the same as here, in America.

Allen turned toward Hekmat aggressively. "What? How can you compare that poor and backward country to America?" he shouted.

"Well, I'm comparing the two countries because I don't feel safe in neither one. I am comparing the actions of murderers in both countries. I am comparing them because the killers in both of them got the wrong perception of the tenets that they invoke to justify their crimes."

"How?" Allen asked curiously.

"I lost my loved ones in both countries. Innocent people are killed there without any justification. The mass murderers, both in America and Afghanistan, are misguided by the misinterpretation of the tenets—the Second Amendment and the Qur'anic verses, respectively."

"Well, before I respond to you about what you said regarding the Second Amendment that you just mentioned, I want to ask you how did you lose your loved ones?"

"My granddaughter, a third-grader, was killed in a school shooting in America. My nephew was murdered in a suicide bomb in Afghanistan."

"Sorry to hear that," Allen said. After a short silence. When was your granddaughter killed?'

"Just around nine months ago," Hekmat said mournfully. "And unlike you said, the shooter was not mentally sick, he was considered by everyone a normal and "decent man." Hekmat drew quotation marks in the air by his fingers."

"And your nephew?" Allen asked.

"My nephew was killed by Taliban for working with American forces as an interpreter."

"Hum," Allen performed an empathetic gesture by pressing his lips and widening his eyes and then gave his new friend and advice. "I am glad you are not in Afghanistan anymore. But here in this country, you better adjust yourself to the American way of life. You need to go with the flow and be prepared to defend yourself against the culprits, get a gun."

"Defend myself against whom?" asked Hekmat, looking straight ahead and not turning to look at Allen.

"Mr. Hekmat, I just said it. To defend yourself against the violence—the crimes of burglary, robbery, and so on! Do you have any idea how many such crimes are happening here every day?" Allen raised his voice a bit.

"I do. But I also realize that these crimes happen mostly because the perpetrators are armed. They commit crimes with the power of guns in their hands. So they are potentially able to rob, burglarize, rape, and plunder the properties and then kill their victims. Also, I know for a fact that approximately 40,000 individuals are killed every year as a result of gun violence in America." Hekmat switched his laptop on and asked his new American friend, "Would you like me to show you the source of this statistic?"

"No, go on!" Allen said.

"Do you know why the crime rate is so high in America?" Hekmat asked but didn't wait for Allen to answer. "It's because owning and carrying a gun is legal here. Hence, there are millions of guns available out there in both the white and black markets. Everyone, including the mentally ill and criminals, has access to them. Guns are cheap and are easy to obtain for almost everyone, both legally and illegally."

"Well," Allen said disagreeably. "It's an opinion, shared, maybe, by a few people who do not take the safety of American citizens seriously." Allen got up and grabbed his carry-on suitcase from the overhead compartment and pulled a book out of it."

"I read that book," Hikmat said as soon as he saw the book in Allens' hand and read its title- *THE GUN DEBATE*. "I even know which part of the book you are going to show me."

"Wait a minute," Allen said loudly. "You might have missed some critical facts regarding what I have been trying to tell you about."

While trying to find the pages of the book he wanted, Allen kept talking. "But, as has been said, the criminals are one step ahead of the victims or, even, the police. For this reason, everyone needs to rely on their own abilities to confront an unexpected crime situation."

"I disagree, Mr. Allen," Hekmat replied quickly. "If you mean everyone should have a gun to defend themselves against crimes, as I just said, you cannot defend yourself with weapons all the time because, first of all, if someone has bad intentions toward you or your property, they will follow you, look for an opportunity, and then harm you when they see a possible opening. Second, if there are random or mass shootings, it is inconceivable that you will get a chance to defend yourself or to subdue the perpetrator who has an R-15, R-10, or AK-45 in his hands. Third, and most important, give me a few examples that show how many gun owners successfully defended themselves with their guns. Of course, there are not many examples.

"My friend, you completely ignore the fact that gun ownership is part of American culture, it is part of our way of life. We feel safe at home with the gun, it gives us peace of mind."

"Well," Hekmat shrugged. "If we accept the notion that owning a gun is a must for self-defense against criminals or for having peace of mind, then every American should carry one. If that's a thing that we should all do, then I ask myself: is it a hunting club that I'm part of or is it a civilized and advanced society of America?" Hekmat gave Allen a challenging look.

"Of course, America is an advanced and civilized society. Here, we have law and order and, as you said, we have the strongest and most equipped security forces in the whole world. However, as I mentioned earlier, bad people exist in this society as well and, to safeguard yourself against the offenders, you need to have the means of self-defense—which is a gun," Allen raised his voice, signaling that he was going to mention additional significant facts in support of his argument. "Furthermore, there is another fundamental reason for gun freedom. If the government resorts to tyranny and disobeys the Constitution, then the people would be able to defend it against governmental abuse. This is very clearly stated in the Second Amendment of the US Constitution," Allen sighed and did not expect Hekmat to dispute his reasoning.

Hekmat thoughtfully listened to Allen and then suggested to him:

"To have a productive conversation on every single issue, let's put the subject of the Second Amendment aside for a moment and talk about the pros and cons of gun freedom first!"

"That's fine. But do remember that Americans are behind their Constitution, especially the Second Amendment."

"The term 'people,' is not exactitude Mr. Allen," Hekmat said readily and eagerly added: "I mean that, by using the word 'people,' everyone usually refers to those people who agree with their point of view. Thus, I can also say that the American people think that the Second Amendment is outdated and that there should be another amendment made to the Constitution to replace or clarify the Second Amendment. I am sure you are aware that the number of people who think that way is not limited."

Allen frowned a bit and pointed to Hekmat with a meaningful gesture requesting him to go to the main point of the discussion as previously agreed upon.

"Yes, in actual life, gun violence is and will be going on, in part, by those who don't have a criminal history or mental illness. It's true that, sometimes, mental illness is the reason for violence, but look at the list of others who commit crimes with the use of guns but are not mentally sick such as thieves, burglars, child kidnappers, car hijackers, individuals involved in domestic disputes, road rage, anxiety related to financial problems, disputes with neighbors, children using their parents' weapons—in all these cases it's the firearm that provides the potential for violence, not a mental illness. In other words, gun possession itself sometimes takes away people's innocence."

Before reacting to what Hekmat said, Allen stopped searching for pages of the book he was looking for. Then, he pulled out his cell phone from his jean pocket. He searched for a name on his contact list and said:

"I have a friend who is a very knowledgeable person about the issue of gun freedom. He is an NRA member. He says that humans kill humans, guns don't."

"Huh," Hekmat giggled loudly. "Sorry to call this notion a stupid one—I deem this idea to present a stupid judgment simply because it blatantly disguises the role that guns play in the commitment of crimes, especially mass murders." Hekmat paused briefly, then added, "Show me a single mass murder example that was committed without the use of a firearm, can you?"

"Well, no. But it's a fact that all mass killings are committed by mentally ill individuals."

"Not necessarily," Hekmat said resolutely. "That's not the case all the time. I studied several cases of mass shootings and reviewed relevant police reports, books, and articles authored by known scholars on specific occurrences. Most of them suggested that the majority of mass murderers do not have serious mental health problems. It's a fact that the supporters of gun freedom label even minor stress or anxiety as a mental illness—something that almost all criminals and even normal people, you and I included, might have. This fact was better revealed by the actions of my granddaughter's murderer as well as by the action of Stephen Paddock." Hekmat paused and stared at Allen expecting his confirmation.

"That's a rare example," Allen said.

"Well, you call it a rare example I would call it the best example. Because this guy poured a barrage of bullets over concertgoers in Las Vegas. He did not have a mental illness record and, I am absolutely certain, as his own brother said that he was bored with his life. This means that he had enough money to have a good life, to go on vacations, to go hunting and fishing, and to gamble, all of which he did. Ultimately, all his hobbies bored him and he began craving hunting humans. Therefore, he stockpiled 24 firearms— AR–15, AR–10, 223 Wylde Chambers, and other "fancy toys" which required a good financial situation. This criminal fired over 1,100 rounds of ammunition within 11 minutes at a crowd of 22,000 innocent people—how could a single "mentally ill" person do that if weapons were not readily available to them?" Hekmat paused, took a breath, and added: "Besides, there are millions of people with mental conditions who live a normal life."

"I said it was an unusual case." Allen reverberated.

"What about the killer of my granddaughter?"

Allen was searching in his mind for a proper answer while Hekmat was gazing at him. When it was his turn, he cleared his throat.

"I don't know. I am not sure if there was an adequate investigation about these guys' mental health or not. Maybe they both were mentally crazy."

Hekmat raised his hand when taking his turn.

"Suppose you are right. Suppose all such criminals have mental sickness, please answer my question!"

"Okay, go ahead!" Allen said with a demeaning smile.

Hekmat took note of Allen's smirk and said, "If these sick people did not have heavy weaponry and if guns were not abundantly and easily available to them, how could 'mentally ill'(drawing quotation marks in the air with his fingers) Paddock kill and injure 481 human beings in 11 minutes?"

Allen remained silent. He said nothing for a long moment. Then, he turned his face toward Hekmat and replied, "Whatever your reasons may be, I still believe in what my NRA friend had said—guns don't kill people, people do."

"Well," Hekmat said in complete disapproval, "no, Mr. Allen, it's the bullet that goes inside a victim's body and shatters their blood vessels."

Allen sighed heavily and summoned the waitress by pressing a button on the arm of his seat. He ordered a glass of wine.

"Sir, the food is coming too," the flight attendant pointed to the food cart just one seat behind.

"Don't you want innocent and law-abiding Americans to own guns to defend themselves with?" Allen asked, his voice raised, indicating his agitation.

"Again, defending themselves against whom, Mr. Allen?"

"Against criminals who have guns and rifles."

"That's the point, suppose the criminals did not possess guns, what would be the point for law-abiding people to have them? Where did the criminals get their weapons from? Why do criminals have such easy access to weapons? Why is owning and carrying a gun not illegal for the general public as a whole? Or, why people are not prevented from carrying guns outside their homes at least?" Hekmat paused.

Allen remained silent too.

Hekmat concluded his lecture by saying: "My point is as simple as this, why can't we have a society where there are no guns in the hands of civilians? Why don't we remove the assault weapons from the hands of civilians, at least? Why can't we prevent mentally ill individuals from acquiring firearms? I am sure if the government so decides, it can achieve this noble goal. I know it will take years, it will require tremendous resources, it will require true will on the part of all politicians but it can be done ultimately."

"Well," Allen said, moving his body in his seat and demonstrating his discomfort by taking a deep breath. "Mr. Hekmat, you are ridiculing the American Constitution."

"No, sir, I am not. I have great respect for the American Constitution, but the Second Amendment is now seriously questionable."

"Let's eat first, then I will listen to your intellectual opinion about the Second Amendment," Allen said sarcastically as he grabbed the lunch tray that the flight attendant held out toward him.

"Ok, enjoy your lunch," Hekmat said, taking his own lunch tray from the flight attendant.

They both consumed their meals in complete silence.

"Owning a weapon is a matter of tradition for Americans. There were times when American citizens were obligated to have a weapon that they could use to fight for the country's independence," Allen said after he finished eating, ordering another glass of wine from the flight attendant.

Hekmat drank the last sip of his green tea, cleared his throat, and answered Allen's question by asking him a question in return, "Yes, I know. It was the time during which America was fighting for its independence, right? And, for that purpose, militias comprised of civilians were formed and considered to be reserves. Now, please tell me, what is the point of gun ownership for civilians today—after independence and democracy have been established, a strong civilian government has been put in place and organized military, police, and security forces have been formed in the country?"

"It's an excellent question," Allen said conceitedly. "The goal is to make people capable of guarding themselves against criminals as well as against a tyrant government."

"So you are saying that anyone who owns a gun is safe and can deal with an oppressive government through armament?"

"Yes, precisely."

Hekmat gave Allen a distressed look and emphasized, "As I said earlier, a gun cannot save you from the danger of someone who is following you. Neither can it protect you if a mass shooter is using a semi-automatic rifle."

Hekmat used Allen's silence to keep talking.

"Please read the statistics, not only about crimes committed by firearms but also about how many people are killed by stray bullets, how many children lose their lives when playing with their parents' guns, or kill their siblings with these guns. Finally, how many people kill themselves or their family members by mistake while cleaning their weapons? Just imagine for a moment, if there were no guns in the hands of civilians—how many lives would be saved? In the meantime, gun freedom has caused such fear that, in some American cities, people don't feel safe even in their homes and on the streets days and nights."

Allen was desperately trying to find a good reason for debating Hekmat. Suddenly, he pointed his hand toward him and asked him to resume the discussion of the Second Amendment.

"Ok, go ahead, please!" said Hekmat, pointing to Allen and allowing him to resume that discussion first.

"As I mentioned earlier," Allen uttered enthusiastically. The main purpose of the Second Amendment is for protection in the case that the government disobeys the Constitution and resorts to dictatorship. It allows the people to deal with the situation and to defend the nation and the Constitution by confronting the government."

Hekmat prepared himself for another long speech. He straightened himself up in his seat as he spoke. "When the founders of the nation made changes to the Constitution and passed the Second Amendment, it was 1791—over 225-226 years ago. Since then, there have been huge changes. First, the rifles of that time were single-shot rifles. They had to be reloaded after each shot. But you know more about that than I do—how modern-day weaponry functions, right?"

Allen nodded reluctantly.

Hekmat continued, "Second, the government now has over one million armed security, police, military, and intelligence forces, as well as the world's most sophisticated traditional and nuclear weapons, which make it capable of crushing any army in the world. How would a civilian army be able to confront such a powerful force today?"

Hekmat paused as he noticed that Allen was looking at his cell phone. "Are you with me?"

"Yes," Allen said. "I am."

"This is important, "Hekmat continued. "Besides, there is a system in place: democracy and the separation of power in America. If the government disobeys the

Constitution and becomes a tyrant entity, the people can use lawful procedures to impeach and remove the government from power. So what would be the need for an armed confrontation?"

Hekmat paused again and, in the meantime, indicated by a hand gesture that he was not done talking yet. After sipping his tea from a fresh cup, which the flight attendant had just brought him, he added, "The other important issue is that there exists a profound disagreement over the interpretation of the Second Amendment. Many law scholars, academics, and judges disagree with the notion that the Second Amendment was meant to give civilians the right to own and bear firearms. However, it was intended to arm the militias for the purposes that you and I mentioned earlier."

"Hold on," Allen stopped Hekmat and asked, "have you ever read the Second Amendment?"

"Of course," Hekmat said assertively, "the Second Amendment comprises just one sentence, and here is the exact wording of it: 'A well-regulated Militia, being necessary to the security of a free State, the right of the people to keep and bear Arms, shall not be infringed.'"

Allen's facial expression indicated suspicion and disbelief.

"Repeat it, please," he asked Hekmat.

After Hekmat did so, Allen continued thinking as if he still didn't believe Hekmat regarding the accuracy of his memory of the Second Amendment.

Hekmat read Allen's mind even before he expressed his uncertainty and had already googled the wording of the Second Amendment on his laptop. He turned the screen of his computer toward Allen, who cautiously read the text.

"So what do you say about it?"

"First of all," Hekmat said, "if you read the text carefully and pay attention to the punctuation used therein, you will realize that it's kind of confusing because of the three commas placed in it. This means that it is not clear whether the founders had the militia in mind or the general public? And even if they did mean that all individuals should have the right to bear arms to defend themselves against the government, this is still not compatible with today's reality. It's outdated and should be changed."

"Why?" Allen asked desperately.

"As I just explained," Hekmat said calmly. "The country has strong democratic institutions for dealing with the removal of a possibly unwanted government. History has proven that the political system enshrined by the American Constitution has been working."

Allen leaned back in his seat and pressed his back to the top of the chair as if trying to take care of the stiffness in his neck. Then, he reopened the book, shuffled its pages back and forth, and then said. Give me a few minutes, I am going to find some essential facts regarding the significance of gun freedom stated right here in this book."

"Sure, go ahead! I am going to take a little walk in the aisle to stretch."

Hekmat got up. He stretched his arms and, before taking a walk, he added, "I am going to use this same book to argue against whatever you are going to say."

Allen didn't care about what Hekmat said and turned a few pages of the book and found pages that he was looking for. He folded them, then waited impatiently for Hekmat to return to his seat.

When Hekmat came back, Allen immediately dictated to him.

"You need to listen carefully, my friend, I am going to read some passages of this book to you, which I am fully confident you would find convincing," he said with an influential gesture and proceeded to read from the last paragraph on page 29. "Gun rights advocates argue that civilian gun ownership constitutes a bulwark against tyranny. More guns mean more freedom..." Allen closed the book and asked Hekmat with a vivid sense of arrogance. "What do you say about this hard fact?"

"It's not a fact, Mr. Allen, it's a myth!" uttered Hekmat in a serious tone. "Gun is a means of taking life, taking freedom—how can it be a savior of freedom at the same time? If gun owners feel safer, it's because they are equipped with a thing that is meant to kill others in order to save their own lives. Still, it's never a sure thing whether they are going to hit the right target or not. Likewise, the noble goal of preventing tyranny cannot be achieved with the nasty culture of gun use. More guns create a culture of violence."

Allen didn't pay attention to Hekmat's argument. He turned to page 31 of the book and read a part of a paragraph.

"A core tenet of gun rights ideology is that "the people" must deny government a monopoly on the use of force. A well-armed citizenry is necessary to counterbalance the state and, if liberty so requires to topple it..."

"Really? Do you really believe that the American people should topple their government using force if liberty requires it? Isn't there a peaceful and democratic way, preserved by the Constitution, of achieving that goal? Can citizens counterbalance the world's strongest, most equipped, and most powerful army? Suppose your answer is 'yes,' then the US will become home to two rival armies, both looking at one another with suspicion and each longing to control the territory. This will ultimately result in anarchy!"

Allen didn't make any comment and allowed Hekmat to go on talking.

"Do you think that the absence of tyranny in so many peaceful countries, such as European countries, Australia, New Zeeland, India, Japan, Canada, Singapore, Check Republic, and other Eastern Eruption countries, means that everyone in these countries has guns in their hands? This is not true at all," Hekmat spoke more seriously.

Allen folded his arms, leaned back in his seat, and closed his eyes.

"I think I need a break," he said with a heavy sigh.

"Ok, let's take a break. I think we have only one hour to Frankfurt," Hekmat said.

"I forgot to ask you, are you going to Kabul too?"

"Yes," Hekmat answered.

"What's your connecting flight to Kabul?"

"The Emirates airline," Hekmat answered.

"Me too. We'll be on the same plane again," Allen said and managed to get up. "By the way, are you done with what you were going to say?" Allen asked, indicating that he had had enough of the discussion.

"Not yet. I have a bit more useful information I'd like to share with you if you don't mind, but I am tired too. Let's take a short break."

They both got up to stretch, taking a walk on the opposite sides of the aisle between the seats. As they were about to return to their seats, the pilot announced that they were about an hour away from the airport and that the weather was cold and windy.

"Where are you going to stay in Kabul?" Allen asked as soon as he returned to his seat and Hekmat was about to sit down in his seat.

"With my cousin. He has a house."

"What does your cousin do?"

"He is a reporter, works for the Afghan National TV."

"Oh, that's good. I want to be friends with local Afghans. Maybe we can meet someday," Allen said, looking at Hekmat for his reaction.

"Of course. He is going to pick me up at the airport."

"Ok, I'll take your phone number and meet you one day—either at my place, which is a place with decent security, or maybe at your cousin's home."

"Sure."

"Ok, getting back to our discussion, you said you have more information for me?"

"Yes, thank you," replied Hekmat looking at the screen of his laptop. "I would like to quote parts of a Washington Post's article written by Christopher Ingraham on June 19, 2018," he spoke a bit loudly in order to secure Allen's attention. "It reads: 'There are more guns than people in the United States, according to a new study of global firearm ownership: There are more than 393 million civilian-owned firearms in the United States, or enough for every man, woman, and child to own one and still have 67 million guns left over..." Hekmat paused and went over the text to make sure he quoted it correctly.

"That's it?" asked Allen in a hurry.

"Yes."

Allen was going through the pages of the book that he was still holding in his right hand. He stopped on page 31 again and commanded Hekmat. "Listen, my friend to the next crucial findings regarding the worth of the freedom of gun," he softened his voice and went on to read from the book enthusiastically "Mass armaments safeguard democracy by leaving to the people a right of insurrection if they judge that their government has gone astray..."

Hekmat turned to Allen and indicated his intention to debate this passage with another recent study. Instead, he immediately thought of a quick answer.

"If that's true, then, according to what you just said, the current political stability and democracy in the US has been there for over 226 years thanks to mass armament, right? If your answer is yes, then are you and your NRA friend satisfied with the current level of gun possession in the hands of civilians? And, again, if your answer is positive, then why are you guys against gun control measures, such as comprehensive background checks and the assault weapon bans for the new would-be gun owners?"

"Well," replied Allen resolutely, "because you can't deprive any US citizen of having a gun they want to own. No reason is a good reason to deprive citizens of gun ownership."

"Well," responded Hekmat rather loudly, "if that is so, then this would mean that you don't care about the negative implications of gun ownership, you don't care about the tremendous numbers of gun violence casualties, you don't care about the one million human beings who have died over the past three decades as a result of gun violence?"

"I'm done," said Allen, indicating his exasperation. "You should educate yourself about the benefits of gun freedom."

Allen put the book back in the pocket of his front seat and stated, "Still, I can't believe in these assertions because I have learned about the positives of gun freedom more than you. As I mentioned earlier, my friend from the NRA is an expert on the matter. He wrote quite a few books and has been acclaimed by several national organizations and research groups. After conducting extensive research studying crime in the cities of Los Angles and Chicago, he concluded that 'more guns means less crime.'"

Hekmat gazed at his new American friend with a slight smile.

"I am sure you have. And I'm also sure that you are aware of the fact that the gun business is a multi-billion dollar business and the NRA is a giant lobbyist and controller of this industry. Like any manufacturer and business that promotes a product, the NRA is also promoting the gun commodity. Unfortunately, the NRA is such a powerful organization that it plays a role in the election of American lawmakers and even the country's presidents, as well as in shaping government policy in the field. Such an opinion is expected from someone who is part of this pro-gun organization."

The airplane started dropping its altitude. Allen gazed at the high rises in Frankfurt, which were now gradually becoming visible, and then asked Hekmat, "What do you do for a living?"

"I am retired now. I worked a government job for a long time."

"Wow, you had a good office job?"

"Yes."

"Do you believe that America is the land of opportunity?" Allen asked.

"Absolutely. I know that a foreign immigrant, like myself, has the opportunity to find good chances and to make a good living here, but it is also obvious that many powerful individuals and bad people abuse the opportunities provided here."

"Example?" Allen asked irritably.

"Well," Hekmat said, "while you and I are having this discussion, there are hundreds of thousands of illegal guns on the streets of America threatening the lives and peace of mind of millions of people. The illegal gun marketers benefit from this situation."

Allen turned his head back to the window and looked outside until the airplane's tires touched the runway.

They walked side-by-side from the airplane to the terminal waiting area.

"I'm going to take a nap here," said Hekmat, pointing to a resting area furnished with a couple of couches.

"Ok, see you later."

On the way to Kabul, they were assigned seats far away from each other. Both preferred to stay that way and to be away from one another after having that long discussion. Allen, using his iPad, spent much of his time taking care of his security business accounts. Hekmat spent the entire flight reading a part of another book, *Politics of Gun Control*, thinking about the subject of his future novel, and then relaxing by closing his eyes and leaning back in his seat.

At Kabul airport, his cousin and best friend, Sultan, waved at him after he collected his luggage and entered the arrivals pick-up area.

A man in uniform, who held a sign displaying Allen's name, was also among the crowd waiting for the passengers.

"Mr. Hekmat," Allen called to him loudly. "Is your cousin here?"

"Yes, Mr. Allen," Hekmat said and pointed to his cousin. "This is my cousin, Sultan. Let me introduced you to him."

After the two cousins performed a warm Afghan-style extensive hugging, Hekmat told Sultan, "This is Mr. Allen, my American friend."

Sultan shook hands with Allen. Both men introduced themselves to each other.

"I would be glad to see you again soon," Allen said to his new acquaintance.

"Sure, you can come to our house any day that you have time," Sultan said.

"I would love to. I love Afghan food, particularly hot Aash," Allan said, smiling.

"Any time," Sultan reacted bulletproof confidently.

"Hot Aash is a perfect treat in this cold weather," Allen smiled again.

They exchanged phone numbers and parted, with Allen driving away in his company's SUV.

Chapter II

The sky was clear. A pleasant late autumn breeze blew. Colorful leaves fell from the trees alongside the road. Hekmat watched the mixture of old and new buildings erected on both sides of the road that lead from Kabul Airport to the city.

"How do you feel in your own poor country?" Sultan asked his cousin teasingly.

"Ah, the familiar atmosphere of my motherland and my dear old friends, like you and Majid—I am going to enjoy every moment of it," Hekmat said cheerfully.

Sultan placed his right hand over his cousin's shoulder and echoed his jubilation.

"We are going to enjoy your company too. We'll refresh our old memories together," Sultan said, pointing to the outside. "The face of the city has changed dramatically, a lot of new roads and buildings were built. After you get some rest, I'll give you a tour of the whole city."

Hekmat didn't react to his friend's offer.

"What do you say?" Sultan asked.

"Well," Hekmat sighed. "You do your work and I'll work on a book I am writing. I'm not interested in seeing the city."

"Writing a book?" Sultan asked irritated. "I thought you came here to visit after fifteen long years, not for writing your book?"

"Yes, I came to be with you guys but need a little time for my book too."

"What is your book about?" Sultan asked in his unique humorous manner.

A brief silence gave Hekmat time to think about his answer.

"What can I say, it's about my granddaughter. She was killed by a gunman at her school. Do you remember that I told you about it over the phone like 9- 10 months ago?"

"Yes, I do. Again, I am sorry for your loss. But what is your book going to do about it?"

"My book is going to avenge her blood," Hekmat said with strong emotion.

"Ah, brother, I wish a book could do that. Nowadays, guns and dynamites talk, not books."

"Right. But that's the only way I can soothe my anguish."

"I know you are an emotional man; I hope there will be no fire shows here to disturb you."

"What do you mean by fire shows?"

"Look at those people," Sultan said as they passed by one of the city's crowded areas.

"What about them?" Hekmat looked at the people— young and old, men and women, children and adults— walking on both sides of the road.

"None of them is sure that they will reach their homes alive tonight. There might be a suicide explosion any minute, anywhere." Sultan paused and then squeezed his cousin's hand. "Don't be scared, you'll get used to it."

Sultan lived by himself in a two-bedroom apartment located in the fourth district in northwest Kabul, which was a relatively safe area. Still, when Sultan left for work the next morning, he emphasized that his cousin to not leave the house without him.

"That's fine," Hekmat said with a half-mocking smile. "It's the same here, too. I wish that I could have a few days without fear in my motherland."

"Welcome to your motherland," Sultan said teasingly. "There is a lot of food in the fridge, like *qabily palaw*, lamb *qurma*, spinach, and *shami kabab*, enough for the three of us," Sultan continued while putting his shoes on.

"The three of us?" Hekmat asked.

"Yes, Majid will be here today, around 1 p.m. He just sent me a text message. Just in case I'm not here on time, you guys don't wait for me to have lunch."

Hekmat gazed at his cousin, inquiring about the reason why he might not be here.

"In my job, you can be sent on an assignment anytime, no matter what."

"Ok. I'll take a nap until then," Hekmat said and walked to his bedroom while yawning.

The excitement about having his other childhood friend, Majid, with him that afternoon kept him up for a while, but eventually the fact that he had not slept since he left California took a toll and he fell into a deep sleep. Even the daytime heavy traffic on the road by which Sultan's apartment was located didn't disturb him. After a few hours of sleep, however, a massive shake and a loud boom, like that of an earthquake, woke him up. A heavily framed tableau slammed on the floor, an old-style heavy chandelier swung, and the glass of the window in his room cracked. He was dizzy for a few minutes and couldn't figure out what happened. He hurriedly got up and looked through the cracked glass of his window onto the road—the traffic was jammed and the people from other apartments and those on the street were staring at the sky, which was covered in dark smoke.

He went to the living room and turned on the TV, expecting to hear about the explosion. It wasn't news time. He placed his arms on the desk and put his head over them, remaining there until the telephone rang an hour later. He looked at the phone screen hastily and picked it up.

"What happened, was it a suicidal attack?" he asked Sultan.

"It wasn't a big deal, don't worry," Sultan said in such an indifferent tone that Hekmat became annoyed.

"How come? The sky is covered with dark smoke and you are saying it's not a big deal?"

"Only a dozen people got killed," Sultan replied simply, in such an unconcerned manner, making Hekmat further upset.

"Sultan!" Hekmat shouted. "Stop joking, where did it happen?"

"Near our home, in front of the women's hospital," Sultan said without any emotion.

"Have you been to the scene? You must have seen everything, tell me exactly what happened?"

"Well, the exact story is typical, like in the past—there are human body parts…heads, hands, and legs scattered everywhere. The ground and the nearby walls are all covered with blood."

Hekmat became upset at the apathetic way in which his friend described the tragedy but remained silent.

"Don't worry; it won't be of any use for your writing," Sultan further ridiculed his friend's passion for writing a book.

Hekmat nearly exploded from rage but managed to continue maintaining his calm demeanor.

Sultan asked him, "What happened to Majid, isn't he there yet?"

"No," replied Hekmat. "It's two already. He should have been here by now, let me call him."

Hekmat called Majid on the phone. Majid's phone rang, but he didn't answer. He tried again and this time he left a voice message on his friend's phone.

"Majid Jan, where are you? Call me please, Sultan and I are waiting for you!"

He still held the phone in his hand, walked up to the window, and imagined the scene outside…*Human heads, hands, and legs are scattered everywhere. The ground and the walls are covered with blood.* He then called Sultan and told him that Majid was not answering.

"Maybe he's still busy with his grandchildren, you know he's crazy about them," Sultan said.

"Look, Sultan, earlier you told me that today's suicide attack was not going to be of any good to my writing— what did you mean by that? I never asked you if it was good or not for my writing."

"What I meant was that there is no benefit to writing at all about these tragedies," Sultan answered coolly.

"What makes you think so?"

"What makes me think so?" Sultan repeated gently.

"First, this is not the first such incident. I've already explained to you—and I'm sure that you also follow the situation in this country from America—that bombs, rockets, dynamite, and bullets are encountered on an almost daily basis by the people here. Innocent human beings die continuously and new tragedies happen daily. Second, all TV stations are going to broadcast the news and all newspapers will carry the story tomorrow. So there is no point in writing a book about it."

"Well," Hekmat said. "There is a big difference between my writing and your news broadcasts."

"I agree. There is a difference between the two, and the difference is that ours is an eyewitness account and yours is fiction—the production of your own imagination. The important thing is that, by the time you finish and publish your book, the story will already be months or even years old and tens or hundreds of such incidents would subsequently have happened."

"That's the point," exclaimed Hekmat. "You write about what you see with your eyes; I explain what every human feels in their heart. I express the feelings that every human gets at the time of such tragedy—you guys announce statistics, I expose the human element of the tragedy."

"Do you really think so?" Sultan became serious for the first time since his cousin's arrival. His voice was mournful and, while trying to suppress his anguish, he continued in an unusually distressed tone. "Which human tragedy do you want to expose, my dear brother Hekmat, how can you do that? When my lovely wife, my two sons, and my daughter, along with my older sister and her four little grandchildren, were killed by a rocket—how will you assuage my agony, how can your book cure my emotional wounds? My life was destroyed. How can your words rebuild my world?"

"You are absolutely right, dear brother," Hekmat said in a soft and comforting voice. "I agree with you a hundred present and share your feelings of sorrow. Believe me, when you told me of your family's tragedy two years ago, my heart broke. It was my family as well, I suffered, too, because of that. No words, nothing, can bring your family back; nobody can rebuild your life. However, one of the reasons I write is to empathize with you and, more or less, to console you and people like you. In fact, that's the only way to find a remedy for my hate against violence and that's the only way to invite humanity to join me and to protest such atrocities."

"Oh, brother!" said Sultan, again in his usual humorous manner. "It's like you are taking medication for yourself and expect me to get better, right?"

"Huh! What a metaphor?" exclaimed Hekmat. "You are again right, Sultan. It really is like medication for me and, therefore, I'm asking you not to hinder me from taking my medication, please!"

"Ok, I won't. But please understand my pain, which I am trying to release through my humor—as I have great respect for your writing and your humanistic feelings, but please spare some of your time for me, I have had no one to talk to."

"Sure, buddy. I am proud of you. You are my family, a wonderful friend, and a dignified man!"

"You are too!"

"Thank you. Are you coming home for lunch?"

"No. You go ahead and eat lunch. I am still working on the reports about the explosion."

"Did you get any information about the number of victims and their names?" Hekmat asked.

"No. The police are going to have a press conference later today or tomorrow morning. I don't think they will have all the names. I might have more information about the casualties tomorrow."

Time went slowly for Hekmat. He tried calling Majid several more times and left him another voice message but received no answer. He turned on the TV, the news hour had passed. He reluctantly started playing chess with his computer and lost three or four games in a row. In the past, he would usually win two or three games and lose two or three games within an hour. But now, he places his pieces on the wrong squares, getting them captured by his opponent. Sometimes he missed significant moves that would have won him his rival's pieces. Then, he spent half an hour walking in and out of his room until his wait was over and it was time for the 6 p.m. news. He switched on the TV and listened to the news with the utmost attention. The report, covering the deadly blast was detailed. It showed the scene of the explosion. Somebody parts of the victims were scattered around. It also named some of the victims based on the documents that they carried with them. Some information provided by witnesses and family members of the victims was also revealed.

"Where are you? It's late?" he called Sultan, who was supposed to be home by now.

"I got stuck with another assignment. I'll be home in an hour or two. Has Majid arrived?" Sultan asked curiously.

"No. He is still not answering his phone. Do you have his son's phone number?"

"No, we never spoke on the phone."

Drops of heavy rain were sturdily hitting the cracked window of the living room. He couldn't see the dark smoky sky anymore. But his imagination did travel to the crime scene. *The blood of the victims must now be flooding the road like a creek*, he thought. He watched the news at each news hour until Sultan came home after 8 p.m. Until then, he tried calling Majid several more times, but his friend's phone was no longer ringing. It was going straight to voice mail.

"Maybe he stayed with his grandchildren tonight too because of the rain and couldn't call us, maybe his phone's battery is dead," Sultan suggested.

"You're kidding," he snarled. "He could use his son's phone to call me and let me know."

"His son is only home on Fridays. He works with the Americans. Today is Saturday."

Hekmat felt a bit calmer. He looked at his cousin and said, "I hope you are right. Still, if there was no other phone in the home, he could go out and use a public phone."

"No," Sultan shouted. "He is not that stupid. Besides being the father of an interpreter, he himself is a target for terrorists. It is not safe for him to go outside, especially in the dark and in the rain."

"Ok," Hekmat was now convinced. "We'll see him tomorrow and ask him why he didn't call."

"I'm hungry and sleepy," said Sultan while yawning and getting up to stretch.

"Me too."

Sultan heated the food. They ate the meal, both longing to go to their beds soon after.

"I have something important to do in the morning and will be leaving for work a little earlier, coming home around noon. Hopefully, Majid will be here by that time," Sultan said as he got up and said: "Good night."

"Good night. Make sure you bring tomorrow's newspaper with you," Hekmat said and went to bed.

He woke up before sunrise. Sultan was already gone. He couldn't wait until Sultan brings today's newspaper in the afternoon. He walked to a nearby store to purchase the paper. It carried information about some of the victims, such as their names, places of residence, and occupations. He placed the paper in front of him and started taking notes. He couldn't afford to look at the bloody faces of the victims. He reviewed their names and information instead. One of the pictures that he unintentionally looked at and which caught his attention was that of an eight- or nine-year-old girl, whose long hair and most parts of her face were stained with blood, made him turn away abruptly. He pushed the newspaper to the corner of the coffee table and then stared at the ceiling of the living room for a while. The little girl's picture, with her long hair and the uncovered part of her face, projected into his mind his own granddaughter's image. This similarity made his heart pound. The little girl's soft tiny pieces of hands and feet, a book, a pen, and a notebook were scattered on the ground, still recognizable despite being stained with blood and dirt. The scene reminded him of the mass shooting at the elementary school in which his Sheila died.

The madness of mass shootings is raging in both of my homes; There, mass murderers dance under the banner of Gun Freedom, and here, they worship the flag of "Holy War". The "lovers" of freedom take lives due to their allegiance to the Second Amendment, while the "devotees" of Islam kill humans for their fidelity to the Quran—other than that, they share the same "values": They don't demand money or jewelry from their victims, they do not ask them for intimacy or sexual favor, and, most of the times, they don't even know their victims' names, identities, religions, languages, nationalities, or the good and bad of their personalities. They slaughter them indiscriminately just for being human beings. He thought to himself while rubbing his left chest with his right hand to soothe the dull pain

"*Salaam,*" where is Majid?" asked Sultan wishfully as soon as he entered his apartment. "Isn't he here yet?" he inquired loudly.

"No, he isn't. I called him several times, his phone goes straight to voice message," Hekmat said irately.

"Maybe he was tired and sleepy after the long trip from Kandahar."

Hekmat stared at Sultan frowning.

"I am going to punish him for this behavior, he should have called us at least and let us know."

Sultan presented Hekmat with today's newspaper that he was holding in his hand.

"This newspaper has relatively useful information about yesterday's blast."

Without grabbing the newspaper from his cousin's

hand, Hekmat glanced at the pictures in the paper half-heartedly, as he was scared of seeing them.

"I bought it as well," Hekmat said and pointed to the newspaper that he had tossed on the coffee table.

Sultan gave his friend an outrageous look as he sat down next to him on the long sofa.

"Didn't I tell you not to go out without me?"

"I couldn't wait to see the report."

"What was the hurry? I was coming home early anyway."

"It's ok. I was so nervous about getting more information about the casualties."

"No, it's not ok, brother Hekmat, you don't know this place. It's hell here. You are an extremely soft target—everyone can easily figure out from your shaved face and fancy clothes that you are here with dollars or euros."

"Ok, ok! I won't go out again without you."

"Promise?"

"Yes, promise." Hekmat extended his hand toward Sultan.

Sultan started looking at the paper and after reviewing the picture of the victims, he pointed to one of them which was showing half of the man's face still visible and asked his cousin to examine the picture.

I can't take it anymore," Hekmat said peevishly. "I am deeply troubled by seeing the little girl's mutilated body."

Sultan placed the paper back in front of himself on the coffee table and read the list of the dead.

"A seventy-five-year-old woman, a young nurse who just got married two weeks ago, a family of four—a husband and wife with their two little children—a little girl and her mother, and a few others whose identity couldn't be verified.

Hekmat couldn't bear even to remain seated on his couch. He got up, walked a few steps, then stood in front of the window through which he could see the pedestrians—men and women, old and young, some carrying their shopping bags in their hands and some walking holding the hands of their children.

None of these people are sure if they will get to their homes alive tonight, he quoted Sultan silently.

Sultan was still looking at the newspaper and carefully examining the picture of the man, half of whose face was covered with blood.

"You must see this picture, please pay attention to the right portion of his forehead and the right cheek," Sultan insisted. "God, do not materialize my assumption!" he then silently prayed as he handed the newspaper over to Hekmat.

Due to Sultan's persistence, Hekmat looked at the picture from different angles carefully. After a second or two, his heart started throbbing. He turned his head towards Sultan, whose face had gotten pale and whose lips were dry. He stared at Sultan without uttering a word.

"It's Majid. I swear it's him," Sultan said, his voice cracking. He rather quickly recognized their mutual friend as he had seen him more recently than Hekmat.

They both leaned back on the sofa, staring at the opposite wall of the room for almost five long minutes as teardrops ran down their cheeks.

"I wish I didn't come here," said Hekmat, squealing.

"Why?" exclaimed Sultan.

"I can't stand the sorrow of losing Majid."

"Me neither."

Another thick silence filled the room.

"We can't escape the inevitable. May God bless Majid! Unfortunately, you and I lost a brother," Sultan broke the silence and placed his hand over Hekmat's shoulder, trying to comfort him.

"God forbid," Hekmat said. He was repeatedly wiping his tears. "I still don't believe it is him."

Sultan remained silent rather than trying to convince Hekmat, although he was sure that it was Majid's body. After a while, he took a deep breath and asked Hekmat, "Don't you have Majid's son's phone number or home address?"

"No, I don't, I told you before. You should have it because you both live in Kabul."

"No, when Majid was here two months ago, he told me about his son, saying that he had been just transferred to Kabul three months ago, but we never met and never talked over the phone."

"We have to find him," Hekmat stressed.

"Of course. But I don't know how—the American interpreters are unreachable," Sultan said.

"Do you have to go back to work today?" Hekmat asked.

"Yes, unfortunately, I have an assignment at 3 p.m. to attend the foreign minister's press conference, and I am the only one from the TV who is available to provide a report on this conference to my boss."

"It's ok. You go to work, but please try to come earlier—I can't bear being alone!"

"Of course, me neither," Sultan said as he got up and said goodbye to his cousin.

Now that Hekmat was alone, his brain was on fire. What he couldn't tell Sultan, he said to himself, *I am the reason for Majid's death; he came to Kabul to visit me.* He felt a sharp pain in his left chest and a general faintness in the rest of his body. He laid down on the couch and was unable to move for a few minutes. He was desperate. He tried to soothe his emotional shock by taking the blame for the death of his best friend.

"Oh God, it's not Majid—or he's not badly hurt," he heard himself daydreaming.

This impossible wish didn't give him time to wait until Sultan returned from work. He ignored his promise to Sultan not to go out without him. He rose quickly and put on his winter coat, walked down to the street, and took a taxi.

"Please take me to Ali Abad Hospital!"

"Sir, are you sick?" the driver asked.

"Yes, my heart is aching."

The taxi driver stepped on the accelerator.

When getting out of the taxi, he prayed, *Please, God do not materialize our guess. May the hospital people tell me that Majid is not among the dead.*

He stopped by a list of the dead persons posted on the board near the emergency department and went through it. Majid's name was not on it. He hastily ran to the security desk, pointing to the board on the wall, and asked the man behind the counter, "Is that the only list for those who died in yesterday's explosion?"

"Yes," the man answered.

His face flushed. His heart started pounding with

hope. Not knowing how to verify whether his wish had come true, he remained motionless until the man in charge asked him.

"Were any of your relatives hurt in the blast?"

"I don't know, my brother was supposed to visit me yesterday, but I never heard from him."

The man pointed to the cooling room and said, "There is one dead body, whose identity couldn't be verified, go look if you want!"

Hekmat strode toward the room. Even though he had last seen his "lost brother" fifteen years ago, he still quickly recognized Majid's dead body. He lost his balance and leaned on the wall of the hospital lobby.

"So, did you recognize the body?" asked the man in charge, who had followed him to the cooling room.

He pulled his hand over his eyes, wiped his tears, and replied, "Yes, I recognize my brother."

"What was your brother's name?"

"Majid, Abdul Majid."

As he held onto the wall, a young man who had just stopped by the security desk overheard Hekmat mentioning Majid's name. The young man looked at Hekmat while trying hard to prevent himself from tumbling.

"Uncle, my father died?" the young man cried.

The last time that Hekmat had seen Majid's son, Zahir, was fifteen years ago when he traveled to Kandahar to visit them. He immediately recognized the young man. He opened his arms to him and groaned.

"Yes, Zahir Jan, my brother has, unfortunately, died. Your father was like my brother; when someone's brother dies, it's like his back breaks. With the death of your father, my back and my heart have both broken."

Zahir leaned his head over his "uncle's" shoulder but was speechless for a few moments. When he lifted his head, he wiped his tears with a handkerchief and said, "Yes, uncle, my father always used the word 'brother' when speaking about you."

Hekmat and Zahir sat down in the waiting room. They shared their feelings of sorrow and common loss empathically until a hospital administrator approached and advised them.

"You guys have until tomorrow to take the corpse from the hospital."

Zahir stopped crying. He put down his head and stayed that way until Hekmat touched his shoulder and asked, "Are you ok, son?"

"Uncle, I have no one else here except you, I need your help," Zahir said and lifted up his head while his cracked voice told a story of deep anxiety.

Hekmat kept his hand over his "nephew's" shoulder and replied with kindness, "Of course, son, I share your sorrow. Tell me, what I can do for you?

Zahir put his head down again as if ashamed of something.

"My father's corpse should be transported to Kandahar, my mother wants my father's body to be buried in our own graveyard there," Zahir murmured in a broken voice, which left his throat with extreme difficulty.

Hekmat quickly and strongly approved of this idea.

"I know, my brother must be put to rest in his parental graveyard, next to Aman, your brother."

Zahir, still silent, shook his head, indicating the existence of a huge problem in this matter. After another long moment of silence, he mumbled, "My wife is ill. I have three small children. And I don't feel safe to travel because of my job, so I don't know how I can take my father's body to Kandahar?"

"Don't worry, son, I am here for you. I can take my brother's body to Kandahar," Hekmat said immediately without thinking about the burdens of this task even for a second.

"Really, uncle? Isn't it going to be too much trouble for you?" Zahir asked in a tone of complete disbelief, which made Hekmat suddenly think about his offer and question himself.

What else can I say? I've got to perform my moral duty as a brother. Besides, I'm responsible for this tragedy, too.

He replied as confidently as possible, "Not at all, son, don't worry!"

Zahir, feeling greatly relieved by the help offered by Hekmat to take his father's corpse to Kandahar, didn't let him worry about the financial burden of the task.

"I will rent a minivan with a driver to take you to Kandahar and, once there, my uncles—my mother's brothers—will help you with the burial and *fateha*."

"Thank you, son," said Hekmat, shaking Zahir's hand. "We'll meet here again tomorrow morning. I'm going to my friend's home to make preparations for the trip."

Before leaving the hospital, Hekmat exchanged his phone number with Zahir.

He shivered due to the bitter cold while waiting for a

taxi on the roadside. The gusty evening wind was hitting hard on his face, making his eyes watery. Losing Majid, however, impacted his emotions so deeply that he even forgot to raise a hand to the taxis passing by, one after another, until a phone call brought him to his senses.

"*Salaam*, Hekmat bro, where are you?" Sultan asked.

"By the hospital."

"Which hospital?"

"Ali Abad."

"Why? What are you doing there?"

"Because the TV said that all victims were transported to this hospital. I couldn't wait to find out about Majid."

"So, did you? Was he among the victims?"

"Yes, I saw Majid's body. He is dead," Hekmat said, nearly crying.

"You stubborn man! I told you not to go anywhere alone," Sultan whispered, silently trying, however, not to further intensify his friend's distress. "We belong to Allah and to Him we shall return," Sultan spoke in Arabic. Then he asked Hekmat, "Are you still there?"

"I'm just about to get into a taxi. Where are you?"

"Home."

"See you in a few minutes."

That night, the two cousins embraced one another. Each made efforts to console the other while coping with the unbearable agony caused by the loss of their mutual best friend.

"I'm going to Kandahar with you," Sultan announced his decision to Hekmat around midnight.

"Why?" Hekmat stared at his friend. "How come you want to go with me? You have to take care of your job."

"I can take a couple of days off. I can't let you go alone to Kandahar!"

"What do you mean by going alone? I won't be alone; a driver is going to be with me."

"What I mean is that the Kabul–Kandahar highway is dangerous. You have come from America. You are a good target both for thieves and terrorists."

"Hmm," Hekmat said. "You make a good point, Sultan. Still, I have no enemy and no one knows who I am, I would just be transporting my brother's dead body—so no one will bother me, I hope."

"You don't understand what's going on in this country," Sultan told his friend in a harsher tone. "I will worry about you. We lost Majid and now I am afraid that if anything happens to you—how will I bear it? It would be better that I accompany you because I know these people, more or less, and can deal with them."

"No, thank you brother, for your sympathy, but don't worry about me. I might have to stay longer in Kandahar because, first of all, Majid Jan's burial and *fateha* alone will take three days. I am also planning to do a pilgrimage to my parents' graves. Therefore, you better stay here and do what you need to do."

Sultan was emotional but gave up arguing with his cousin when he realized that insisting wouldn't help. He rose to go to his bedroom and extended his hand to Hekmat.

"Ok, I'll stay, but I strongly advise you to listen to me!"

"I am listening to you, what do you want to tell me?"

"Make sure you don't carry American money or

any paperwork whatsoever that shows your American identity!"

"You're right; I will not carry any such thing with me and I will change some dollars into Afghan money tomorrow."

"One more thing," Sultan said firmly.

"What?"

"Grow your beard starting today and also wear our ethnic outfit, which I will give you!"

"Do you think that will save me?"

"Yes, these things do make a difference." Sultan sounded positive. "Tomorrow morning, I am also going with you to the hospital to see Majid Jan's face for the last time."

"Goodnight. Hopefully, we will both get some sleep."

Hekmat closed the door and went straight to his bed.

A good friend is part of one's life. The next morning, while Zahir and the driver were loading Majid's body into a minivan at Ali Abad Hospital, Hekmat and Sultan stood at the side, quiet and traumatized. Tears ran down their pale faces and white mustaches as they watched a part of their lives leave them forever.

It was around noon that Majid's body was placed in the vehicle and ready to move. Zahir kissed the hands of both of his father's best friends. Sultan also hugged Hekmat and, raising both his hands, prayed for him.

"Wish you a safe and sound return back to Kabul—be very careful Hekmat bro!"

"I sure will," Hekmat pressed Sultan's hand a few times and said goodbye to him.

"Listen," Sultan said, almost running after the minivan as it started moving. He went closer to Hekmat, who was in the passenger seat, and whispered in his ear, "Make sure you don't come alone from Kandahar, keep the driver until you are done and ride back with him or come by airplane, although I know that sometimes there are no flights for a whole week."

The road between Kabul and Kandahar was full of potholes. Since the Soviet invasion of Afghanistan and until the present day, it was severely damaged by the use of military tanks and by roadside bombs. Before that, it used to be a seven-hour trip, but now it took them more than twice that to get to Kandahar. They needed to spend the night at a roadside restaurant to get some rest and sleep. They arrived at their destination the next morning.

At the beginning of the trip, both Hekmat and the driver were silent for hours. Hekmat's mind went to the times when he and Majid were six-year-old kids. They had become friends as young children and remained friends until today. He recalled the days when they had walked together to school and played on their streets after school. He entertained his mind by recollecting their shared sweet memories of having picnics and parties, helping and making sacrifices for each other in times of need, caring for and respecting one another during their over fifty-five years of friendship. This remembrance brought tears to his eyes. The driver noticed that Hekmat was wiping his tears with a paper tissue but said nothing.

"Do you have children?" Hekmat asked when he saw that the driver began yawning, trying to stretch his arms and neck and thus signaling tiredness and sleepiness.

"Yes, I have four kids."

"Good. How old are they?"

"My daughter is ten and my sons are eight, five, and two years old."

Jaafar seemed to be in his early thirties and he spoke Farsi with a heavy Hazaragi accent.

"What's this dead person to you?" to shorten the long trip, Jaafar also wanted to prolong the conversation and asked Hekmat his first question.

Hekmat sighed heavily.

"It's my brother. He died in a suicidal attack."

"May God bless him, was he your only brother?"

"No. I do have one other brother but, to tell you the truth, he was my childhood friend—he was as close to me as a brother."

Jaafar remained silent for a moment, then turned to Hekmat.

"Very good, although it's strange that you are helping a stranger in such a big way," Jafaar said in a tone of appreciation.

"There is nothing strange about it. As I said, we were childhood friends; we were buddies for fifty-five years."

"Well," the driver said vehemently. "Nowadays, even a brother won't help a brother. You are taking a friend's dead body from Kabul to Kandahar—I mean, what you are doing is something hard to believe."

It was around 10 p.m. when they arrived in Shar-e Safa city. Both felt sleepy. They stopped at a restaurant by the highway, where they ate dinner and spent the night in a rental room that the restaurant had offered to the travelers.

"We should leave early in the morning so that we can

arrive in Kandahar while it's still cold in the morning or the corps is going to further decay," Jafaar suggested.

"Right, I agree. We will leave early in the morning."

They left before sunrise and, by 10 a.m., they arrived at Majid's parental house, which was located on the Manzal Bagh road in the eastern part of Kandahar.

It was mid-December; the cold weather did not allow the corpse to perish quickly. Majid's two brothers-in-law and several other relatives waited by the house to transfer Majid's body from the minivan to the funeral vehicle. Then, they transported the body to the nearby mosque so that the corpse could be washed and services performed. Hekmat and Jaafar both felt tired and sleepy. They stayed in the minivan and took a nap.

After resting for about two hours, the driver woke Hekmat.

"I am leaving to go back to Kabul."

Hekmat rubbed his eyes. Still leaning back in the seat, he asked Jaffar, "Why? We were supposed to go back together."

"When will you be going back?"

"I don't know. I have to attend the funeral and the three-day, *fateha*, after that we will see—if there is nothing else for me to do, then we can go back to Kabul."

"I can't stay that long. I'm leaving now, my job is over."

"Oh no, brother, how can you leave without me? We came together and go back together," Hekmat told the driver in a friendly tone.

"I can't. I have to go, I have to work," Jaafar insisted.

Hekmat held his journey companion's hand in his own and spoke to him in an indulgent tone.

"Listen, brother, I am somewhat of a stranger here. I don't want to take a bus to Kabul and there is no flight to Kabul for a week. Please stay with me until I am done with my friend's, *fateha*, then we will go together!"

"That's not my problem. The guy in Kabul gave me money only to get you and the corpse here."

"Let's be together on the way back to Kabul so we won't be bored with the long trip."

"I can't stay here for three more days. I'm a poor working person. I have four kids. I need to make money."

"Okay, let's do this," Hekmat said softly. "I will pay you an additional 15,000 Afghanis if you stay with me until the *fateha* is over."

The driver adjusted his Mazari hat over his head and, during a short silence, he calculated the offer. Finding it fair, he said, "That's fine. I know you are a good man. You brought your friend's corpse from Kabul to Kandahar and I will stay with you due to your respect."

"Thank you."

By the time that the coffin was ready, a crowd of Majid's family members, friends, neighbors, and acquaintances grew considerably. It was around 1 p.m. when the hearse arrived and the corpse was loaded into it. Majid's widow, her older brother, and his wife got on the vehicle as well. The rest of the funeral party—an estimated one hundred men—divided into groups and got into private cars, minivans, and SUVs belonging to some of the mourners. Likewise, four individuals joined Hekmat and Jaafar to ride with them to the cemetery.

The procession, led by the funeral vehicle, moved towards the Old Edgah—the site of the official Eid prayer—next to which the cemetery was located, some ten miles from Majid's house.

Among the group of people riding with Hekmat, at least three were his age or older. However, none of them seemed familiar to him. He left Kandahar forty years ago. Over the years, he traveled back to the city only once, fifteen years ago, solely to pay a short visit to Majid. During the four decades, the country fell apart—starting with the civil war—and most of his friends, relatives, or acquaintances had either died or had left the country as refugees since then. Therefore, he did not expect to see any people he knew here. Everyone in the vehicle said a brief "*Salaam*" to one another and went on reciting prayers for the deceased.

"May God reward him a place in heaven; he was such a nice and decent man," said one old guy with a long white beard, wearing a black turban and a silk gown— unique to religious authorities—a long white colored *shalwar kamis* and holding a set of fancy marble beads in his right hand. After the man lowered his hands from prayer, he addressed Hekmat, "May God bless you for bringing Majid's body here so that he can be buried in his own graveyard by the side of his mother and father." The man pulled his hand over his long beard and asked, "Do you have a family relationship with him? I have never seen you before."

"No, Haji Sahib," Hekmat replied in a saddened voice. "Majid and I were friends since childhood. We were good friends for over fifty-five years and, to me, he was like a brother."

The man gazed at Hekmat in amazement.

"Fifty-five years? Where did you know him from?"

"We were classmates from first grade until the end of high school."

"But he went to Mirwais High School?" the man uttered hastily, wondering where Hekmat himself went to school.

"Yes, I went to Mirwais High School, too."

The man stared at Hekmat more directly and asked him again, "What's your name?"

"Hekmat, Hekmatullah."

The old man, whose upper lip was covered by a white mustache, smiled slightly and—staring at Hekmat—said with utmost excitement, "Oh God, you are Hekmatullah Jan? Don't you recognize me? I am Esmatullah? I was also your classmate. I was with you guys together from grades seven to twelve!"

Both men stood up, moved toward each other to the middle of the minivan, and hugged each other firmly. When back in their seats, Esmatullah wiped his hand over his long white beard and said, "I got old, Hekmat Jan. My face is covered with white wool; that's why you didn't recognize me."

"Don't worry, Esmatullah Jan. I am not younger than you. We are the same age. But I am glad to see you alive; life is such a wonder—that I am seeing you now after more than forty years," as Hekmat spoke, he tried to conceal his contentment at meeting another one of his classmates.

As a gesture to indicate he appreciated his friendship, Hekmat moved and took an empty seat next to Esmatulla. The two old buddies talked about what a good human being Majid was. Also, they shared their memories of their time together all along the way until they arrived at the cemetery.

At Majid's parental graveyard, there was an even larger number of people waiting for the funeral caravan to arrive.

"It looks like your brother was a popular man," Jaffar whispered to Hekmat as they got off the minivan.

"Of course," Hekmat said with emphasis.

With the help of Majids's brothers-in-law, Hekmat carried the coffin over his shoulder from the funeral vehicle to the graveyard. He stayed by his "brother's" body until it was placed into the freshly dug hole. He took turns, together with Majid's family members and other close friends, pouring dirt over Majid's body, signifying his closeness to the dead.

"I think that a part of my soul is being buried," he whispered into Esmatullah's ear, who was standing next to him.

It was cold and windy. Hekmat felt uncomfortable with the weather but couldn't endure moving farther away from Majid's body. Esmatullah and he stood next to each other, while others erected the tomb over Majid's grave and organized the rocks on it. A few more people joined them and Esmatullah introduced his old friend to them.

"This is Hekmatullah, my high school classmate. We are meeting again after more than forty years."

One of the newly joined individuals, also around 60 years old, moved closer to Hekmat and opened his arms for him, exclaiming, "*Salaam*, Hekmatullah Jan! I am Abdul Wahab, we were neighbors, we were friends—you and I used to play together. Do you remember me?"

Hekmat recognized his childhood playmate rather quickly and opened his arms for him. They hugged each other for a long time. While they still held each other, a loud noise shook the ground and tossed them both to the middle of the graveyard. The dust and dirt that flew everywhere were so thick that even those who were not struck by the blast were unable to see the others for a good three-four minutes.

When Hekmat opened his eyes two days later, he found himself in a hospital bed. His right arm, right leg, and head were wrapped in a white bandage. An artificial breathing tube and a vein infusion apparatus were attached to his body. The wounded person to his left was groaning loudly, which annoyed him. He wished that the patient was taken out of the room so that he could be without that extra headache source. The groaning went on for a long time. He turned his head toward his noisy neighbor with tremendous difficulty. Looking at him from the corner of his eye, he recognized his old buddy—Esmatullah.

"How are you?" he asked using sign language and without uttering a single word.

"I am…in extreme pain…I think my head is exploding," Esmatullah replied in a broken voice, wheezing and coughing at the same time.

He asked Esmatullah another question in sign language, which he didn't understand.

"Abdul Wahab?" he whispered that name, but Esmatullah didn't hear and didn't bother to ask him about what he said.

The large room was full of wounded people; some were lucky to have separate beds, but the rest were lying on the floor, wrapped in blankets. Almost everyone was groaning and wheezing, Hekmat included.

For another twenty-four hours, Hekmat wasn't conscious enough to remember what had happened. He once thought it was a bomb or a rocket dropped from the air over the funeral.

"What was it, brother?" he asked Esmatullah when he gained a bit of energy to talk the next day.

"You didn't see it? It was a suicide attack."

"A suicide attack on a funeral? Why? Who would do that? A lot of people must have died?"

Neither Esmatullah nor he was capable of further discussion. Both closed their eyes.

The next morning, when a male nurse came by with a pain killer and a glass of water, he asked him, "Where is a patient by the name of Jaafar?"

"There is no patient here by this name," the nurse replied.

"He must be somewhere in this hospital. He is my driver and we were together at the time of the explosion."

"I know the names of all the wounded; there is no one by this name. Your driver might be among the dead."

"How many people died?" he asked the nurse.

"Eleven."

"And wounded?"

"Twenty-three."

"Oh, God, this poor man left four kids behind," Hekmat said aloud.

The nurse heard him but said nothing and left the room.

The discomfort caused by his wounds and the stressful noise of other wounded in the room did not allow him to fall asleep. His throat was bitter and felt severe headache and body ache. He closed his eyes for a few seconds. Soon, the voice of a female nurse, who was talking to another patient, drew his attention. He asked her a question to which he already knew the answer.

"When will I get discharged from the hospital?"

"I don't know, the doctor should know this. You need more treatment because your right shoulder is badly damaged," the nurse said and continued attending to the patient.

"What did they do with the dead?" Hekmat asked the nurse, having Jaafar in mind.

"They are in the cooling room, awaiting their family members to come and get them."

"If someone has no family here, then what happens to them?"

"They give such corpses to medical students for disfigurement and experiment."

"Oh, God! Poor Jaafar, his family won't be able to see his body. I'm not going to let that happen to him," he muttered to himself and quickly spoke to the nurse again. "Listen, sister, can you do me a favor? One of my relatives is among the dead, his name is Jaafar. He might have his identification or his vehicle registration in his pocket bearing his name. I would like to take him to his family. With whom should I talk about this?"

"Mr. Sabir is the person in charge. I will let him know that you want to talk to him."

"Yes, please, tell him as soon as possible before they give away my relative's body for medical experimentation."

No document was required to prove a relationship between Hekmat and Jaafar because the hospital authorities liked to see corpses leave as soon as possible. Thus, the hospital authorities approved Hekmat's request to take Jaafar's body out of the hospital. For this reason, they even discharged Hekmat from the hospital on the sixth day after his admittance. However, he still needed more hospital medical attention. Hekmat was happy to leave earlier.

On the day of his release, his head wasn't hurting as badly. At the same time, his right shoulder and right leg were still in plaster and ached. He knew he couldn't drive to Kabul himself—he needed to hire a driver to take Jaffar's body in his own minivan. Before leaving the hospital, he was allowed to mark Jaafar's body to be ready for pick up.

During his stay in the hospital, Majid's brother-in-law would check in on him from time to time and today he picked Hekmat up in his car, then drove him to his house, where he also met Majid's widow.

"May God give you your health back and may God award you with His mercy for being like a brother to my late husband," Majid's widow said, with tears continually running down her cheeks. "He always spoke your name with such respect and adoration, as if you were his own brother. Thank you for bringing his corpse back to me to so that I can pay my respects to his shrine whenever I wish." She wiped her tears with her black hijab.

The next morning, Majid's younger brother-in-law, a 55-year-old civil engineer, helped Hekmat find a young man who would drive Jaafar's minivan, along with his corpse, back to Kabul.

The young man had a short beard and he frowned at Hekmat as he said, "I would like to travel to Kabul because I've never been there before, but I'm going to lose a lot of money because it's going to take two days and two nights both ways. It's too much time for me to be away from my children."

"What do you do for a living?" asked Hekmat.

"I own a minibus and transport passengers in the city."

"How much do you make a week?"

The guy scratched his head and estimated his weekly earnings at 25,000 Afghanis.

Hekmat placed his hand over the young guy's shoulder and addressed him softly, "That's okay, my friend, let's go to Kabul, I will pay you enough money.

"How much?"

"I am going to pay you 25,000 Afghanis. Is that ok?"

The man remained silent and thought about it.

"If you go with me, you can both see Kabul and make the same amount of money you would make in a week in only four days," Hekmat said in a friendly tone.

The young man did a quick calculation in his mind and agreed to the deal.

"Okay, pay me 10,000 first, so that I can leave some money for my family."

"Do you have children?"

"Yes, a girl and a boy. I go with you because you are

respected, but I've never been away from them for that long."

Hekmat thanked the young man and asked him to meet him by the National Bank in the afternoon so he could get the 10,000 Afghanis.

Surviving the horrible suicide attack incident was worth celebrating. He thought he was reborn. Nevertheless, publicly, the tragedy of Majid's death did not allow him to rejoice. Also, he felt apprehensive about Jaafar, whose death had left a wife and four little kids behind. He felt guilty about his death as well. Everyone in Majid's brother-in-law's house, where he spent the night, was in mourning. However, he was more than mourning—he considered himself to be the reason for both tragedies—the death of Majid as well as that of Jaafar.

He hardly closed his eyes during the night, wondering who the attacker was and why they bombed the funeral. Who was the target, what was the reason that terrorists had Majid and his family on their list?

In the morning, he asked Majid's brother-in-law, who was the principal organizer of the funeral, these questions.

"That's a good question, but I don't know the answer," his host replied.

"Don't you think that you or other members of Majid's family were the targets?"

"I don't think so, because we never had any dispute with anyone and never felt anything that would justify such a conclusion."

After finishing breakfast, he asked Majid's brother-in-law whether he could take him to his parents' graveyard for a quick pilgrimage and then to the hospital a bit earlier so that he could say goodbye to his classmate and friend, Esmatullah.

"No problem."

That morning, before Hekmat left for the hospital, Majid's widow, wearing black and teary-eyed, came again to her brother's house to say farewell to Hekmat. She also had a request—a wish—to express to him.

"Brother Hekmat," she said, sounding as weak as if she had spent all her energy on crying since the day her husband died. "My late husband called you brother and loved you as his brother. Thus, you are my brother, too. Now, our son, our daughter-in-law, and our grandchildren are going to America. They need your care and kindness. If you want to make your brother's soul happy, if you want to make your sister happy, please treat them as your own children. I leave them first in God's hands and then in yours. Be both their father and grandfather, please."

"Yes, sister, no doubt about it. I already made that promise to Majid. He was my brother and you are my sister, sincerely. Your son and his family are my own family. I promise you too, I will treat them and take care of them as if they were my own children and grandchildren," Hekmat spoke honestly and emotionally.

Hekmat walked with a cane. When his host dropped him off at the Ali Abad Hospital, he went straight to his high school classmate's bed and asked him, "Brother Esmatullah, what do you think, who was the target of the attack on Majid's funeral? I'm not familiar with this place, nobody knows me—so who, among the funeral attendees, was on the mind of the attackers?" Hekmat asked him, after inquiring about his health condition.

Esmatullah still groaned in pain due to severe headaches. "I think you were the target," he said in a brittle voice.

Hekmat blinked in astonishment. "Are you sure? Why do you think so?"

"Because I know all the other people who live here, work here, and attend such gatherings all the time—you were the only new person among us."

"But I don't live here and no one was aware of my coming over. Besides, I never had any kind of hostility with anyone here," Hekmat uttered humbly.

"Oh, brother, nowadays things are different. You might think that no one knows you and no one knew that you would be coming here, but they would already have a case for you and would be plotting against you. You said Majid was like a brother to you, right? And they wanted to kill Majid's brother as they killed his son, Aman."

Esmatullah's opinion was nonsense to him and he had no reason to believe it. He wished him a quick recovery and said goodbye to him.

That day, around noon, Majid's brother-in-law and the young driver loaded Jaafar's body into his minivan. They placed him over the same wooden boxes that they had used to convey Majid's body from Kabul.

At the beginning of the trip, the driver, who was not familiar with the condition of the Kabul-Kandahar highway, tried to drive faster. Unlike the city, where the traffic was jammed most of the time and it was often difficult to drive faster than 10 miles per hour, he was excited to enjoy driving at highway speeds. Soon, however, he noticed the potholes, cracks, and bumps on the road and expressed his concern.

"It looks like we'll be on the road for a week before we get to Kabul!"

Hekmat's mind was absent. He was engaged in an imaginary debate with Esmatullah, who had suggested that he was the only possible target of the suicidal attack.

I don't think so. If I was the target of the killing, then the question is—why? Why would anybody want to kill me? I know no one here and have no problem with anyone, he was immersed in his thoughts so much that even his lips were moving.

"Sir, did you hear me?" the young man asked, sounding humorous.

"Sorry, what did you say?"

"I said that this road is badly broken. I think it will take us a week to get to Kabul!"

"No, not a week. We came from Kabul in less than 24 hours—but we do have to spend the night somewhere along the way."

The driver felt assured about the length of the trip.

"You said the dead man is your relative, right?"

"Yes…but he is not, actually…he was the driver of this vehicle that you are now driving. He transported my friend's body with me to Kandahar."

"I see," the young man said with a sigh. "Poor man. Do you know if he had a family?"

"Oh yes, he was married and had four little kids," Hekmat paused briefly. "He told me he was the only breadwinner of his family. I feel very sorry for his wife and children."

"Oh God, how hard it will be for his wife and children to live without a man and a father."

"I know, hopefully, we'll be able to find his family to hand over his body to them."

"What? You don't know where they live?" the driver asked seriously.

"God willing, we'll be able to find them. He told me he was living in the Chandawol area."

"Was he sick to die?"

"No, brother, he got killed in a suicide attack when we were burying my brother."

They both remained silent. The vehicle suddenly slowed down near the city of Qalat—almost halfway to Kabul—and a dim light appeared at a distance of approximately 1,000 feet. Hekmat hadn't slept enough for nearly a week, not since the day he and Jaafar had left Kabul.

Observing the light, Hekmat was delighted and told the driver, "We should make a stop in this city, have our dinner, and stay for the night."

The driver, a 22-year-old man, whose mind was occupied with what was ahead, didn't respond to Hekmat immediately. After a second or two, he squeezed his eyes and stared more seriously at the road ahead for a bit.

"Oh God, please help me. It seems like my life is gone with the wind!" he uttered in a deeply worrisome tone.

Hekmat also looked ahead at the dim light.

"Why? What's going on?" he anxiously asked.

"They blocked the road," the driver said with tremendous apprehension.

"Who blocked the road? Who are they, what do you think they want?" Hekmat turned to the driver.

But the driver preferred to recite a prayer for his rescue instead of answering Hekmat's questions. As they approached the light, which was coming from a heavy-duty flashlight, the young driver stepped on the brake and stopped the minivan.

"What's your name?" the guy who first reached the vehicle walked straight up to Hekmat and asked him. "What's your name?" the man shouted again as Hekmat delayed his answer.

"Hekmatullah," he answered anxiously.

The armed man, wearing a traditional *shalwar kamis*, a white turban, and *patto*—a traditional Afghan wrap—smirked.

"Hekmatullah?" He lifted Hekmat's chin up with his fingers, looked him in the eyes, and said irately, "Now you altered your name, ha? You liar!"

In astonishment, Hekmat gazed at the man who now pointed a handgun at him.

"No, brother! I haven't altered my name. Here is my *Tazkirah*, you can see for yourself that Hekmatullah is my true name," he replied softly.

The man violently pushed his hand back along with his ID booklet and roared, "I don't want to see your *Tazkirah!*

Nowadays, every bastard is carrying a fake *Tazkirah*. I know you are the one who worked for Americans!"

"What? I never worked for Americans."

"Don't lie to me you son of a pig, let's move—get out of the car!"

"For God's sake, I'm taking this Muslim's dead body back to his family."

The man pressed the muzzle of his gun to Hekmat's head and yelled, "Get up, or I will blow your head off!"

Hekmat sighed heavily, touching the man's beard in a gesture of begging.

"This poor driver is unfamiliar with Kabul; he doesn't know where to take the corpse."

The driver who was silent until this moment suddenly realized his own problem. He swallowed his saliva and humbly said to the armed man, "He is right brother, I've never been to Kabul, and I don't know what to do with this dead man."

"You shut up—go, run away, and don't look back or I will put a bullet in your skull!"

The armed man pulled Hekmat out of the minivan by holding the upper neckline of his woolen winter coat.

They have followed you, your life is in real danger, Hekmat said to himself and, as a last resort, he once again begged the man.

"I am innocent, for God's sake, please let me go!"

"You know," the Taliban fighter looked into Hekmat's eyes, "we were looking for you in the sky, but God gave you to us on the earth. Let's move!"

The militant kicked his captive on the right shoulder, which caused a fierce scream to escape Hekmat's mouth irrepressibly. His shoulder wound, caused by the blast in Kandahar, reopened, and a stream of blood flowed down his body. When the armed man released his collar, he had already passed out and his body fell on the muddy ground.

When Hekmat opened his eyes in the middle of the night, he saw that he was locked in a tiny room with shabby walls. He was taken to a remote village by the name of Mizan, located on the outskirts of Qalat—the capital city of the Zabul province. It was brutally cold; enormous drops of rain and harsh wind penetrated the room through the cracked and ratty door, striking his injured shoulder. He was one of the three "guests" housed in this room, which was barely large enough to fit one full-sized bed. The guy who guarded the room searched him all over. He confiscated his cell phone, his wristwatch as well as all the Afghan currency cash he had on him.

Thank you, Sultan, he silently praised his cousin for advising him not to carry anything that could reveal his American identity.

Hekmat was suffering from a severe headache, chest pain, and body aches—the burning pain in his right shoulder and right leg were especially unbearable. He repeatedly squeaked and moaned, which made his jailers uncomfortable. Two days later, they rinsed his wounds and put a bandage on them, then moved him to a separate, smaller, cave-like room that smelled of rot in which there was a piece of worn carpet thrown on the floor. His new guard was a young man who appeared to be no more than 16 or 17 years old. This young man was a harsh and ruthless person. He used very insulting language when communicating with Hekmat.

"Maybe you are a big dog; that's why Maulawi Sahib put you in a separate room," the young guard would address him in this ill manner several times a day. Each time, when Hekmat looked up at him but chose to remain silent, the guard would add, "They should have finished you on the first day."

The person in charge of his interrogation introduced himself as the attorney of the Islamic Emirate and said that his name was Maulawi Samander. He seemed to be in his early fifties, a short and heavy man with a flat nose, a long pepper and salt beard, and a full mustache. He stood in front of Hekmat, who was lying on a threadbare carpet in the corner of the tiny room. He asked him in a heavy thunder-like voice, "How long did you work for Americans?"

"What are you talking about, Maulawi Sahib? I never worked for the Americans."

"Don't lie to me, old man, everyone is aware that you used to work for the American AID Company in Kandahar."

"I swear to God I never worked for AID."

"Your name is Mohibullah, you lived in Deh Khwaja—we know all about you," the investigator spoke in a heavy and menacing tone.

"No, sir, my name is not Mohibullah. My name is Hekmatullah—look at my *Tazkirah*."

"Your *Tazkirah* is fake; you are a dishonest person as

well," Maulawi Samander roared. "What do you do for a living now?"

"I'm retired, I do nothing."

"You liar pig, you are now in the hands of the Islamic Emirate! Tell me the truth or I will send you to hell straight away!"

The Taliban attorney kicked Hekmat in his left thigh hard enough to make him scream. Maulawi Smander didn't wait for Hekmat to stop groaning. He continued his interrogation:

"I know that you once lived in Karachi. Then you went to America and now you are back here to spy for the Americans. What are their plans here? Tell me all that you know!"

"I am not spying for the Americans and I have no idea what their plans are," Hekmat uttered persuasively.

"Ok, if you don't want to confess, I'm going to do this to you," Maulawi pulled an old pair of slip joint pliers out of his jacket's pocket and put his right index finger in it.

"What are you doing brother? You are a Muslim, too—for God's sake don't cut my finger!" Hekmat cried.

"You traitor, you are afraid of losing your finger because you will no longer be able to write reports for the Americans, ha? You escaped death in Kandahar—we wanted to bury you along with Majid—that bastard."

Thus, Maulawi revealed the motive of the Kandahar blast and Hekmat just realized that Esmatullah was right about it. Hekmat was scared. If they cut his right index finger, he would never be able to write or type his novel. He stared at the attorney of the Islamic Emirate, who was still holding the pliers in his hand and waiting for Hekmat to confess.

He murmured, "I am not writing a report for the Americans, I am going to write a book."

"Aha, you are a scholar, writing a book. What's your book going to be about?"

"My book is going to be about the killings, this nonsense war, and human tragedies—how long is this going to go on?" Hekmat spoke in a soft tone. While looking Samander in the eyes, he added, "Now I would like to ask you a question, if I may?"

Maulawi looked at Hekmat in astonishment and let him ask his question.

"What sin did Majid commit that you guys killed him?"

Maulawi released Hekmat's finger, put the pliers on the floor, and harshly answered him, acting as if his prisoner had asked an insulting and inappropriate question.

"Did you forget that he was also working for the Americans, like you? Don't you know that he was spying for them, like you?" Maulawi paused. He grimaced with rage and continued, "We couldn't get him in Kandahar because he was hiding with the Americans, so we finished him in Kabul."

The Taliban attorney combed his mustache with his fingers.

"Now, it's his son's turn, since he is also working with the Americans in Kabul," he added arrogantly.

"Why did you kill his other son in Kandahar?"

"Hmm," Maulawi roared. "His son tried to be a hero. He tried to apprehend our jihadi soldier—but our boy was quick to explode himself. Majid escaped that time."

"In Kabul, you guys killed eleven other innocent people, why did you kill them?" Hekmat asked his question without hesitation.

"Get lost, you stupid man, you can't interrogate me! Where can we find you—the infidels—alone? We get rid of you bastards wherever we can get you and we don't care who else we hit along with you."

Hekmat pointed both his hands toward the interrogator.

"But you guys are Muslims, you believe in the Quran. Allah says—in the *Almaedah* chapter of the Quran—that 'if there is one innocent human killed, it's like the whole humanity is being murdered.'"

"Huh, you infidels know about the Quran and Ayah too!" Maulawi Samnader yelled. "In Islam, the killing of a *moamin*—a faithful Muslim—is *haram* but not killing infidels. You can't call any non-believer a *moamin!*"

"I'm not, but the people you murdered—both in Kabul and Kandahar—were all *moamins!* They were devoted Muslims. I saw them myself, they were Muslims."

Hekmat was speaking in a calm and composed manner. The Taliban prosecutor, in the meantime, became mad because he couldn't stand his prisoner's argument.

"You are stupid! How do you think that the Taliban can't distinguish the *moamins* from the *non-moamins*? How can the servants of the puppet government and their family members be considered to be Muslims?"

"That's not true," Hekmat objected to his prosecutor. Then, he leaned against the wall and pressed on his right thigh, which was still painful from the kick it received from Samander. He exhaled heavily. "I personally saw, with my own eyes, everyone you killed or injured during the attack on Majid's funeral in Kandahar. They were true Muslims. I heard them as they loudly recited the Kalimah-e Tayibah of La ilaha ilallah—there is no god but God. Also, a driver by the name of Jaafar—who had transported Majid's corpse to Kandahar with me—was a poor working guy. He performed the five daily prayers before my eyes when we were on the road together on our way to Kandahar and during our stay there."

Hekmat paused momentarily and, looking straight into his interrogator's eyes, he made him wait until he had finished all he had to say.

"I also saw the pictures of those innocent people you killed along with Majid in front of the women's hospital in Kabul—a pretty little girl, an old woman, a nurse, and a family of four with two children. I'm sure that none of them were working for the Americans. Neither they nor their family members were government employees."

"Listen to me, you pig, you need to understand," Samander once again put his fingers under Hekmat's chin and rumbled, "Do you have a brain or no? Jihad is like a jungle on fire. It burns both dry and wet stuff together."

By now, Hekmat lost his patience. He no longer cared who he was talking to because he realized that it was just a matter of time before they would finish him. He asked his jailer, "So you mean to say that you guys kill innocent people, even real Muslims, to achieve your goals?"

Maulawi remained silent for a moment. He sat dawn on one corner of the shabby piece of carpet, face-to-face with Hekmat. Then, he spoke in a mock calm manner, reflecting his deep rage.

"When the enemy is hiding and mingled in a crowd of people, how can we separate the good guys from the bad guys? We have to sacrifice some people, in the name of Allah, which is permissible in Islam."

"What? It is permissible to kill a Muslim for the sake of Allah?" Hekmat asked with utmost seriousness. "If you think so, show me any Ayah from the Quran that says so—if you can't, then you are nothing more than murderers."

Maulawi's upper lip and mustache started shivering. His eyes popped out of their sockets and he ground his teeth but stayed quiet, breathing heavily out of profound anger.

Hekmat sensed his prosecutor's rage very well. Since he was convinced that there was no way that he would be leaving this "hell" alive—and since he heard from his young guard that he was only being kept alive for a reason—he did not care much about Samander's anger. He asked him one more question.

"Are those kids who stick explosives on their bodies and perform suicide attacks, Muslim?"

"Without any doubt," Maulawi said with a sense of pride after taking a deep breath. "They are real Muslims. They sacrifice their lives in the name of Allah."

"But they are small boys. You deceive them. You brainwash them and promise them a place in heaven after death. You prepare them to kill themselves—which, in itself, is murder."

"It's not murder; it's the ultimate sacrifice needed to

punish the enemies of God, like you, and to win a certain stay in heaven."

Hekmat rubbed his injured shoulder and then spoke.

"Look, Maulawi Sahib, I believe that you are a wise man and, for this reason, I'm encouraged to ask you a question."

Hekmat pulled himself together and waited for Samander's reaction. The attorney sighed, then nodded positively with a smirk. Hekmat put his question forward.

"If someone, Majid, for example, recited the Kalima-e Tayibah—the word of Purity—and said that there is no God but God…and if he also performed his prayer before your eyes…would you still call him an infidel and kill him?"

"Of course, we would kill him. Because he was a hypocrite. He served the Americans and spied for them. Hence, even if he were standing in a niche-mihrab and prayed, we would still have finished him," Maulawi stated with arrogance.

"Okay," Hekmat was heartened by Maulawi's mistaken answer and continued more aggressively. "First of all, whenever you want to punish anyone for committing a sin or a crime, then—according to the Islamic Sharia law—that person should first be tried and convicted in a court of law, and only after that the person can be punished, right?'

Maulawi nodded agreeably.

"So how do you guys receive your court orders—or how does your court pass their judgment to allow you to kill a group of people whose names you didn't even know? Second, working for the Americans or other non-Muslims is not a sin—if you think it is, then show me where it says so in the Quran? Third, in the world, there are billions of Christians, Jews, Buddhists, and people with no religion at all—do you think that God has authorized you guys to kill them all? Are you God's agent for killing His creatures in His name? And why would you kill any human who doesn't obey you? Is following God's directive less important to you than having your own orders be followed?"

Maulawi had exhausted his patience. He took a deep breath and, while standing up, spoke words of warning to Hekmat.

"It seems to me that you are a very dangerous man. I don't know why they are delaying your execution—I hope that I will get the verdict soon and shut your big mouth once and for all."

"Ok, if that is the case, then sit down—I'm going to tell you the truth!"

The Taliban prosecutor was encouraged by what Hekmat promised and sat down again just across from Hekmat on the carpet.

"Ok, tell me the truth, the whole truth!"

Hekmat once again pressed his shoulder wound with his hand and addressed Samander in a taunting calmness.

"Look, Maulawi Sahib, I would first like to ask you a question. Suppose that my name *is* Mohibullah and suppose that I did work for the Americans and you have decided to kill me. Why would you waste so much of your time and resources to train a suicide bomber—who would kill other innocent people—just to get rid of me through a suicide attack? Why don't you just terrorize me, alone?"

The prosecutor habitually combed his long beard with the fingers of his right hand. He sighed heavily before answering Hekmat's questions in a loud voice.

"This matter is beyond your grasp. Do you think we're so stupid? You want our boys to be captured if you have a pistol and hand them over to the Americans? And you want the Americans to get them confessed and then execute them? That's what you want us to do? We are not idiots."

"I don't have a pistol, I never held one in my hand and I don't know how to use one," Hekmat said.

"We don't know which infidel has a gun and which one doesn't. But our soldiers of Islam are ready to make their sacrifice for Allah. They are entitled, without any doubt or uncertainty, to be placed in paradise."

Hekmat pulled himself a bit closer to Samander and coolly asked him, "How do you know that your soldiers of Islam will go to heaven for sure?"

"Do you deny the fact that the Quran says that if anyone makes a sacrifice for the sake of Islam or the sake of Allah, they will be placed in heaven?" he asked his captive in a thunderous voice.

"If that's the case," Hekmat stated in a calmer tone, "then you claim that your soldiers of Islam—who took the lives of Majid and so many other innocent people—are going to be placed in heaven for sure, right?"

"No doubt, God willing,"

"Ok, so you're admitting that God agrees that His innocent servants should be killed by your hand, and then He rewards your soldier for doing so?"

Hekmat raised his voice a bit as he completely forgot with whom he was speaking at the moment. He didn't even give his jailer a chance to react to his harsh words. He asked his next question without hesitation.

"If by killing Majid, Jaafar, or that little girl and old lady, your murderer can earn the stay in paradise, then why don't you, yourself, make the killings—so that you can also be in heaven with *Hoors* and *Ghilamns* sooner?"

Maulawi grunted like an elephant. He reached into his pocket and pulled out his handgun.

"Lā ḥawla wa lā quwwata illā billāh—there is no might nor power except in Allah," he said in Arabic and swallowed his rage by doing so. He slowly got up and said in despair, "I have no idea why the verdict of your execution is delayed, I will talk to the Great Mullah Sahib myself about you today."

Then Samander left.

Like the Taliban prosecutor, Hekmat, too, had no idea why the Taliban leader was keeping him alive for so long. However, he was confident that, sooner or later, his life would end at the hands of his jailers. Despite his perception, his burning desire to write and to fulfill his promise to Sheila, Majid, and Jaafar would not allow him to concede to the loss of his dream.

Two days passed. Neither Samander nor any other executioner showed up. He felt that his physical and emotional wounds were getting better or, maybe, he had completely lost hope that they would improve—therefore, they weren't bothering him anymore: they became numb.

The number of prisoners in this small and filthy room, in particular, and in the whole prison, in general, was increasing—the jailers became busier. They no longer had time and patience to attend to the old ones. They transferred Hekmat from the tiny room to a big one, where a larger number of detainees were kept.

"Now you have lost your significance. We got more dangerous thugs than you. So you will stay in this room with your buddies until the day your execution verdict arrives," Maulawi Samander, who supervised his cell transfer, told him.

Hekmat's burning desire to write was still alive within him. This desire was the only source that nurtured the tree of his life, which threatened to dry up. Thinking about his novel was luxurious entertainment and it was soothing his mind. He tried to use every available opportunity to think about the character or characters of his novel, its central conflict, and its plot—in the context of his experience with the suicide attack and at the Taliban jail. In order to memorize his thoughts, he would repeat them every now and then.

"Get down everyone, it's a raid, turn the lights off!"

It was midnight when one of the Taliban night guards screamed. Except for one or two militants, the rest of the jailers and their captives were asleep when they were suddenly bombarded by large-sized bullets from a helicopter, which fiercely and indiscriminately targeted the prison. The helicopter circled the prison and made crazy attacks like a hungry wolf trying to smash the body of a dead sheep.

Some people were killed either asleep or awake and some were injured. Hekmat was among the second group. He fell to the ground when he got hit by the debris from the shattered walls of the room. He felt a burning pain in his injured shoulder and passed out.

"I knew that the American bastards had a spy among us."

Just before he fell unconscious, Hekmat saw and heard a wounded prison guard shout these words while pointing his finger at him.

A few hours later, some cells of his brain came back to life and he remembered the incident, envisioning his death at the hands of that mad armed man. Still, he wished to be killed by a bullet coming from a gun instead of being stoned to death in public by the Taliban. He considered himself dead meat. Any minute now, he expected to receive a gunshot from the large rifle that his antagonistic captor always carried.

Tomorrow morning his entire brain awakened. The fear of the Taliban did not allow him to open his eyes.

I better play dead so I don't have to see the face of my executioner. Let him shoot me, he advised himself. *How dear life is! I wish for those who take other people's lives to experience the same feeling as I do now.*

So he played dead and kept his eyes closed until he smelled that the environment he was in, had changed.

Chapter III

The noise and the smell around him told a different story from that of the Taliban prison; people were walking back and forth constantly, speaking in lower voices. With each passing minute, Hekmat's fear of being called insulting names or getting shot by the scary-looking militants diminished. He felt further assured as he sensed an IV tube being attached to his right arm and a respiratory pipe to his nose. He opened his eyes carefully and, with some surprise, observed the white walls of the room, which further encouraged him to look around with fully opened eyes. To his disbelief, instead of the armed Taliban, there were nurses and doctors in white gowns walking around.

You ripped the shroud again, your dream of keeping your promise to little Shaha got rescued, he thought joyfully. Now confident of his safety, he closed his eyes for an extended period to get some rest. When he reopened them a few minutes later, a male nurse was attending to a patient next to his bed. With great effort, he forced his voice to leave his mouth.

"Where am I?" he asked the nurse.

"In the Zabul Civilian Hospital," the nurse replied.

He examined his own body by moving his legs, arms, and neck; everything was fine except that every movement came with excruciating pain.

He remained in the hospital for two more days. During that time, he saw a doctor only once and that one visit by a doctor changed his fate—he recognized the doctor and hoped that the doctor would recognize him as well. Since he hadn't shaved for the past two weeks, his face was covered by white hair. Still, the doctor gazed at him diligently and after hearing his name and his voice, asked, "What's going on brother, what happened to you?"

"*Salaam*, Doctor, how are you?"

"I am fine. Tell me, how are you doing and what happened?"

The doctor was aware of the fact that Hekmat and the other wounded who were brought into the hospital last night had come from a Taliban prison. He wanted to hear more about the story from this patient.

"Aren't you doctor Patyal?" the patient asked enthusiastically, instead of answering the doctor's question.

"Yes, I am. Your face looks familiar to me and I think that I've heard your voice a lot before—who are you?"

Hekmat smiled slightly. Before he said his name, the doctor removed his reading eyeglasses and asked him, "Aren't you Hekmat, my high school classmate?"

"Excellent memory, doc, thank you."

"You're welcome. Now, tell me your story. What happened to you?"

"Do you remember Majid?" asked Hekmat.

After searching his memory for a short while, the doctor nodded.

"Majid, the good poet?"

"Yes. Majid, our classmate."

"What about him?"

"He was killed in a suicidal attack when he came from Kandahar to Kabul to visit me. I transported his corpse back to Kandahar and there another deadly explosion occurred during his funeral in which I was hurt. Afterward, on my way back to Kabul, the Taliban captured me, and then I was severely injured when their hideout was bombed by American helicopters…Now, here I am."

"Wow, it was God's mercy that you survived all these fatal events."

"Yes, of course, it was. I think my shoulder is badly broken. If it is not possible to have it treated here, please send me to Kabul. I would greatly appreciate it."

The doctor examined his patient's injuries, demonstrated his empathy, and nodded approvingly.

"Yes, your shoulder injuries are critical. I'm going to make the recommendation that you are transferred to Kabul."

The next morning, when a couple of nurses delivered his wheelchair to an army helicopter, one of them asked him, "Is the chief physician your friend?"

"Who is the chief physician?"

"Dr. Patyal."

"Oh, yes. He is my longtime friend, thank God I met him here after so many years."

Visiting my homeland cost me my innocence. I am to be blamed for the deaths of Majid and Jaafar. Majid traveled to Kabul to visit me and save me a trip to Kandahar. I was the one who kept Jaafar in Kandahar to accompany me back to Kabul. And now, Zahir is on death row, the executioners of the Taliban and the ISIS are after him. If I don't inform and protect him, I will be responsible for whatever happens to him, too. He thought to himself. He couldn't wait to be discharged from the hospital in Kabul and then find Zahir.

When a doctor at the Jamhoreyat Hospital examined his injuries, he told Hekmat that his shoulder was badly damaged.

"What do you think doctor, how long will my shoulder take to get better and I will be free to go home?" Hekmat asked quickly.

"I can't tell right now. We have to take an X-ray to see how the injury is doing and only then will we be in a position to tell you more about it. If your shoulder needs surgery, then, of course, we will need to do it," the doctor concluded while removing his statoscope from his ears.

Three hours passed since they took his X-ray, but to Hekmat this felt like three days. He spoke to a nurse who happened to be in the room with another patient.

"Do you know if the doctor has looked at my X-ray?"

"Not yet. You must wait; the doctors are very busy," the nurse answered apathetically.

The clock on the wall is dead, he thought. Each time that he looked at it, it showed that only 4 or 5 minutes had passed.

"How long shall I wait, it has been such a long time?" he complained.

"It hasn't been a long time; you can see that the hospital is full of patients and wounded, the doctors are busy," the nurse answered harshly.

A few more hours went by but there was no news about his X-ray results. He felt like he was being strangled and needed to take a walk outside to get some fresh air—but he had no energy to do so. Trying to move his body, he would feel a punitive pain in his hand, shoulder, and leg. He pressed the red button requesting help. It took an hour for a nurse to appear by his bed with a glass of water and oxycodone.

"Any news about my X-ray?"

"Not yet," the nurse said, putting the medication in his left hand and holding a glass full of water to his mouth. "Drink all!" came the command.

He gulped the entire glass of water and then asked the nurse softly, "Do you know how it will take to get my X-ray results?"

"Maybe the doctor will have a chance to look at it in a little bit."

One hour later, the nurse returned to his bed with good news.

"The doctor has looked at your X-ray and said that your shoulder has a fractured bone and should remain in the plaster for a longer time. You should continue taking the medication regularly, but no surgery is needed."

"Thank God," Hekmat shouted. *God, protect Zahir from the danger of terrorists.* He prayed silently.

The oxycodone began working. His pain subsided and his eyes closed. The four to five hours of sleep that followed gave him some energy and relief from pain and headache. He tried slowly and carefully to stretch his arms and legs and felt good about it, despite being painful.

His minor physical recovery, however, brought back

his emotional distress and the agonizing thoughts of self-blame. He was desperate to find a way to alleviate that pain. Writing a book to reveal the innocence of Sheila, Majid, and Jaafar would contribute to awakening greater human awareness about these crimes and it was the one remedy that he hoped for. However, at this point, saving Zahir's life was a more urgent duty to be fulfilled. He was the only one aware of the danger that his "nephew's" life was in and the only one who could help save his life.

The next morning, the nurses were running back and forth in the hospital lobby. The cries and groaning of the newly wounded people who were just brought in woke him. Everyone, the doctors, and the nurses seemed to be in a panic—they desperately tried to attend to the numerous new patients, most of whom were in critical condition. For this reason, the hospital staff ignored the older patients, Hekmat, among them.

Hekmat asked a couple of nurses to do him a favor—to contact his cousin Sultan, who worked for the Afghan National TV. No one would do that. He then decided to leave his room out of desperation. He took a walk in the lobby and moved slowly and carefully toward the end of the long hall. A policeman who stood in front of a room caught his attention. Hekmat approached him.

"*Salaam*, may I ask you a question?"

"Yes, go ahead."

"Are you on duty here or visiting someone?"

The policeman pointed to a patient on a bed in the corner of the room.

"Yes, I am on duty. Why?"

"I thought that if you were going back to the city, I could ask you to do me a favor."

"What favor?" the police soldier asked.

Hekmat moved closer to him.

"I have no one here in Kabul, except for a cousin who is working for the National TV. His name is Sultan. If you could go to the TV station and inform him that I am in this hospital, I would greatly appreciate it."

"I wish I could do that, but I am guarding that prisoner," the policeman pointed to the man lying on a single bed in the room, covered by a blanket. "Don't you have his phone number?"

"No, my phone—which has his number in it—is lost."

"Sorry, I can't do anything to help you."

"That's alright," Hekmat started walking back to his room when a strange, squeaky and cracked voice stopped him.

"Mohi…bullah!"

Hekmat looked around because he neither recognized the voice nor knew anyone by the name of Mohibullah. This time, as he continued to move forward, he heard his own name.

"Hekmat…ulltah!"

Once again, he looked around but saw no one.

The policeman walked closer to his prisoner and warned him.

"You can't talk to anyone here!"

"Please let me see him, it looks like he knows me, please let him talk to me," Hekmat asked for permission from the armed guard while looking at the prisoner attentively.

"Only two minutes, ok?" the policeman emphasized the word "two" and pointed to the person on the hospital bed, whose entire body was covered by a blanket except for his head.

Hekmat moved near the bed and addressed the guy lying on it.

"Who are you bother, I don't recognize you?"

It was hard to hear the patient's voice, his chest was congested and his words were mixed with groaning. Hekmat extended his hand to remove the blanket from the patient's mouth, but a harsh voice stopped him.

"Don't touch him, his entire body is burned!" the policeman commanded Hekmat.

Hekmat removed his hand from the blanket and gazed at the patient's eyes, still unable to recognize him.

"What's your name, brother?"

"My name?" the voice was shaky and mumbling.

"Yes, your name."

"Maulawi… Saman…der."

Hekmat moved closer to his former jailer, looked him in the eyes, and whispered to him, "I am glad that you are alive so that you can taste the pain of wounds, too."

The Taliban interrogator inhaled and exhaled several times, with which came severe wheezing and groaning. He could hardly keep his eyes open and after a few slow blinks, he talked with his eyes closed.

"Do you…see that…Americans kill…their friends… and other…innocent…people…too?"

"Why do you blame them? Because you see them

as *Kafirs*? You are saying that *Kafirs* have no mercy for Muslims…but you guys claim to be Muslims—so why do you kill you Muslims?" Hekmat asked.

"You are…blind to the…truth…we didn't…kill you…but they…wanted to kill you…even…though you are…their friend."

"I'm wondering why you didn't kill me—since you believed that I was a spy for the Americans?"

Maulawi half opened and closed his eyes a couple of times as if he were demonstrating his rage by doing so. When he was able to present his answer, he uttered it with his eyes closed.

"Maybe…God didn't…want you…to die… although…I received…the verdict of your…execution… on the night…of the raid…it was just a matter…of minutes…I was…about to get up…and finish you…when the…damn…helicopter…attacked us."

"Why do you think that maybe God didn't want me to die in your hands?"

"Maybe…you were…innocent," Maulawi replied, without thinking.

"No doubt about it. I was and am innocent. But what about the other people, the little girl, the women, the children, the young and old men that were killed in your suicidal attacks in Kabul and Kandahar—were they all sinners?"

"Maybe their *ajal*—the absolute moment of death determined by God—had arrived."

"What? Are you the angels of death? When God wants to take His creatures' lives, you guys receive His order to fulfill them? That's what you think you people are?"

His eyes closed, Malawi mumbled in a cracked voice, "Someday...maybe I will...be dead or alive...my boys will...get rid of you...and Majid's...other son...God willing."

"You want to murder another innocent man?" Hekmat said outrageously.

"No," Maulawi Samander mumbled. "Everything... is in God's...hands. We do...what He says."

Hekmat was caught by extreme apprehension.

This pig is for real, they have plans to kill Zahir. He thought and moved closer to Samander.

"You can't find him."

Maulawi turned his looks toward him and performed a humiliating smirk with his half-open eyes and whispered: "You pigs... can't escape ... the sword... of Sharia."

The policeman cut off the conversation between the two, asking Hekmat to leave.

The day of his discharge from the hospital arrived. They gave him crutches to use to get to the taxi stand outside the hospital. The nurse checked his blood pressure in a hurry and rushed him out of the hospital.

On the way to Sultan's home, he asked the taxi driver to take him first to a cell phone store, where he purchased a new cell phone, then gave the driver directions to his residence.

"Can you go faster, please?"

It was five in the afternoon. He was anticipating that Sultan would already be back home from work. The radio in the cab announced the time for the evening news.

"According to the Kabul Police Authority, today's

suicide attack left 57 people dead and 112 wounded." The newscast added, "Most of the casualties, which included children and women, were civilians." It went on, "The victims of the blast were taken to the Jamhoreyat Hospital.

He listened to the cab's radio with distrust.

"Is it true?" Hekmat asked the driver.

"Yes, it happened around noon. Didn't you hear it before?"

"No, I was at the hospital, just came out."

"There were two blasts, not one," the driver said. "The second one happened a few minutes after the first one."

"Really? Was it true that so many people got killed?"

"Oh, yes, it was like a blood bath. Thank God I had just passed that point a minute before the first explosion or I would have been dead already."

"How? Tell me the story," Hekmat moaned extensively due to the pain in his shoulder.

"I feel like I was reborn," the driver said thankfully.

"Where in the fourth district are you going to?"

"Near to the women's hospital, my cousin's apartment is there."

"You sound ill, are you okay?"

"My shoulder and my leg hurt, I have a lot of pain."

When the cab stopped in front of the two-story apartment building, Hekmat asked the driver to go upstairs to the second floor and see whether his cousin was home. The cab driver rang the bell a few times but there was no answer.

"I have no other place to go to, please stay here with me until my cousin comes home, I will pay for your time."

"Don't you have his phone number or the key to the apartment?"

"No, my friend. I have returned from a trip to Kandahar."

It got dark. The driver wanted to go home but Hekmat didn't know what to do on his own.

"Don't you have another friend or relative in the entire city?" the driver asked curiously.

"Well," Hekmat said with a heavy sigh. "I know one more person, but I don't have his phone number or home address."

"That's hard," the driver said. "It's getting late, I have to go home. My family is waiting for me. If you don't have a place for the night, I can take you to my house and bring you back here tomorrow."

Hekmat looked at the driver suspiciously and remained silent.

"I know, brother, it's not the time to trust a stranger. Since you have no place to go, you have no choice but to trust me. You look like you have come from a foreign country. I am offering you to stay at my home tonight— the choice is yours."

"Let's go ask that shopkeeper, he might have an idea," Hekmat suggested.

Hekmat got out of the car with difficulty. He walked up to the small local grocery shop and spoke to the man sitting behind the register.

"*Salaam*, brother. Do you know Sultan, who lives in those apartments?"

Hekmat pointed in the direction of a four-flex apartment building.

"May God award him a stay in heaven, he died in the

Shahre-Naw explosions this morning," the shopkeeper, a white-bearded man, said regretfully.

"What? Who are you talking about?" Hekmat asked with panic.

"I am talking about Tour Jan, I mean Sultan, who lives there in one of those apartments. I've known him for at least ten years," the man stressed.

"Oh, God, the merciful!" Hekmat shouted aloud.

He became confused and dizzy. He leaned his back on the stone wall and took a deep breath. He waited by the wall for a few seconds to suppress his desperation. Then, he turned to the driver who was standing by his side in the shop.

"You are right brother, I have no choice but to trust you. Thank you for your offer and let's go to your home."

A customer who had just entered the shop gazed at him attentively.

"Here you are," said the man looking to be in his late fifties. "*Salaam*, brother Hekmat."

"*Salaam*," Hekmat replied coolly. "Sorry, I don't recognize you, who are you?"

"I am Sultan's brother-in-law, Abdul Ghafar," the man said, also sounding mournful. "I know it has been a long time since we last saw each other; maybe you've forgotten me."

Hekmat thought briefly, then leaned one of his crutches against the wall and gave the man a brief hug.

"*Salaam*, brother, Abdul Ghafar," Hekmat said and blinked a few times in an attempt to conceal his tears. "What happened to Sultan, is it true?"

"Unfortunately, yes. He lost his life in today's suicide attack."

"I am such an unlucky man, I've lost Sultan, too," he said while grabbing his crutch.

"Sultan—may God reward him a place in heaven— was worried about you. What took you so long to return to Kabul?"

"It's a long story. I am devastated. My back and my heart are broken for the second time," Hekmat said as extreme sadness resonated in his voice.

"I know, first you lost Majid and now Sultan."

"Did you go to the hospital to see his body?"

"Yes, but they wouldn't allow us to see him today. I will go there again tomorrow."

Losing a friend is always hard. Losing a childhood friend is a misery. Losing the only friend is a catastrophe. Hekmat lost all at the same time. Sultan's death made him forget the pain in his shoulder.

"Let's go to your room. You might need to get rest." Ghafar said.

"I can't stay in this place alone."

"You won't be alone. I'll stay with you."

Hekmat thanked Ghafar and turned to the cab driver.

"Thank you, brother, for your patience and for offering me a stay at your house tonight."

Hekmat handed 1,000 Afghanis to the driver.

"Will it be enough for your fare and time?"

"Yes, it is. Thank you."

That night, Ghafar stayed with Hekmat in Sultan's apartment. They shared their sorrow and spoke of the good memories they had of their mutual family member and friend. Also, Hekmat asked his host whether he knew how to find Majid's son Zahir. Ghafar was not much of help in this matter.

The next morning Hekmat and Ghafar went to the Jomhoreyat Hospital and viewed Sultan's face. Hekmat stayed by his best friend and cousin's body for a long time, finally leaving with tears running down his cheeks.

"Look for a hotel for me in a safer area. I want to get a hotel room," Hekmat told Ghafar on the way back home.

"Brother Hekmat, you can stay here for a few more days. I own this place and have no plans to sell it right away."

"No, thank you. I told you, I can't bear to look at Sultan's empty chair in the living room."

"You won't be alone. I'll be here for a few days because I need to find a tenant or a buyer for this apartment, so you can stay with me until then."

"Ok, if you are going to be here, I'll stay. Thank you."

"You are welcome," Ghafar said. "I hope you don't get bored while I am out during the day."

"Don't worry. In the afternoon, I would like to go to the Ali Abad Hospital to see whether they have any record of Zahir's contact information from the day we received Majid's body from the hospital."

"I think, you should stay home because it's not advisable for you to go out alone because of both your safety and your health," Ghafar told him.

"Hmm," he looked down, then nodded in agreement. "That's what Sultan told me too."

Hekmat was too weak to attend his cousin's funeral. *Let Maulawi Samander be disappointed*, he told himself because he thought of the Taliban prosecutor's threat against him and Zahir as real. Therefore, he felt comfortable not attending his beloved cousin's funeral because, this way, he saved his life and the lives of other funeral attendees from a probable suicide attack. However, after Ghafar left the house in the morning, staying at home proved to be unbearable for Hekmat because he was increasingly worried about Zahir's safety. He felt like he was being tortured by not doing anything to save his "nephew's" life.

Despite the sensible advice from Sultan, as well as Ghafar, he decided to go to Aliabad Hospital. He shaved his beard for the first time after he had left for Kandahar and then took a taxi.

"Please take me to Aliabad Hospital."

"Sure," the cab driver, an old-looking man with an entirely silver beard and mustache said. "Are you okay brother, you sound ill?"

Hekmat took a second to answer.

"What can I say, brother? I feel sad because of these nonsense killings. Only recently, I lost two of my brothers in the *entihari*—suicide attacks."

"I feel sorry for you. But yes, this is the everyday story here. Why are you going to the hospital?"

"Well?" Hekmat said and then remained silent.

The cab driver looked at him in the rearview mirror.

"Your voice and face look familiar."

"I don't know, I don't remember seeing you before."

"Do you have someone in the hospital to visit?" the driver asked curiously.

"No. One of my brothers was kept at that hospital after he was killed by a suicide explosion and his son and I picked up his body."

Hekmat stopped short of explaining the reason for going to the hospital.

The driver once again looked into the rearview mirror and took a good look at his passenger.

"Ok, so what do you want to do there now?"

Hekmat felt embarrassed by the driver's curiosity. He sighed heavily and said in a lower voice, "Brother, I must have a reason for going to the hospital. I don't feel comfortable being questioned. Please take me there faster."

The driver chuckled and asked, "Do you remember the Kabul Energy Authority?"

"Yes, why? I worked there for five years," Hekmat said while trying to get a full view of the driver's face in the mirror. *He is not anyone that I know*, he thought.

"Here, thank you," Hekmat said and extended his hand, which held a 100 Afghani bill, toward the driver as the taxi arrived at the hospital.

The taxi stopped. The driver also quickly got out of the cab and opened the door for his passenger. Hekmat managed to get his crutches out of the vehicle, stepping out slowly.

"Thank you," he said.

The driver smiled.

"Hekmatullah Jan, I am Naqib, Naqibullah—your

former coworker," the driver said, opening his arms wide and moving closer to Hekmat.

Hekmat looked at him closely.

"I can't believe it's you, Nagibullah Jan," Hekmat cheered.

He held both crutches in his left hand and slowly open his right arm for a hug.

"Sorry, my shoulder is hurt," he said.

The two men looked at each other in the eyes, smiling.

"No wonder you didn't recognize me. I got old, am driving a taxi, and my face is covered with white cotton," Naqib said, wiping his long white beard with his right hand.

"Don't say that my friend, we are the same age," Sultan said pointing to his own short white ungroomed beard.

"Now, tell me, what are you doing at the hospital?"

"Well," Hekmat said with a heavy sigh. "I am desperate to find my friend's son, who is living in Kabul. I don't know his address and I don't have his phone number."

"Ok?"

"My friend, Majid, was killed in a suicide attack here in Kabul and was kept for two days at that hospital until his son and I picked up his body. I'm hoping that they have his contact information and will give it to me."

"You just said that your brother was killed by a suicide attack?"

"Yes, Naqib Jan, Majid was my childhood friend, and—to me—he was like a brother."

"Ok, let me park the cab in the parking lot, then we go together."

They went to the front desk. Hekmat inquired about the information he needed.

The person in charge, a heavy, tall man in a blue uniform, examined him from head to toe.

"We don't give away anyone's information. Everything here is confidential," he responded flatly.

"I'm his uncle—you might have my information too."

"It's not important who you are. We simply don't give that information to anyone," the guy repeated resolutely.

Hekmat moved away from the desk in disappointment and pointed to Naqib.

"Let's go. He says it's confidential and won't give it to us."

Naqib got closer to him and whispered in his ear, "You should have let me ask him for the information."

"Why? What's wrong with me?"

"You know, here they look at your suit and boots— your freshly shaved beard with your nicely trimmed mustache and western dress. Everyone knows you have dollars or euros in your pocket," Naqib teased but was serious, at the same time.

"You mean, they want money?"

"Of course. Here, you can't do anything without money."

"Ok, you go talk to him and let me know how much they want," Hekmat moved around the corner in the lobby and let Naqib talk to the man.

After Naqib and the man talked, the man left his desk.

"He wants to talk to his boss. I am hoping…" Naqib told Hekmat in a combination of whisper and sign language.

The man returned to his desk in a little bit and whispered with Naqib. Naqib approached Hekmat.

"Let's go, they are not doing it," Naqib said frowning. "They want five hundred dollars."

"Is that what he said?" Hekmat asked.

"Yes."

Hekmat stopped Naqib from exiting the hospital.

"Let me go talk to him."

Hekmat walked with the use of his crutches up to the front desk and addressed the man behind it.

"Listen, brother, give me my nephew's phone number. It's very important. Otherwise, we'll talk to the head of the hospital," Hekmat said in an authoritative tone.

"It's a big responsibility to give away someone's phone number," the man in the uniform replied.

"He is my nephew. I am not asking for anything illegal," Hekmat stated while moving away from the desk. "Where is the office of the chief physician?" he asked, looking determined to talk to the hospital boss.

The guy was hesitant, not sure if the customer was serious.

"He is not here today," he said.

"Never mind, I can find him," Hekmat said and indicated to Naqib to follow him to the second floor.

"Here, sir," the man ran after them with a piece of paper in his hand and handed the paper to Hekmat.

"Thank God, I got it," Hekmat said with utmost delight after grabbing the piece of paper from the man's hand without paying him anything. He immediately dialed that number from his cell phone. There was no answer. The second time he left a voice message.

It was Thursday. He knew Zahir was off on Fridays only. So he didn't expect a call back from his "nephew" that day.

"If you know where he works, we can drive there now, Naqib proposed.

Hekmat gave Naqib a suspicious look before getting into his cab.

"He is working for the Americans as an interpreter. Please, keep this a secret."

"Sure, don't worry."

"I might need you to help him in the future after I leave for America," Hekmat said.

"Of course. I'm worried about you, too," Naqib emphasized.

"Ok, I'll try to ride with you whenever I want to go out."

"Right. What day do you have time to be my guest?" Naqib asked.

"Well, let me find my nephew first. Then, I'll have peace of mind and maybe one day I'll go with you to your home."

Chapter IV

Losing Majid and Sultan inflicted an enormous blow on Hekmat's emotional stability. His physical health was also impacted—his blood pressure elevated. Constant chest pain, stomach pain, and a lack of apatite became part of his everyday life. He now considered himself to be a hopeless and lonely man in a country in which he was born and raised. He was mindful of the fact that friends can neither be purchase with money nor be attained through beggary. He believed that taking refuge in writing his book was now the only means through which he could cope with his severe frustration and loneliness. This was his only sanctuary, where he could calm his soul's grievances. However, his peace of mind was primarily dependent on ensuring that Zahir was safe. He must do whatever was in his power. Likewise, having the chance to help Zahir and his family was the only—albeit faint and ambiguous— glimmer of joy and hope that was left in his mind. He also hoped that, in this manner, he would soothe his feelings of guilt and somehow recuperate his destroyed innocence.

Zahir worked for Americans in Kabul to support his wife and three little children. Because of his job, he was now facing a death threat from the Taliban, and without any doubt, ISIS as well. As a first-hand witness of this threat, Hekmat was extremely anxious and determined to protect this young family at any cost.

After speaking with Zahir over the phone on Friday,

he obtained his home address and told him that he would visit him and his family in the afternoon of the same day.

"Listen, son," Hekmat told Zahir on the phone. "Don't go out of your home today, okay? It's important."

"Why, uncle, what's going on? I have shopping to do."

"Wait for me, we'll go shopping together."

In the early afternoon, he called Naqib on the phone and asked him to give him a ride to Zahir's house.

Hekmat rode with Naqib and, on the way to Zahir's house, he bought some cookies and fresh fruits.

"I will introduce you to my nephew—please help him with their shopping, doctor visits, or whenever they need transportation," Hekmat asked Naqib.

"I sure will. But, God forbid, times are evil. Murderers smell the existence of interpreters wherever they are. Just last month, they killed one interpreter and his older brother during daylight in the safest area of the city—in Microryans."

"Really?" Hekmat immediately visualized Zahir being shot and killed while shopping in the market.

"Oh yes, these kinds of things happen here very often," Naqib emphasized.

"God forbid such a thing. That's why I'm asking you to help him with their errands as much as possible."

"God willing," Naqib agreed.

"I know that he may not be able to afford the taxi fare so often, but don't worry about it, I'll pay you whatever it costs," Hekmat said.

When they arrived at Zahir's place—a small one-story shabby house located in the eastern part of Kabul—Hekmat was greeted by the entire family as everyone, adults and children, was waiting for him in front of the house. He kissed the kids on the cheeks, Zahir and his wife kissed his hand as a usual way of showing respect to seniors. He pointed to the cab driver and said to Zahir, "This is Naqib, my friend and coworker from forty years ago. He is a good man and I trust him. I already told him to help you with your transportation needs."

"Uncle, I can do my shopping using the city bus, why would I bother Mr. Naqib?" Zahir said and walked towards the cab, which was parked on the road, and shook hands with Naqib.

"No, son, I advise you to use his help whenever you do shopping—you just call him and he will be there for you,"

Zahir seemed unconvinced as to why he should be using Naqib's taxi for his shopping and how he would be able to afford the taxi fare, which was much more expensive than other public transportation.

"I will explain it all to you later at home," Hekmat said as he read Zahir's mind.

It was cold. Hekmat had left his crutches in his hotel room and walking was a slow and arduous process for him. Zahir insisted that he stayed at his home while he and Naqib did the shopping. He agreed and went inside the home. He sat down on the mattress that lay by a wall in the living room.

"You look ill, uncle, what happened to your legs?" Zahir's wife asked.

"It's a long story daughter. I will tell you all about it when Zahir comes back from shopping."

That night, Hekmat enjoyed being at his "nephew's" home and chatting with a family that he would call "my family" for the rest of his life. The husband and wife were kind and respectful to him. The children played and hot Aash, a favorite ethnic dish—a soup of homemade noodles, red beans, and chickpeas topped with sautéed ground beef, liquid whey, and aromatic herbs—was cooking for dinner.

"Son, your father—may God place him in heaven—told me why you took this job. Do you think it is a sure thing that you will go to America?" Hekmat asked Zahir after they ate dinner.

"Yes, uncle, I took this job precisely for that reason. I want to secure a better and safer future for my children in America."

"Is it guaranteed, that they will send you and your family to America?" Hekmat asked inquisitively.

"Yes, uncle. They have already sent hundreds of interpreters with their families to America to live there forever. It's just a matter of working with them for two years—after that, they will send my family and me to America on a special immigrant visa."

"But I heard that their policy has changed lately.

"Not in my case. The change will affect newcomers to this job."

"Good, I'll be so glad to see you living close to me in America," Hekmat said.

"Yes, we will be glad too to live closer to you so that you can help us learn where to send our children to school and how to get a job," Zahir said enthusiastically.

"Sure, I'll help you as much as I can," Hekmat said sincerely. "In America, it's important to have someone to help you establish your life and get adjusted to the new culture and a new way of life."

"Of course, we'll certainly benefit a lot from your experience and knowledge of that country," Zahir said with increased excitement. "Some friends are saying—and I am sure that you know better than me—that America is the land of opportunity. I hope I can work and make a good life there so that my family will live in peace and security."

Hekmat looked at everyone's faces. They sat near one another on a mattress, resembling a typical happy Afghan family.

"Of course son, America is the land of opportunity. There you can live a decent life if you work hard," he nodded in agreement.

"I'm determined, to work hard. Although my English is not bad, I plan to go to school to further improve it and go to university there."

"Yes, that's a good idea."

"Where in America do you live, uncle?" asked Fahima, Zahir's wife, who was particularly excited about moving to that country soon.

"In California."

"Oh, good! Everyone says California is a nice place, with many jobs. We are going to come to California, too," Fahima exclaimed with a big smile of jubilation on her face.

"Certainly, daughter, make sure you tell the Americans to send you to California."

"Zahir already did," she said happily. "Two more months and my children will be going to schools in sunny

California," she added while pressing her arms around two of her youngest children who sat next to her.

"Is it true that you will be done in two months?" he asked Zahir.

"Yes, uncle," Zahir said elatedly.

"When will you be going back to California?" Fahima asked.

"Well, I wish I could go back sooner." Hekmat sighed heavily. "I'm so sad and anguished here because I have lost my two brothers—your father and Sultan."

"Sultan was your cousin, right uncle?" Fahima asked.

"Yes, daughter. He was my cousin but also my best friend. To me, he was like my brother, the same as your father-in-law was. But the thing that I'm now worried about the most is you—you are the target of the Taliban, they are seriously after you," he said, looking at Zahir.

"How do you know that uncle?"

Hekmat looked at the kids, the oldest of whom were playing in the corner of the living room, and made sure that they were not watching. Then, he pulled the right sleeve of his winter coat up to show the adults the white plaster on it.

"You know, on my way back to Kabul, I was captured and beaten by the Taliban. Then there was a helicopter raid on their hideout by American forces, which hurt me badly."

"No wonder it took you so long to return to Kabul. Are you okay now?" asked both Zahir and Fahima unanimously.

"Yes. I am doing better now. My shoulder does not ache that much anymore. But the doctor told me yesterday that I must wait a few more days before getting on an airplane." Hekmat pulled his sleeve back down and added, "When I was in the hands of the Taliban, one of their commanders, who interrogated me, told me that they killed your brother and father because they worked for the Americans and that now it was your turn for the same reason. They are murderers, we must take them seriously."

"Oh God, take us to the safety of America as soon as possible," said Fahima while holding both of her hands up in the air in prayer.

"One of the reasons I am here today is to tell you about that," Hekmat said. "You should never take the bus or walk outside your home until the day you leave for America!" he continued in a serious tone.

"So what shall I do uncle? Every Friday, I have to do the shopping for the week because Fahima is unable to do it," Zahir said anxiously.

Hekmat thought of something, then said, "I can do your shopping while I'm here."

"What about after you leave? We are scared uncle," Fahima said anxiously.

"Naqib will help you, I told him. Either give him the list of the items you need or sometimes you can ride with him, but always look after you," he insisted.

The husband and wife looked at each other, a big question on their minds, *how can we afford the taxi fare every Friday?*

"I know that nowadays the taxi fare is high and hard for you to afford, I will take care of it," Hekmat read their minds.

"Uncle where are you staying here in Kabul?" Fahima asked.

"I still stay at my cousin's house, but now that he is no longer alive, I don't want to stay there alone. I want to get a hotel room."

"Why should you pay for a hotel room? Come stay with us until you go back to America," Fahima said.

"She is right uncle, I will have peace of mind if you stay with us. Fahima is especially scared during the nights that I am not home."

"I would love to. But the problem is that I still have pain in my shoulder and right arm. I cannot move around freely. When staying with my lovely grandchildren, I have to be in a good mood and in good health to play with them," he smiled slightly.

"You are right uncle, our children are kind of bouncy. We pray for your quick recovery," said Fahima

"But please, uncle, come here every Friday while you are still in Kabul," Fahima said.

"Of course. I'll also call you during the weekdays. In case you need any help with shopping or any other urgent matter, just let me know, ok?"

"Thank you, uncle."

As requested by Zahir's mother, Hekmat didn't tell the couple what happened at the funeral in Kandahar. She didn't want her son and his wife to be anxious about their families in Kandahar. Therefore, while Hekmat was still at their house the next morning, Zahir called his mother on the phone and told her that uncle Hekmat spent the night at his place.

She asked her son to give the phone to him.

"*Salaam*, brother, how are you? I'm glad that you are with my son," she said.

"I'm fine, sister. Of course, that's what I promised— that I would check on them all the time."

"Yes, thank you. I hope you're doing better. Please check on my grandchildren very often. They would be missing their grandpa— you be their grandpa now and consider my son and my daughter-in-law as your own children as well!"

"Sure, don't worry sister. As I said before, I'll give them all my love and attention for as long as I live."

"Thank you and May God give you long life and good health!" Majid's widow said and then asked him to give the phone back to her son.

"Don't worry son, I'm sure that your uncle will never leave you alone. He promised me that he would help you and your children." The old lady tried to comfort her son.

Zahir was almost half of Hekmat's age. However, at this young age, he behaved like a wise and mature man. He was a well-mannered gentleman, polite, down-to-earth, as well as a smart and educated person. Like his father, he was tall and had a strong figure with an open forehead, bright eyes, and a straight nose. He treated Hekmat like his true uncle. To Hekmat, being around Zahir brought to his mind the good memories of his "brother" Majid. Hekmat considered Zahir both as a family member and as a prudent friend, with whom he could spend time talking and chatting.

Due to a measure of safety and security, Zahir was not allowed to travel in the city. His employer, the American

Provincial Reconstruction Team, was quite strict about this. Any violation of this rule could cost him his job. His spouse was a housewife and she didn't drive. Therefore, Hekmat was of tremendous help to them both for completing their shopping and providing them with fatherly love and care. He, too, enjoyed being there for them, visiting them every Friday, and—through them—getting a glimpse of the kind of family life that he had grown up with.

On the sixth day after Sultan's death, he packed up his stuff. He asked Ghafar, who was also planning to leave for his home in Paghman that evening, to take him to a hotel in the Wazirabad area, near to Zahir's house. Ghafar insisted that he could stay in this house until it is sold, but it didn't affect Hekmat's decision.

"Thank you. As I said before, I can't be here alone and look at Sultan's empty chair in the living room," he told Ghafar.

"When are you going to leave for America?" Ghafar asked him.

"I don't know. Maybe I'll stay here until Zahir is done with his job and moves to America."

"Why?"

"Well, I don't feel good about leaving before that because, as you know, he is a target for the anti-American and anti-government groups. I have to help him with shopping and so on."

"Hmm," Ghafar said. "You are right. I heard that just in the past few months one or two interpreters were killed."

Ghafar took him to a small-sized hotel, located in

a relatively clean and safe area within only a couple of miles of his "nephew's" house. He felt good about it and checked on Zahir's family by calling his daughter-in-law, Fahima, on the phone almost every day.

At the same time, when he settled in the hotel room, the pain in his shoulder and leg gradually subsided. His mobility improved a bit, but still, for the reason of his safety, he couldn't take a walk outside, which was his favorite type of exercise. He started thinking again about his passion—his dream of writing—as his anger against bullets and dynamite surfaced again.

The next Friday morning, he called Naqib to pick him up from his hotel room. Before going to visit Zahir's family, Naqib drove him to a bakery and a toy store. When he entered his "nephew's" house with two plastic bags full of cookies and toys in his hand, all the kids—seven-year-old Sheila, four-year-old Shapor, and two-year-old Sara—screamed in excitement. Everyone grabbed a full fist of cookies and a toy. From now on, the children called him "grandpa," as their father told them to. Each of them claimed that he was only his or her grandpa.

"He greatly enjoyed that title."

"Congratulation, uncle, you can walk without crutches now," both husband and wife said.

"Yes, thank you."

He enjoyed his time with the family. He established a particularly emotional bond with little Sheila —as soon as he had learned her name. Not only did she have the same name as his own granddaughter but was as cute and as charming as his little Sheila had been, whom he missed very much. Her long hair, which covered her rosy cheeks and which she would throw over her shoulder to the side without using her hands, would make him long to take her into his arms and kiss her repeatedly. He wished Zahir was done with his job today and that the family could fly with him to the USA tomorrow.

The next evening, he was at Naqib's house for dinner. The two old coworkers shared their memories. They told one another stories from the time after they had separated from one another until now. They had become friends while working at the Kabul Power Authority around forty-five years ago. They had much in common to make them friends—both were honest and hard-working, both disliked and fought corruption in their workplace, and both liked listening to Indian classical music.

Hekmat openly expressed his anxiety over the fact that the Taliban were after Zahir because he worked for the Americans.

"I know, I've heard of several such cases. These poor interpreters live in fear. But I will do everything possible to protect him."

"Thank you. I will wait a few more days to see what happens, then I'll let you know what I'm going to need from you."

"Ok, anytime, my friend," Naqib said resolutely. "Would you like to have a tour of the city tomorrow? That way you will kill one day of your time."

Hekmat thought about it briefly

"Not a bad idea. Actually, I would like to pay a visit to Kabul University. I hope to run into one of my classmates or friends there. I believe one or two of them worked at the Faculty of Law and Political Science as assistant professors."

It was a sunny and mild day. The first two-story building of Kabul University that was across the road from where he got out of Naqib's taxi was the Faculty of Law and Political Science. He walked straight up to the second floor of the building as he was very familiar with the place. Before looking for offices of professors, he went to the other side of the L-shaped lobby, where classes were located. The classrooms were full of students and teaching was in progress. He snuck through a little door window into the first classroom and gazed at the last row of chairs, where he used to sit during his four years of study.

"You sit in the last row because you don't want the class to see your dry lips, wrinkled face, and sleepy red eyes," one of his classmate buddies had told him jokingly at the time.

But his reason for doing so was something else.

"No, I chose the last row because, whenever I ask my professors a question or I'm answering their questions, I want to speak loudly and clearly so that the entire class can hear me. I like that."

While still looking through the little window, he heard somebody in the back asking him.

"May I help you?"

He turned around, gazed at the man in a dark- blue suit, white shirt, and burgundy tie. He didn't recognize the man.

"I am looking for Professor Basharmal Sahib," he whispered, feeling ashamed for sneaking into a classroom.

"Basharmal Sahib is no longer here," the man said but quickly looked at Hekmat in the eyes and put his hand over his shoulder. "Wow, Hekmat Jan, is that you?"

Hekmat, still staring at the man, blinked a few times. Finally, he recognized the man and said, "Be careful, Farooq Jan, my shoulder hurts!"

"Why, what happened to your shoulder?" Farooq asked while holding his former classmate's left hand and walking him to his office around the corner.

"Never mind, it's a long story. How are you doing? I'm so glad to see you alive!"

Farooq opened his office door for him and took a seat next to him on a long sofa instead of sitting on his chair behind the desk.

"I'm also glad to see you after such a long time," he said and did a quick calculation. "Almost thirty or thirty-two years, right?"

"Yes, almost thirty-two years," Hekmat replied while reading the name tag on the desk, *Dr. M. Farooq, Dean of the Faculty of Law and Political Science.* "Congratulations, where did you do your doctorate?"

"In France."

"I know you deserve to be the Dean here as you were one of the smartest and most intelligent students."

"Oh, no kidding, Hekmat Jan—I was nothing compared to you."

"Tell me, who else from our classmates or professors is still around?"

"Not many, some have died and some went to foreign countries, like yourself."

"What about Basharmal Sahib, our psychology professor?"

"He died when his home was hit by a rocket, may God bless him."

"Oh, I'm so sorry to hear that. He was such a nice instructor," Hekmat said sadly. "He was such a good person, too."

"I know. I remember that he liked you, too." Dr. Farooq said. "So, are you still living in America?" Farooq asked but hastily left the office before Hekmat could answer, returning a few moments later with a teapot and a cup. "Sorry, Hekmat Jan, you came at a bad time. I have to go to an assignment in half an hour."

"That's ok. Where are you going?"

"I have to go to the entrance exam training center and I will probably be there until late in the evening."

"What's that?"

"The high school graduates from all the provinces are here to take their entry exam for the university, which is going to be the day after tomorrow. The president of our university has instructed me, along with one other professor, to go and help familiarize the students with the rules and procedures of the exam," Farooq explained while he poured green tea into a cup and placed it on the coffee table in front of his friend. "Tell me, where are you staying in Kabul?"

"In a hotel."

"Why in a hotel?" Farooq asked with astonishment. "You have no one in Kabul, no family or friends?'

Hekmat's face turned pale and his lips started quivering. He said nothing.

"Why, what happened?" Farooq realized something terrible must have happened to him.

"Do you remember my cousin and friend Sultan?" Hekmat asked in a sorrowful tone.

"I sure do. The one who was studying journalism at the same time you and I were students."

"Yes. He died in the Shahr-e Naw suicide attack last week."

"I'm sorry to hear that. I was going to ask you about him. He was such a humorous guy."

"It's so unfortunate," Farooq said. "Listen, Hekmat Jan, give me your phone number and the hotel address— you pack up your stuff by 5 p.m. tomorrow. I am going to take you to my house in Microryan."

"Why should I pack up?"

"Because you are going to stay with me as long as you are in Kabul."

"No, Farooq Jan, I don't want to be a burden for you."

"No, you won't be a burden for me. I have a two-bedroom apartment and I live by myself. I will tell you my story, the sad story of my family tomorrow, okay? I have to leave in a couple of minutes."

"Well. What can I say?" Hekmat murmured.

"Please don't say anything, I know you are bored."

"Ok, buddy. Thank you for your consideration."

"You said your hotel is in the Wazirabad area?" Farooq asked while he put on his winter coat.

"Yes."

"Let's go, it's not too far. I will drop you off by your hotel."

"No, thank you. I have a taxi waiting for me outside."

"Ok then, see you tomorrow at 5 p.m.," Dr. Farooq said, held Hekmat's left hand, and walked him to the door. "Let me introduce you to professor Sohail."

Hekmat read the sign on the door, which said, *Dr. Sohail, Head of the Criminal Psychology DPT.* Farooq knocked on the door and entered the room.

"*Salaam, ustad,* this is Hekmat, my former classmate."

The 75-year-old professor with long silver hair and a penetrating look put down the book he was reading on his desk and stood up. He walked over to Hekmat and they shook hands.

"I am privileged to meet you, sir," said Hekmat, putting his left hand on his chest as a sign of respect.

"Me too," the professor said and asked his guests to take a seat.

"Thank you, *ustad,* I just wanted to introduce my buddy to you and to invite you for dinner at my place tomorrow night. He will be there, too."

"What time tomorrow?"

"Will 6 p.m. work for you?"

"Fine. The same address, yes?"

"Yes, sir."

Farooq and Hekmat left the professor's office and walked together to the parking lot.

"You called him *ustad,* master, did he teach you after we graduated?" Hekmat asked.

"He didn't. At the time that you and I were students, he taught at Yale University in America. He is a very knowledgeable person and here he is considered to be a living reference. Especially when it comes to the subject of criminal psychology, we are all learning from him and that's why everyone calls him *ustad*,

"Interesting. I look forward to meeting with him tomorrow night, I have an important issue to discuss with him," Hekmat said enthusiastically.

"What issue?" Farooq asked.

"It's about a tragedy that shook an entire town in America. A man went to an elementary school and killed children, his own daughter among them. To this day, no one has any idea what the motive of the killer had been. I did a lot of research but haven't succeeded in figuring out why that man—who was educated, enlightened, hardworking, and family-oriented—would murder his only child, a pretty little girl. I'm hoping that the science of psychology might have an answer to my question. Since he lived in the US and is an expert on the subject, I'm sure I'll learn something from him, which is something I've wanted for a long time."

"Why are you so interested in this issue of motive?"

"Huh," Hekmat sighed heavily. "My lovely granddaughter was also among the dead."

"Oh, really? I'm sorry to hear that. I'm sure that Dr. Sohail will offer a scientific analysis on the subject."

After the two friends parted from each other, Hekmat observed changes in his mind and body. For the first time in a long while, he noticed that he could walk faster than before. His head felt lighter and without any ache. When he stepped out of the building, he sensed the freshness of the air that reminded him of the wonderful time when he was a student at this faculty. He was able to take the long walk to the parking lot, where Naqib was waiting for him.

"Very good, you walked a long way without your crutches," Naqib told him as he got into the cab.

"Yes, I feel a lot better."

"Let's go to my house for lunch, ok?" Naqib asked.

"No, thank you. You go to work and make some money. I want to get some rest."

The rest of his day was long but full of excitement. He took a nap and ate his dinner around 5 p.m. He couldn't wait to be together with his classmate and friend and to have a discussion with Dr. Soahil tomorrow. Time was going slowly; he tried to make it pass faster by reading a book and reviewing what he had most recently written. Around 7:00 p.m., he took a break from reading the book and stretched by walking up and down the stairway from the second floor, where his room was located, to the hotel lobby on the first floor. He happily noticed that the pain in his shoulder and leg had diminished considerably. He continued walking and took brief breaks alternately until the clock showed it was 8 p.m. Then, he switched on the TV.

"The suicide attack today took the lives of 50 and injured 70 high school graduates who have come to the capital to prepare for taking the Kabul University entry exam."

This was the first piece of news. While leaning back on the sofa, he listened to the news absentmindedly. When the camera focused on the pictures of the crime scene, it resembled a war zone—more than a hundred bloody heads, hands, feet, as well as shoes, hats, exam papers, booklets, and pens were scattered around. Hekmat's eyes were now pinned to the screen. However, his mind was processing the scene as if it had happened in the past. He took a deep breath and continued to stare at the TV screen.

50 dead and 70 wounded, these young boys and girls had brought their love for education here, along with their hopes for a better future. Now, everything is gone with the wind, he thought. All of a sudden, he remembered that this was where Dr. Farooq was headed when they parted, where he was supposed to train the high school graduates about the rules and procedures of the university entry exam. He quickly turned his face away from the TV and laid on the sofa, feeling a sharp pain in his skull. He rubbed his head but the sharp pain in the central part of his skull persisted. He reached a bottle of baby aspirin, recommended by his doctor for the prevention of heart attack and stroke, and took one tablet with water.

Samander and his comrades must be celebrating their victory and must consider themselves to be nice human beings, or good Muslims, or devoted soldiers of Islam, or genuine Mujahidin, or true patriots, or proud national heroes. He thought. *Oh, God, please save Farooq!*

He hurriedly dialed Farooq's number—it went straight to voicemail. He repeated the call three times in a row; it was the same story all three times. His heart began beating faster and faster as the mere thought of losing another friend seemed unbearable to him. He couldn't do anything to find out more about Farooq's fate—he didn't have his home address. His helplessness further aggravated the pain in his chest and skull.

That night was one of the worst and most stressful nights of his life—he couldn't fall asleep nor was he in the mood to entertain himself by thinking about his novel. He turned and tossed in his bed until past 2 a.m. The bloody bodies of Farooq and 120 young boys and girls were dancing in his imagination.

The next morning, he woke earlier than usual. Without eating breakfast, he ran out of the hotel. He took a taxi to Kabul University, without even bothering to call Naqib—his trusted cab driver—for his own safety. After getting out of the cab and despite his injuries, he virtually ran to the Faculty of Law building. He wished that he would find Farooq standing at the entrance of the building or walking in the stairway or appearing behind a corner of the lobby. On the second floor, he strode to Dr. Farooq's office and violently pulled the knob. It didn't turn. He pushed the door; it was locked. He knocked on it once, twice. There was no answer. He then moved to the next door, which was the office of the Assistant Dean of the Faculty, and inquired about his friend.

"We are sorry to say that our Dean was among the victims; they took him to the hospital but couldn't save his life," the person behind the desk—the Assistant Dean apparently—said with sadness.

Hekmat went back to the lobby and desperately looked for Dr. Sohail's office. He missed the big sign on the next office door- *Dr. Sohail, Head of the Criminal Psychology DPT.* He once again knocked on the Assistant Dean's office and asked about the professor's office.

"Next door," the Assistant Dean pointed to the corner.

Hekmat knocked on that door but it didn't open. He pushed the door and found that it was locked. He went to the Assistant Dean's office for the third time.

"I am terribly sorry for bothering you again, can you please let me know about the day and place of Dr. Farooq's funeral and *fateha*?"

"Sure. Give me your phone number. I will call you as soon as I receive that information from his family."

This time he left the faculty of law building with a different kind of "gift"—instead of Farooq's invitation for dinner, he got the news of his friend's death. He didn't even feel like answering Naqib's phone call the first two times he called. The third time, he was ready to share his feelings.

"*Salaam*, brother, how are you?" Naqib asked.

"Traumatized, destitute, desperate, and sad," he replied loudly.

"What? Why, brother, what's going on?"

"My friend that I told you about last night, Dr. Farooq, was among the victims of yesterday's explosion."

"Oh, I'm sorry to hear that. I was happy that you finally had a friend to stay with. Where are you now?"

"At the university."

"Do you want me to pick you up?"

"Yes, please. I can't even walk to the road to take a taxi."

When Naqib arrived, he found Hekmat sitting on the ground by the entrance door of the Faculty of Law, his back leaning on the wall. Despite Naqib's insistence, he refused to go with him to his house. He preferred to go to his hotel room and be alone.

He spent almost the entire day in his bed. Toward the evening, he got up, went downstairs, and ordered a meal from the hotel restaurant. While still sitting in the waiting area, the TV set on the wall across from him announced the 6 p.m. news hour. He turned away from the TV screen, scared of seeing the same bloody scene again.

For the first time since coming to Afghanistan, he received a phone call from Allen. When his phone's screen showed Allen's name, he answered the call taciturnly.

"Hi, Allen."

"Hi, buddy, how are you? I've been expecting a call from you to get together and enjoy hot Aash at your cousin's place someday."

"Sorry, I didn't get a chance to give you a call. Actually…"

"I know you are busy with friends and family, but I really want to spend some time with you and your cousin," Allen cut Hekmat off enthusiastically.

Hekmat remained silent.

"Are you busy?" Allen inquired.

"Yes," Hekmat said emotionlessly. "Everyone is busy. Some are busy making weapons and bombs. Some are occupied carrying out the killings. Some are engaged in digging graves, while the rest of the people are busy attending funerals and services. This is what life is all about in the two nice countries that I belong to."

"Wow, you have strong emotions Mr. Hekmat, what's going on, what are you busy with?"

"I'm busy mourning the loss of my friends and family."

"Who? Who did you lose?"

"Whom did I lose?" Hekmat said angrily.

"Yes."

"Majid, Jaafar, Sultan, and Farooq, I can't further explain who they were."

"Oh, God, I'm sorry to hear that," Allen said emphatically. "Is there anything I can do for you?"

"No, thanks."

"When are you planning to go back to the US?" Allen asked.

"I don't know. I have a dilemma."

"What kind of dilemma? Can you share it with me?"

"Well," Hekmat mumbled. "Remember that in the airplane I told you about my nephew, who works for Americans as an interpreter? He and his family need my help for a few weeks until he finishes his contract and leaves for the US."

"Yes, I do. But what kind of help does he need? Is it financial or what?"

"No, it's not financial. You know, working for Americans is risky. Terrorists like the Taliban, ISIS, and others are after them."

"Right, I know that. But how can you protect them without a gun, do you need one?"

Hekmat was mad. "I will think about it," he replied, wishing to end the conversation with Allen.

"Yes, Mr. Hekmat, think about it seriously. If you want to get one, I can help get you a good one."

The idea of going back to America as soon as possible and purchasing a last-minute ticket had been on his mind since yesterday. He wished to escape the suffocating atmosphere of the country in which violence had taken all his friends and connection. He had nightmares at night in which he and Zahir were blown up in suicide bombings. Therefore, he wouldn't even consider attending Farooq's funeral. The burden of announcing his decision to leave for America to Zahir weighed heavily on his nerves.

How shameful it will be, he thought.

Hence, he decided to allow himself some more time to sleep on this idea or, at least, to let the element of time lessen his feelings of shame more or less. He took an aspirin and went to bed.

The next morning, when the first phone call came in, he felt panic. He thought it was the Assistant Dean of the Faculty of Law telling him about the time and date of Farooq's funeral. But it was Zahir on the phone checking on him.

"*Salaam* uncle, how are you? Did you enjoy staying with your classmate and friend last night?"

He didn't feel comfortable talking about that tragedy at the time.

"Ok, son, how are you and your family?" he replied.

"We are fine, uncle. I am home and waiting for you."

"Ah, son, I am tired and stressed a bit," he said in a gloomy voice.

"Why, what happened?"

"I can't even talk about it right now. Do you need anything from the markets today?"

"No, uncle, Fahima did the shopping early in the morning."

"Why didn't you call Naqib?" He asked Zahir.

"It's ok, she only needed a couple of items. We'll do a bigger shopping trip next week."

"In this case, I will come over next Friday, for sure."

Zahir was silent. Hekmat overheard Zahir's wife, Fahima, saying, "Let me talk to him!"

"*Salaam*, uncle, please come for dinner; my children want to see you, too. I am going to cook our ethnic lamb soup, which I am sure you will like on this cold night!"

"Ok, daughter, I can't disappoint you. I will be there by dinner time," Hekmat said after a brief pause as he couldn't resist the love of "his" family, especially the wish of the little kids. "But listen, daughter," he continued, "I have an American friend who likes Aash, can you cook Aash instead and I will invite him for dinner?"

"Of course, uncle. I have everything I need to make Aash," Fahima said happily.

"I want to ask Zahir, too, about bringing my friend?"

"He overheard you and is saying, yes, please, bring your friend, too."

"Ok, I'm going to give him a call. I hope he agrees. If I don't call you back, it will mean that he'll be coming over for dinner."

Allen accepted Hekmat's invitation to join him for dinner at Zahir's place.

"Sure, buddy," Allen told Hekmat on the phone. "Even though, due to security reasons, we are extremely careful about going to our Afghan friends' homes—but, of course, I trust you and gladly accept your invitation."

"Good, thank you. Please pick me up from my hotel, we will go together."

After the hot Aash was served and consumed, Allen expressed how very much he enjoyed it. He praised the couple for already speaking English. He told them that they were going to have a wonderful life in America and that their children would live in peace and security.

"I have to leave. Thank you for your tasteful Aash, I loved it." Allen rose and spoke to Hekmat before saying goodbye. "Think about what I told you the other day."

"I will," Hekmat replied, not bothering to disclose what was discussed between the two of them.

The guest left. The family was enjoying the company of their uncle, whose support was crucial to them in their future life in America. After listening to the sad experiences that Hekmat recently went through, Fahima spoke.

"Oh, God, we are so sorry for you, you lost so many of your friends."

"Thank you, daughter. Now, you are the only ones I have. May God protect you against all hazards and please be careful until you leave for America.

"Uncle, we are so happy that we have you. We feel like our father is sitting with us," Fahima said and Zahir echoed his wife's feelings.

It was green tea time as usual after dinner. Fahima filled her "uncle's" cup and placed it before him, then brought a platter of *fereney*—a traditional dessert made of milk pudding topped with minced cardamom and pistachios.

"Uncle, what do you think if, in America, I go to school in the morning and Zahir cares for our children until I return home, and then he goes to work in the afternoon? I want to learn English and then get a good job, maybe nursing?" Fahima asked so excitedly as if she were already on an airplane headed to the US.

"What if I want to go to school, too, to improve my English?" Zahir said nervously.

"Well," Fahima said proudly, "in America, men and women are equal and both can go to school and work. I want to have a good job there."

"It will be a while until you learn English well enough and qualify to get a job," Zahir argued. "I will do both things—study English and support you until after my English is good enough for me to find a well-paid job. Then you can go to school."

"There is a way out of this problem," Hekmat intervened, addressing the couple. "You can both go to school and Zahir can work at the same time. The adult school has classes in the evening, too. He can go to work during the day and then, in the evening, you can both go to school together."

"That's good; I'm happy to learn more English," Fahima said and looked at her husband. "I also have a bachelor's degree as he does."

"Yes, we were classmates at the Faculty of Economics at Kabul University," Zahir said.

"So that's where you guys found each other, ha?" Hekmat asked with a smile.

"Yes, uncle. but I am one year older than her," Zahir commented.

Looking for the right moment to announce his decision to leave Afghanistan, made him miss this explanation.

A phone call interrupted their discussion and made Zahir shout.

"*Salaam*, mother, how are you?"

"I'm fine son, how are you and Fahima and my lovely grandchildren?"

"We are all doing well. Listen, mom, uncle Hekmat is here too, in our home."

"Good, is he okay? I want to talk to him later but wanted to let you know that your uncle Suleiman is going to have a work-related trip to Kabul next week."

"Really? That's wonderful news, mother. We missed him," Zahir said excitedly. "When is he going to come?"

"He said that he was going to call you and let you know about it. I think he mentioned that he will leave a week from today and might be there for two months." Zahir's mother was happy both because her brother was going to be with her son and grandchildren for a while and also because Hekmat was visiting them too. "Let me talk to brother Hekmat."

Hekmat overheard his brother's widow and thought to himself, *that's great, they will not be alone, now I can leave for America with my mind at peace.*

Zahir handed the phone over to Hekmat.

"*Salaam*, sister, how nice it is to hear from you."

"Yes, brother, I'm glad you are there with my son's family and checking on them."

"Yes, of course. I will miss them if I don't see them every Friday."

"God bless you. I am delighted that they will have you in America to help them and take care of them, especially my grandchildren."

"Certainly, sister, I will be with them and help them with all the means at my disposal."

"As I told you in Kandahar, I leave them first in God's hands and then in yours. Your brother's soul, Majid's soul, is looking down upon you!" The lady said in a weepy tone as if she was begging Hekmat to care for her grandchildren and their parents once they are in America.

"I know, sister, don't worry, I will never disappoint my brother's soul," Hekmat said categorially, then said goodbye to Majid's widow.

After Zahir's mother hung up, Hekmat surprised the couple by announcing that he would be leaving the country next week.

"I'm glad that you will not be alone. I had such a hard time thinking about going to America and leaving you alone."

"Thank you, uncle, we will miss you," both the husband and wife said.

Realizing that their shopping and errand trips will still remain a problem and that, even with Suleiman being with them, Zahir might still need Naqib's help with transportation, Hekmat thought of something and shared it with the couple at breakfast the next day.

"Even though your uncle is going to be here, I think that during the day he will be busy with his official business. I urge you to use Naqib's help for your transportation," Hekmat said while drinking his green tea. "I am going to ask Naqib to take you anywhere you need to go shopping or anything else. I know your income is not enough to pay for all the taxi trips and it's expensive too, so I am going to give Naqib some money—enough to give you a ride two times a week for the two months that you will be here."

"That is too much money, uncle?" Zahir said.

"That's ok. I can afford it."

On the day of his departure, he discussed with Naqib what he told Zahir and Fahima. He put 500 dollars' worth of Afghan money into an envelope and gave it to him to help Zahir with his family's transportation needs.

"This is too much, my brother," Naqib said after counting the money.

"Well," Hekmat said, pressing Naqib's hand in a friendly manner. "Too much or not, it's yours now. After I leave, please, you be their uncle in my place and care for them as the children of your brother."

"Of course I will, Hekmat brother, don't worry."

Chapter V

Leaving his homeland this time seemed to him to be as hard as it was for a bride to leave her parent's house forever. He was emotionally tied to the souls of his lost friends as if each one of them—Majid, Sultan, Jaafar, and Farooq—begged him, *Dear Hekmat, don't go, stay here and pay a visit to our graves sometimes!* He felt like the fragments of his inner self were scattered across the country—a part of him was buried in Kandahar, two pieces in Kabul... and God knows where poor Jaffar's body was at this point. Was it buried somewhere, like a normal human being, or was it thrown somewhere in the desert and torn apart by animals?

When the aircraft took off and gradually gained altitude, he looked through the window down at his country of birth, whispering silently, *what a gift you gave me, my motherland!*

When the airplane became entirely engulfed in the cloud, he leaned back in his seat. In a matter of seconds, his mind went back to the subject of his book. Remembering the disastrous events that took his loved ones from him intensified his hunger for writing. He deeply wished to expose the crimes committed against Sheila, Majid, Sultan, Jaafar, and Farooq. His thirst for writing was no longer just a hobby or a dream or a mandate—but it became a debt that he owed to the memories of those who would live in his heart forever. His mind went back, thinking about the subject of his book—the motive of Sheila's killer—until the end of the first part of his journey.

He enjoyed his stay at the Frankfurt airport during the six-hour stopover, where he felt safe for the first time in the past five weeks. He spent most of the time relaxing on a couch and taking slow walks in the long halls of the airport.

After he became exhausted from walking and thinking at the same time, he took a short nap, which didn't last long. A phone call from Afghanistan interrupted woke him up. Zahir and his wife spoke with him and wished him again a safe trip back to America. Before he hung up the phone, Zahir's wife asked, "Uncle, can you please look for a safe area in California with a good school for our children?"

"Yes, daughter, I will. Make sure they send you to northern California," he said, stressing the word "yes."

God, help me find a safe area and a good school for my grandchildren.

The six-week time period before Zahir and his family arrived in California was full of mixed feelings of excitement and anxiety. He was excited about the day of "his family" arrival but was also anxious for the very same reason as well—finding a safe area with a good school for little Sheila who was already of school age. Enrolling Sheila in the same school where his granddaughter Sheila was killed, was not an option as he didn't feel comfortable with it. Therefore, he ruled out the idea of looking for a rental place for them in his neighborhood. Looking for an apartment in a safer area, close to a highly rated elementary school and also near an adult school was the criteria of his search, which kept him pretty busy.

Using Craigslist, he found two to three addresses daily and drove to each one of the prospective rental apartments to check the area and to get information about the schools nearby. Within a week or so, he had seen quite a few places that seemed relatively nice and met the criteria of his first and foremost concern—a good school for "his grandchildren."

Time started to go by faster. Zahir and his family were arriving in a few days. He started to clean and organize his own house. He did the shopping, which included buying cookies and other goodies for the kids, as he wanted the family to stay with him for a few days until they had some rest and could choose a place from the list of apartments he had prepared for them.

"What time and day are you arriving?" he asked Zahir over the phone.

"On Tuesday," Zahir said, implying that they would be in California in four days.

"What time? What's your flight number?"

"I don't have the ticket with me right now. Why, uncle?"

"I want to pick you up from the airport."

"You don't have to. The International Rescue Committee arranged that for us. They said that they already found an apartment for us and are going to help us with some houseware too."

"Did you tell them to take you to my city, Richmond, or somewhere near?

"Yes, but they said that they made arrangements for us in Oakland."

"That's ok. But I want you to stay with me for a few days until you adjust."

Zahir remained silent. Hekmat heard Fahima saying something.

"Uncle, Fahima says 'thank you,' but we don't want to bother you with our messy kids," Zahir repeated what Fahima had said. "You know uncle, women like to have their own place."

"I know. That's fine," Hekmat said knowing that insisting would not work. "Call me when you get to your new home here."

"Sure, uncle."

———

Zahir and his family were now in California. On the day of their arrival, Zahir told Hekmat over the phone that they were housed in a two-bedroom rental apartment in the city of Oakland and that the IRC helped them with some food items as well as with some basic houseware items.

"I am glad you are here. Get some rest and don't buy more stuff for your home. I have some houseware items for you, too. I will bring them over in two or three days after you get settled a bit," Hekmat told his "nephew" over the phone while writing down his address.

Two days later, he loaded his Toyota sedan with some new houseware items and toys as well as cookies and candies. When he arrived at their address, it was already dark. He parked his car on the street and walked up to the gate of a large apartment complex. Zahir and his wife were waiting for him by the entrance. They gave him a warm welcome and directed him to their apartment on the second floor.

"Where are the kids?" he asked while walking along with the couple to their home.

"They are home," Zahir answered.

"Why—you guys left them home alone?"

Zahir and his wife looked at each other and Fahima murmured, "We just left them home."

Hekmat was enjoying being with the family that he considered to be his own and, more so, he loved the cheerful faces of the children when they were playing. After getting a little rest and sipping a cup of green tea, he asked the family to help him carry the stuff from his car.

Fahima stared at her husband first and then asked Hekmat, "Where did you park your car, uncle?"

"On the street, just around the corner."

"The manager told us we have a parking space inside, but every day somebody parks their car in our space," Fahima expressed said unhappily.

"It's alright when you get your own car, we will take care of that," Hekmat assured them. "Let's bring the stuff."

Fahima once again gave her husband a meaningful look.

"Ok, uncle, Zahir, and I will go with you; the children can stay here," she said hesitantly.

"Why can't the children go with us? There is a bit

too much stuff; they can help, too. Besides, we shouldn't leave them home alone."

This time a bitter smile appeared on Fahima's lips, she gazed at Zahir and silently asked him to explain to their "uncle" why she was unwilling to take their children out with them.

"It's ok, the children can go with us," Zahir said, ignoring his wife's concern.

But the dubious exchange between the couple made Hekmat question the reason for it. After a short silence, he asked Fahima why she was hesitant. She didn't answer but did seem worried.

"Is there a problem with taking the children with us?" Hekmat asked, staring at Fahima.

"Uncle," she groaned. "Late last night, there was gunfire just behind our apartment. Our neighbor told us today that a man's dead body just lay there until the morning. My children are scared to go out."

"Actually, she is more scared than the children are," Zahir said mockingly.

"Hum," Hekmat said and, after thinking briefly, he pointed to Zahir and continued, "Let the two of us go and bring the stuff—maybe two trips will be enough!"

Hekmat got an idea, realizing that this family had already been touched by the gun problem. After delivering the stuff from his car, he opened the toy bag and gave the toys to the children. They were cheerful. Each one grabbed a toy and some cookies and candies. The couple was also pleased to receive the much-needed kitchenware, a new landline telephone, a couple of curtains, and four colorful blankets for the children that he had brought.

"Thank you, uncle, for buying us so many things," Fahima said while pouring more green tea into his cup.

"You are welcome, daughter. It's nothing."

"I wish we never hear another gunshot here—or I will be very unhappy that we came to this area," she spoke in a severe tone.

"Don't be scared that soon, bad things can happen anywhere!" Zahir addressed his wife.

"Why not? A gunshot is a gunshot, it kills. How can we raise our children in a place in which bullets fly in the air and people can be killed just behind our apartment?" Fahima said in a shaky voice.

"I agree with you both," Hekmat intervened, then continued with a slight sigh. "It's true that America is a big, rich, and powerful country. Still, this doesn't mean that there are no bad people here and that bad thing does not happen here." Hekmat was mindful of the fact that he should prepare the newcomers to accept the harsh reality of gun violence in their new country. "It's the other way around, a lot of bad things can happen here and a lot of bad people exist here. So we have to watch after our children and ourselves."

Fahima dried a couple of teardrops that had made their way down her face, and spoke in a worrisome voice, "If my children are afraid to go out of the house, how can they go to school? We thought that we will be living in peace in America, but it is the same as in Afghanistan"

"Don't cry. We can look for another place with the help of our uncle!" Zahir tried to comfort his wife, topping her on the shoulder.

"How much is your rent here?" Hekmat asked Zahir.

"It's $1,800 a month."

"Did you pay?"

"No, the IRC paid the rent for one month. They also paid the security deposit, but we have to pay rent for the next month."

"How can we afford to pay rent when we have no income?" Fahima told her husband so seriously that it seemed as if they had never spoken about this before.

"I will try to get a job. You don't need to be so anxious about it so soon."

Hekmat was drinking his tea one sip at a time while keenly listening to the discussion. After he emptied his cup of tea, he spoke in a calm and assuring tone.

"Don't worry, daughter. I will think about finding Zahir a job, which is, of course, the most important thing for your family."

"Please, uncle, do something about it, you are the only one we have here. Please help us," Fahima said.

"Sure, daughter. I will try my best,"

"Uncle," Zahir said. "Our neighbor downstairs is also an Afghan—he drives a taxi. He told me that the company he works for needs more drivers, can you help me get a driving license?"

"Sure. Can you drive?"

"Yes. I have six years of driving experience, I drove my dad's car. My Afghan driving license is still valid."

"Good. Here, you will need to get a driving permit first and you need to study for the test."

"Yes, that's what the neighbor told me. He gave me the DMV booklet."

"Good, study the booklet. On Monday, I will take you to the DMV to get you a driving permit," Hekmat said while looking at his wristwatch, signaling his intention to leave.

"Uncle, don't go, please stay with us tonight!" Fahima said.

"No, daughter, I have to go home. I will come on Monday."

"Uncle, if you think our place is small, it might be— but our hearts are not. We have plenty of space for you in there," Fahima insisted.

"Thank you daughter, that's very kind of you. Still, I think I should leave you guys to have some time alone and to get comfortable."

"We are comfortable with you, uncle," Zahir said. "Unless you don't feel content with our children?"

"Oh no, son, I love children. Being with your beautiful kids makes me feel especially happy."

"It's Friday, please stay overnight!" both husband and wife said at the same time. "You can have the smaller bedroom. Sara will sleep with us. Shapor and Sheila can use the living room. You brought us enough blankets," Fahima added.

After Fahima was assured that her "uncle" would be staying overnight, she got up, went to the kitchen, and started to cook something for dinner.

"I know, uncle, you like Aash; I am going to make it for dinner."

"Of course, I do. I can still remember the delicious taste of the Aash that I ate at your house in Kabul. But I'm wondering, did you already find all the ingredients here?"

"Yes, the Afghan lady downstairs took me to an oriental store this morning and I bought some stuff, including beans, liquid whey, and spices, because I knew you were coming over tonight."

"Thank you, daughter, so much."

"Uncle, how much money is the government going to give us?" she asked after returning from the kitchen.

"Well," Hekmat sighed slightly. "The money that the government is going to give you will not be enough to pay for your rent and other expenses. Therefore, it would be best that Zahir looks for a job as soon as possible and, in the meantime, you can try to learn English quickly because you can work then, too."

"If Zahir is working, they won't give us the money?"

"It depends on how much money Zahir is going to be making. I think that you shouldn't count on that money. But you can apply for medical, which is very important."

"How can we apply for medical?"

"On Monday, I will take you to the social services office, too, and there you can apply for medical."

"There is another big problem, uncle," Fahima said anxiously. "Yesterday, after Sheila and Shapor heard about the dead body in the parking lot, they didn't want to go out to play; they were scared. I don't know how they would feel about going to school."

"How far away is the school?"

"About a 15-minute walk. I walked over to school today to measure the distance," Zahir replied and added. "It's still early for their school, we can enroll Sheila in school next year and the rest are still little.

"How old is Sheila?" Hekmat asked.

"Seven," Fahima answered. "We didn't send her to school in Kabul because we thought we would be going to America soon, so no need to enroll her in school there.

"But here you can't keep her home at this age because it is the law that children must be enrolled in school at the age of six."

The couple stared at each other in astonishment.

"Can't she walk to school by herself?" Fahima asked in disbelief.

No, daughter, no," Hekmat replied in a sharp tone. "An adult should walk or drive children to the school. It's not safe to let a child walk to school alone."

"That's strange. I never thought so," Fahima reacted.

"Don't they have a school bus for children?" Zahir asked.

"No. They provide transportation only for students with disabilities."

"Oh, God, it will be me walking her to school because Zahir will be working!"

Zahir touched his wife's hand.

"You will be ok, you can do it. You are a brave woman."

"God knows, I am as cowardly as a child," Fahima murmured.

Human needs are countless; the most essential among them is the need for love and affection. Especially the unconditional love of children, their sweet smiles and innocent fondness can rekindle the desire of living in my lonely heart.

This was what Hekmat believed in and what he longed for. He fantasized most of that night about the joy of having a fatherly and grandfatherly relationship with the children. He spent the rest of the night in comfortable deep sleep.

In the morning, at breakfast, Zahir and his wife were looking at each other and searching for an answer to the question they had in their minds ever since they arrived in the US.

"Uncle, you've been living in America for a long time. Where is your family? We want to meet with them" Fahima finally asked.

Hekmat had been expecting them to ask this question, so he readily answered it with a sigh.

"I have two daughters; my youngest daughter and her husband moved to San Diego just six months ago because she got a better job there, and my older daughter is living in New York with her husband and three children."

"How far is San Diego?" Fahima asked nosily.

"Very far. More than five hundred miles from here."

"So, you live alone?" Fahima asked and immediately added, "Sorry, uncle, I should not have asked you this personal question."

"No, it's all right, daughter. Your guess is right. God took my lovely wife from me."

Knowing the answer to their question, Fahima told Hekmat, "Uncle, you are a great asset to us. If you would like to live with us, we would be more than happy. We will try not to bother you with the care for our children."

"She is right uncle, we would be delighted to have you with us in the house. We would not feel good to see you living alone at this age," Zahir backed his wife.

"As I said before, children wouldn't bother me. Thank you for your sympathy, but I'm ok living alone, especially now that I have you in America and can visit you whenever I wish."

On his way home, even though he felt good about the couple's proposal, he found himself satisfied with his answer. He was ok with constantly attending to the family even though he lived around 30 miles away from them. However, he was hesitant to compromise his privacy and seclusion as well as the comfort of being alone so that he could work on his dream book.

For the time being, he tried to focus on getting Zahir a driving permit, taking care of their medical application, and enrolling everyone in the school. He planned all these things for Monday. During the weekend, he was in a relatively better mood. His physical health condition allowed him to take a walk to Sheila's elementary school, to refresh the memory of his lovely granddaughter, and to reiterate his promise to write a book in her memory.

Finally, it's time to resume the research and the writing, he thought.

Sunday was a bit cold day. He cooked chicken soup for lunch and afterward, he took a nap. Around 3 p.m., he received a telephone call from Fahima, which he excitedly answered.

"*Salaam*, daughter, how are you?"

"Uncle, my daughter and I were nearly killed by a bullet just five minutes ago!" Fahima was panting and groaning.

"Why, what happened?" Hekmat asked, terrified by the news.

"Sheila and I were walking home from a grocery store, close to our home. Two men were shooting at each other and the bullets flew by our heads!"

"Thank God, you were not hurt. Where are you now?"

"We just got home. Sheila is in shock, she is shivering and crying, what should we do?"

"Where is Zahir?" he asked.

"He's here, he's depressed, too."

Hekmat paused for a moment.

"I'm coming over. I'll be there in an hour."

"Yes, uncle, please come. We are all miserable!"

Seven-year-old Sheila was still shaking. She wouldn't take her winter coat off despite the heat inside their apartment. She pressed himself in her father's arms and didn't move even when Hekmat arrived at the house.

"I don't know uncle how we can continue living here!" Fahima said with tremendous nervousness. "My heart is still pounding!"

"Did you forget Afghanistan so soon? What about the mass killings that took place every day?" Zahir argued with his wife.

"In Afghanistan, there is a civil war going on—there aren't enough security forces, it's a backward and poor country, there is no law and order! What about America? It's the most advanced and richest country in the whole world, can't they do something about the guns?" Fahima cried.

"Don't be scared, there are a lot of nice places in America. Someday we will move to a good area," Zahir said while pulling his hand over his daughter's head who was still seeking safety in his father's arms.

While silently agreeing with Fahima, Hekmat tried to assure the couple that he would do everything possible to help them move to a better place when the time comes.

"What about the school, uncle? I can't let my children go to school here," Fahima said while wiping her tears.

"I don't want to go to school," Sheila lifted her head, crying and looking terrified.

"I have a college degree and was hoping to learn English so I could get a job here. But with these shootings—how can I go to school? I am scared even inside my home," Fahima said after she washed the dinner dishes and returned to the living room.

Hekmat was compelled to stay with the family overnight because both the husband and wife insisted. He was silent, thinking, and gazing at the children now and then. Around 10 p.m., Fahima told him that his bed was ready as she noticed that his eyes had become red and drowsy.

"Thank you, daughter. Goodnight, everyone," he said, trying to get up, but a heavy gunshot's sound from a distance pinned him to the mattress that he was sitting on.

Sheila and Shapor who had just fallen asleep on a mattress in the corner of the room woke up out of fear and start crying.

"Oh God, it sounded like a military-type rifle!" Zahir exclaimed.

"I think so, too," Hekmat said. "Maybe it was an AR -15 or an AK- 47."

"What's that uncle?" Zahir asked.

"Those are semi-automatic military-type weapons."

"So you think it was the police firing?" asked Fahima, looking confused.

"Don't know. Criminals also have access to these kinds of rifles."

An extended silence filled the room. Even the children were quiet.

"What do you think, uncle, what kind of life are my children going to have here? They will become crazy, won't they?" Fahima said as she got up to go comfort the kids, trying to put them back to sleep.

"How is your area, uncle? Is it possible to look for an apartment close to your house?" Zahir asked.

"It's possible. I can look but the rent is higher there."

"How high?"

"Maybe $2,000 for a two-bedroom apartment."

"Wow, we can't even afford $1,800 a month, how can we pay $2,000? I know my children are going to starve to death due to our poverty!" Fahima screamed.

Hekmat was silent. He stared at the ceiling of the room for a few seconds, and then said, "Let's go to sleep now, we will talk about this in the morning."

That night, Hekmat didn't fall asleep until 2 a.m. He spent hours thinking about this young family. He repeatedly asked himself, *how can I afford to see Majid's grandchildren live in misery? How can I let Majid's son and daughter-in-law live such a gloomy life?*

Kindness is a remedy that performs two jobs—it cures the ailment of the "ill" and satisfies the conscience of the "healer," he thought.

It was this feeling that had taken him to Afghanistan to be with his friends and their families for a while. However, he returned home with deep emotional wounds, the wounds of losing his best friends, and the wounds of self-blame, which eroded his soul ever since. Now, by having Majid's family with him, he saw an opportunity to seek a cure for his emotional wounds by helping the family.

In the morning, when Fahima announced that breakfast was ready, he was already prepared to go to the living room. She served her "uncle" a cup of *sheer chai*—hot milk tea with cardamom and honey. Like last night, he still looked thoughtful and sipped his milk tea quietly.

"Uncle, are we going to apply for medical today?" Fahima asked.

"No, daughter."

"Are you and Zahir going to the DMV?"

"No," he replied, sipping the last drop of his *shear chai*. He seemed serious.

The husband and wife looked at each other in bewilderment.

"It's Monday. That's what you said the other night, uncle. You don't have time or what?" Fahima asked desperately.

Zahir was looking at his "uncle" with his mouth opened, scared that he had changed his mind and was no longer willing to help them.

"You will apply for both medical and driving permit with your new address. I want you to move in with me at my house, if you like," he said, sounding sharp.

The couple looked again at each other, but this time their mouths were open in a smile.

"Are you sure, uncle? Do you own your house?" Fahima asked, not believing at all what she heard.

"Yes, daughter, I am positive. And yes, I do own a humble house."

"Does your house have enough room for us?"

"Yes, my house has three bedrooms and two full baths. Enough for us all."

"That will be a huge favor and kindness, uncle," Zahir said, sounding cheerful.

"You guys start packing up right now and also give a notice letter to the management of this complex—I know you might lose the deposit money."

"If we can live with you, that's ok. The deposit money is not important," both husband and wife said.

"Mommy, where are we going?" asked little Sheila.

"We are going to move to our uncle's house? Grandpa's house," she replied cheerfully and pointed her hand toward Hekmat. "His house. You call him grandpa, he is your grandpa."

Hekmat allocated the master bedroom to the couple.

He stayed in the small bedroom that he was used to sleeping in, which had a window facing the street. The third bedroom went to the kids.

After the move was complete, Fahima looked around the house. She liked it. She especially loved the convenience of having a full bathroom inside her bedroom, something she had never seen before. This house had a family room as well as a living room—another aspect that excited her. She also loved the large backyard with roses, and an orange tree, and a lemon tree in it.

"I think that now I am living in America," she said to her husband with a big smile.

Hekmat made appointments and arranged for them to get medical. Zahir got his driving permit. Hekmat started giving him driving lessons and practicing with him several hours a week. Their older child, Sheila was enrolled in the school close to his house. Although he was still carrying the bitter memory of his own Sheila's death at the school, Hekmat so far concealed that information from the couple as he didn't feel comfortable revealing it to them. He had no other choice but to enroll the kids in the same school because there was no other school in the zone. He took upon himself the task of walking Sheila to and from school every day. Zahir and Fahima started going to the adult school in the evenings, using the bus for their transportation.

Zahir got his driving license two months later and, soon after, he started working for a taxi company at which his former Afghan neighbor also worked. He was energetic, hardworking, and a dedicated contractual employee for the company. Besides driving a taxi from 6 a.m. until 5 p.m., he also attended adult school and did homework with his children in the evenings.

Fahima, who wished to become a teacher, was also ambitious about learning English and was hoping to get a job of her choice sooner. In addition to doing house chores and caring for her three kids, she never missed her English class and always did her homework on time.

The couple adjusted rather quickly to a new way of life in America. They regularly watched the news on American TV channels. They tried to follow Hekmat's suggestions on eating healthy food. They abandoned consuming deep-fried beef and potatoes. They also started doing daily exercise using a manual treadmill that Hekmat owned. For their children, they ordered Mister Roger's "Neighborhood" DVDs. Soon, the kids were singing "Won't You Be My Neighbor?" Everyone in the family was starting to enjoy their new life.

Now, I can concentrate on my search for the motive and my writing, too much time was wasted, Hekmat told himself, wishing he was able to make up time for almost four months that he had lost. He no longer felt lonely. The fear of being followed by Samander's boys no longer existed. He felt like his wish to serve the soul of his lost friend, Majid, was coming true. Therefore, he revived his old schedule—following his search for the murderer's motive who killed his Sheila, and working on his book mostly in the pre-dawn hours when there was no noise of any kind and no phone calls. He would go to bed around nine and let Zahir and Fahima do their homework. He would wake up around 4 a.m., having slept for six or seven hours, and would sit down in front of his computer. On weekdays, besides walking Shala to her school and back, he would take an hour-long walk in the nearby park, allowing himself time and space to relax and be secluded with his thoughts.

One day, Zahir had made good money at work. When he returned home, a big smile was visible on his lips.

"*Salaam*, uncle, you were right when you said that honesty brings joy even if no one witnesses you."

"Of course, son. Tell me what happened," Hekmat said curiously.

"Today, I dropped a lady at the SFO. When I left the airport, before entering the freeway, I stopped by a gas station to fill my tank. I noticed that the passenger had forgotten her purse in my cab. I quickly grabbed the purse. It was open and a passport and airplane ticket peeked out of it. I hurriedly jumped in my cab and drove back to the place where I had dropped her off. The lady, whose hair was partly gray, was wandering around, staring at each and every taxi, hoping that I would return to give her the lost purse. When I got there, she was looking the other way. I called out to her, 'ma'am,' and held the purse up in my hand. Would you believe it, uncle? When she looked at me, she was motionless and speechless for a moment, then she virtually ran towards me, grabbed her purse from my hand, and hugged me. When I tried to run back to my car because the police were rushing me to move, she pulled out a hundred dollar bill and her business card from her purse and handed them to me, saying, 'I am coming back next week, call me please, thank you very much,'" Zahir said cheerfully.

"Very good son, you did the right thing. Call her a week later to see what she's going to say."

"Ok, uncle."

"He is a good man," Hekmat said, looking at Fahima that night when everyone was present in the living room. "I wish his father were alive to see his honest, educated, and hardworking son."

"Yes, uncle. He is really a very honest, man and a good father to our children."

"Thank you both for your compliments," Zahir interrupted. "I don't deserve them."

The next morning, the kids knocked on Hekmat's bedroom door as usual. He ignored them. They started pounding on the door, but he didn't answer. The kids wanted him to play with them. Whenever he was out in the living room, little Sara wanted to sit in his arms, Shapor would climb over his shoulders, and Sheila liked to play the *closed-fist game* with him.

He overslept that night and h felt too idle for getting up at the usual time. He continued ignoring the kids until Fahima knocked on his door.

"Uncle, breakfast is ready. If you don't mind, I would like to go to the Afghan store for shopping today."

"Ok, daughter, I'm coming," he said. "What are you going to buy?" he asked Fahima once he was out in the living room.

"I am going to buy Basmati rice and Afghan bread. The children missed them."

"Oh, those are good things, I like them too."

"Yes, Zahir also mentioned them last night, he is hungry for these things."

"Why don't you wait until tomorrow, I'm going to get my car back from the mechanic, then I can take you to the store?"

"It's alright, uncle, the Afghan lady from the next street and I go together by bus, she is familiar with the area."

"Good, you already made friends in the neighborhood, ha! I was not aware that we have another family from our country here," Hekmat said.

"Yes, she said they just moved here a month ago."

"That's why I didn't know. They moved here while I was still in Afghanistan."

"Do you anything from the Afghan store?" Fahima asked.

"No, thank you. What time will you be back?"

"I don't know. We are going to leave at 10 a.m., so maybe we will come back by 1 p.m."

Hekmat walked Sheila to her school first, while Fahima stayed home with Sara and Shapor. After Fahima left, he made himself busy playing with the two little ones until they got tired. Around noon, he fed the kids with the leftovers from last night's chicken soup and then tried to put them to sleep. He needed time to think about his projects, the search, and the writing, which he thought were long overdue. But, in the absence of their mother, the kids were cranky. They started crying and asking about their mother, making him uncomfortable.

He took them to the park and let them play, while he sat on a bench, thinking.

Time was going by quickly. Around 1 p.m., little Sara started crying, signaling that she was hungry. He took her and Shapor back home. Fahima was not back yet. With each passing minute, his worry increased.

They might have gotten lost, he thought of Fahima and the other Afghan woman.

He tried to convince himself that they couldn't be lost. He put the children to sleep and turned on the TV to kill time. Around 2 p.m., he grabbed his cell phone to call Zahir to see whether he had any idea about Fahima's whereabouts. However, he immediately told himself, *that's not a good idea because he might be driving and my call can cause an accident.*

Before going to pick up Sheila from school, he ran to the neighbor's house to inquire whether the lady who went shopping with Fahima had returned. He rang the bell once, twice, and three times then knocked on the door heavily—but no one answered. It was 5 minutes to 3 p.m. when he hurriedly woke Sara and Shapor and went to bring their sister from school.

"Where is my mom?" Sheila asked as soon as she entered the home.

Hekmat put his hand over her head and assured her, "She will be home soon, with hot Afghan bread and Basmati rice."

After serving the kids some milk and cookies, he started walking—first in the living room and then in the backyard—and thinking about his "daughter-in-law" as his anxiety grew.

It was almost 5 p.m.

I should have bought Fahima a cell phone, so I could call her now, he reprimanded himself.

He went back to the living room and turned the TV back on, tuning to the ABC evening newscast.

"There was a mass shooting on a public bus in the vicinity of North International Boulevard in Oakland this afternoon around 1 p.m."

Another mass shooting, another gift of gun freedom, thought Hekmat and continued to listen to the news at the same time, while half of his brain was worried about Fahima who was more than late and the other half was documenting yet another example of the destruction of human lives by the gun business.

The newscast added, "The Oakland Police Department said that eight people have died—six women and two children—and another six are injured. The victims have been transported to the Oakland Medical Center."

"Oh, God, save Fahima," he said aloud as his brain just connected the dots of the situation...*bus in Oakland, 1 p.m., six women, Fahima still not here, now 5 p.m.*

Still, he was trying to process the news in his mind the way he wished, *Fahima might not have been on that bus at that time.*

On the TV screen, he carefully and fearfully reviewed the crime scene, which was crowded with police vehicles, ambulances, and fire trucks.

"Uncle, is Fahima home?" Zahir called and asked in a shaky voice.

He held his cell phone away from his ear for a second to give himself time before answering Zahir's question, whose shaky voice told him that he had undoubtedly smelled a tragedy.

"No, son, she went to the Afghan store in Oakland this morning."

"I know that. What time did she leave?"

"She left at 10."

"Can you please go and ask the Afghan lady that Fahima went shopping with?"

"I did, but nobody answered the door."

"Can you please go again?"

"Ok, son, I'll go there right now," he murmured, panicking within as he knew that if the lady was back home, Fahima would be, too.

"Please call me back soon because there was a shooting on a bus in Oakland, I just heard the news on my taxi radio."

"Ok, son, I am on my way."

"What happened uncle, what did the lady say?" Zahir called again, not even two minutes after his first call.

"No one is answering the door; I'm here, ringing the bell," Hekmat said, his voice shaking worse than Zahir's voice.

"What doorbell are you ringing, do you know their house number?"

"The second home on the opposite side of the next street."

"That's not the one, uncle! It's on the same side of the next street, like our house."

"Oh God, let me run to that house."

He ran to the other house as fast as a child runs after his mother. An old lady from the house answered the door and said, "My daughter is not back either, I don't know why. I thought she went to your house with Fahima."

"She didn't. I hope everything is fine," he responded hurriedly and then informed Zahir of the neighbor's response.

"You stay with the children, I'm going to go to the Oakland Medical Center to see whether she is among the victims!" Zahir said, sounding genuinely nervous.

"God forbid, please call me back as soon as you find out anything about her."

He was still dressed, with his shoes on, and he hadn't eaten since the morning. While visualizing the bloody body of Fahima, he quickly tuned to a few more local TV channels, hoping to hear something specific about his Fahima. There was nothing. But all the channels reported that it was just another horrible incident of mass shootings.

"Uncle, my life is gone with the wind—my family has been destroyed!"

When Hekmat received this phone call from Zahir, he was unable to believe him.

"Why, son? God forbid, where is Fahima?"

"She is dead! She was shot in the head!" Zahir was crying aloud.

He couldn't follow what Zahir said next. He suffered a blackout. He walked from the living room to his bedroom, holding his hand on the wall. He laid down on his bed, now envisioning Fahima's bloody body more precisely—with a huge gunshot wound in the head.

Gun Freedom again took innocent lives. The stupid gun advocates claim that guns don't kill, people do. He started an imaginary clash with Allen. But since Allen was not there, he automatically projected the sorrow of losing Fahima onto himself and started suffering from self-blame again.

Had I not brought them to my house, Fahima would now be alive.

He couldn't stay in his bed long enough to swallow his agony and sadness because the kids were crying in the living room—asking for their mom.

Chapter VI

Fahima's death took a huge toll on the life of the family. Zahir lost his enthusiasm; he no longer wished to achieve his dreams. Becoming a widower at the age of 32, he considered himself to be without a lifemate forever. He categorically rejected any suggestion about getting remarried that his fellow taxi drivers would sometimes give. From that point on, he would miss going to work one or two days every week. His sadness gradually progressed into a severe depression.

For months, the children cried, mentioned, and asked for their mother. Little Sara, especially, would not go to sleep without mentioning her mom and extensively sobbing every night. Shapor would always follow his little sister and cry, too. Sheila was suffering inside. All three were confused by the meaning of death—a strange thing that took their mother from them.

Hekmat felt the impact of this tragedy no less than the other family members. More so, he felt ashamed before the soul of his deceased friend, Majid, and his widow, to whom he had promised that he would take care of their son's family at any cost. For weeks, he wasn't able to even think about what he promised to his own Sheila. He was as sad and as emotional as a father can be who had lost a beautiful, young, and educated daughter.

He lost his ability to get enough sleep. It affected both his physical and mental health. His doctor prescribed Mirtazapine tablets to help him with his depression and to allow him to get some sleep at the night—or he would be facing the danger of a heart attack or stroke.

When would America be able to cope with its gun madness? He thought.

Sitting by his computer for the first time three weeks after Fahima's death, he tried to narrate an idea that would provide an answer to this question. He switched his laptop on and opened the "novel" file. His eyes stared at the screen for several long moments because his weary mind wouldn't allow his fingers to touch the keyboard and type even a single word.

My dear Sheila, I am losing my mind. There are so many things happening in my life. They keep me from fulfilling my promise to you. He whispered to himself. *But I will try, with all my bones and blood to fight the murderous empire of the gun business.*

The two men in the family divided the home chores among themselves, such as caring for the children, walking them to and from school, shopping, cooking, cleaning, laundry, and so on. Besides going to the adult school in the evenings on weekdays, Zahir drove a taxi six days a week. He was off on Mondays and stayed home with his children. Hekmat was responsible for almost everything else—caring for the children, walking them to and from school, cleaning the house, cooking, washing dishes, and doing laundry. On Mondays, while Zahir babysat at home, Hekmat was able to go out and do the shopping. He volunteered for this division of work in order to allow Zahir enough time to work and to attend adult school to improve his English language.

Devoting much of his time and energy to caring for the children and doing chores, Hekmat believed that he was doing the right thing. He enjoyed his dedication to and sacrifice for Majid's grandchildren. He considered this responsibility to be a way of soothing the pain caused by his inner self-blaming. He also hoped that this would provide him with peace of mind and allow him to resume working on his projects.

However, with all his dedication to the promise he had made his granddaughter, the circumstances forced him to, at least for the time being, give precedence to dealing with the implications of Fahima's death. Her children needed fatherly care and attention, her husband needed family support, and her murder itself needed to be investigated. Therefore, on days and nights, his mind was preoccupied with two compulsory questions to solve.

The crime of the bus shooting was perpetrated, according to the police report, using an AR-15 semi-automatic gun. This fact prompted Hekmat to continue his research related to the psychological influence of possessing a stronger weapon in the commitment of crimes.

One of the Oakland police department reports said that, after shooting people on the bus, the murderer tried to escape. However, when surrounded by the police force, he tossed his AR-15 rifle away, pulled out a handgun, and shot himself in the head. The report also said that the criminal was a 35-year-old man from Los Angeles with a long criminal past. Despite a court order that barred him from possessing a firearm, the police found one more shotgun, an AK- 47, in his home.

Unlike some other criminals, this immoral man still wished to live, but he took his life only after the police surrounded him and left him without the possibility to escape arrest. Therefore, he was not a mentally ill person because he still loved life. And no doubt, he had a motive for the shooting.

This was a common analogy shared by many individuals, Hekmat included. He was again holding an imaginary debate with Allen.

Gun advocates are blind, they don't realize or don't want to realize these facts.

The motive of this crime remained unknown as well. However, based on his findings and the analyses of numerous criminal cases, Hekmat firmly believed that whatever the shooter's motive, the possession of a murder weapon was an underpinning factor in the execution of such crimes. Because the weapon is a tool for hunting—for killing. It's a thing, the same as everything else, which incites a human mind to use it for the purpose it was manufactured for. In other words, human nature is such that things are acquired for specific purposes—human beings enjoy using things for the purposes they were intended. For example, a wristwatch and a wall clock are used to find out the time, a radio is used to listen to news and music, and a telephone is used to communicate. Similarly, a gun is manufactured for its envisioned usage—to hunt and kill living creatures. That's what a gun is built for—killing. It's a fact that all gun owners are not criminals. Still, the reason that they are able to commit violence is the fact that they own guns—and guns affect their personalities.

"Superiority and inducement" are the constituents of the human mind that need to be satisfied. Guns provide a potential for criminal-mindedness. Who can deny the fact that some criminals feel good and get satisfaction for their feelings of "superiority and inducement" from their possession of a weapon? It's a fact that some crazy criminals do enjoy watching the bloody bodies of children, men, and women that they have hunted, which provides them with a perfect motive for using their guns.

Still, to be more candid about his theory, he desperately needed to find out the underlying scientific foundation for drawing his conclusion regarding the role of gun ownership in the commitment of crimes. He went ahead and ordered a few more books on Amazon in order to further his knowledge about the genetic, social, economic, ideological, and emotional causes of criminal mindedness and to promote awareness of the real faces of mass murderers and serial killers in America. He selected the following books: *Applied Criminal Psychology: A Guide to Forensic Behavioral Science* by Richard N. Kocsis, *Strait Talks About Criminals: Understanding and Treating Antisocial Individuals* by Stanton E. Samenow, *The Myth of the Out of Character Crime* by Stanton E. Samenow, *Serial Killers: The Method and Madness of Monsters* by Peter Vronsky, and *Another Day in the Death of America* by Gary Young.

After the day of Fahima's death, Hekmat had become a perfect babysitter, a good cook, a capable housekeeper, and a professional caregiver. He excelled in managing his time. Besides doing all his tasks on time and efficiently, he also made time to pursue his goal to read books and conduct his research. At the age of 63, fulfilling motherly tasks allowed him to look into the world of children more deeply and, sometimes, to put himself in their shoes—being a child without a mother. He would say to himself, *it's frightening, thank God I didn't lose my mother when I was a child.*

One day, he took a break from reading books and doing household chores. It was a beautiful and sunny day in early May. He took Sara and Shapor to the neighborhood park after they had lunch at home. He sat on a bench, watching the little kids playing, running around on the climber, or the spring rider. He breathed fresh air and enjoyed watching the kids have fun. He wished that they were happy inside as well.

"Hello Mr. Hekmat, this is Allen, I am back in San Francisco. How are you?"

A phone call from Allen came at the perfect time.

"Hello, Mr. Allen. I'm grieving the loss of my daughter-in-law."

"What happened to your daughter-in-law?" Allen asked apathetically.

"She fell victim to the generosity of the Second Amendment!" Hekmat said loudly.

"What do you mean?" asked Allen compassionately.

"She died in a mass shooting."

"Oh, I am so sorry to hear that! Tell me, how and when?"

"Almost five months ago. It was the same madness. She was among the victims of a bus massacre, didn't you hear about it?"

"I'm not sure. It's so sad that your daughter-in-law was killed, too. But that has nothing to do with the Second Amendment."

"Mr. Allen," Hekmat said in a serious tone. "I'm sorry, I can't afford to listen to your justification of the gun tyranny."

"Huh!" Allen said mockingly. "I don't blame you, are sad. But I'm sure the shooter was a sick man, a mentally crazy thug."

"Listen, Mr. Allen," Hekmat replied in a relatively harsh tone. "First of all, the killer wasn't a mentally ill person—no police report or forensic analysis indicated that. Second, suppose that he was a sick person—how would a sick person shoot fourteen people if he didn't have a gun? Let's suppose, for a moment, that the machine gun he used was not easily available to that crazy thug—how would he have taken so many lives?"

"So what do you think that the killer's possible motive was?"

"His motive was obvious—a desire to hunt…to hunt humans," Hekmat raised his voice and Allen allowed him to throw his frustration out. "What I can also say about this particular murderer is that, after the shooting, his desire for hunting humans was not yet gratified, and—unlike some other criminals—he did not feel the need to take his own life right away. He tried, however, to avoid being captured and wished to hunt a few more innocent lives. He killed himself only after he was surrounded by the police."

"He would've been captured anyway, even if he didn't take his life."

"No doubt about it. But would that capture bring back the eight lives he took? Will there be any measures taken to avoid such disasters from happening again? I know that some people, including your NRA friend, may have shown their sympathy for the dead and the wounded—some may even have cried for them—but will there be anyone who can genuinely protest against the destructive nature of the gun lobby?"

Allen felt his friend's anger. He tried to say something to him in the hope of pacifying his rage.

"I have some good news for you, Mr. Hekmat!"

"Good news? Are guns going to be banned in America?" Hekmat said sarcastically.

"Not exactly, but it's something in that direction."

"Ok, please tell me about it!" Hekmat said his voice already reflecting his doubts.

"First, the good news," Allen said triumphantly. "Efforts are being made in Congress to ban the sale of all semi-automatic guns and all those guns that can fire more than ten bullets." Allen cleared his throat and continued to explain the importance of the measure under discussion in Congress. "It's a historic step forward, one that will change the culture of gun ownership in America."

Hekmat held his cell phone away from his ear until he succeeded in swallowing his anger.

"Is it? Is it really a historic step forward, Mr. Allen?"

Hekmat said in a loud, sarcastic tone, indicating his vivid desperation.

Allen realized his friend's sarcasm and allowed him to go on.

"First," Hekmat continued. "Congress also passed a similar law in 1994, which expired ten years later. It did not bother to extend it. Second, during those ten years, the mass killing rate did not decrease because there were already thousands and thousands of such weapons in the hands of people, both legally and illegally. Just in this period of time, there were 32 mass shootings, including some of the deadliest ones—such as the ones at the Westside Middle School, the Arkansas shooting on March 24, 1998 that killed and injured a total of 15 people, the Columbine High School massacre on April 20, 1999 that took 14 lives and injured 24 others, the massacre at Thurston High School in Oregon on May 21, 1998 that killed and wounded a total of 29 people, the mass shootings at two day trading firms in Georgia on July 27, 1999 that killed 13 and injured another 13 people."

Hekmat sighed heavily, and so did Allen.

"Last but not least," continued Hekmat, "what about the guns that take ten or fewer bullets? My question is, are those ten or fewer bullets made of chocolate—or are they also made of gun powder and metal, the same as all other bullets? And are the people who get killed by these ten or fewer bullets not considered to be human beings or what?"

After this lengthy statement, he expected his American friend to cut off the conversation and say goodbye to him.

But Allen went on to present his second piece of good news instead.

"I know how you feel and I am sure that you will like the second piece of good news I have for you. Congress just passed a law according to which new gun buyers are required to undergo a more thorough background check than before. This is the law that you wished for, right? What do you say, Mr. Hekmat, is it something that will make you happy?"

"Huh," said Hekmat without delay. "It is. But do you really think Mr. Allen that the senate will pass this law? Do you believe that the NRA, the gun dealers, and the lobbyists will do nothing to prevent it from getting passed? I don't think so." Hekmat sighed. "I am certain that these kinds of ideas will be flying in the air for years and will never take on a form in the actual law. Because these groups will use all their power to bribe the senators and other government authorities for their purposes. They won't allow there to be a chance for this 'good news to be realized even though it would not do any harm to the validity of the Second Amendment."

Before he finished talking, Hekmat looked at his wristwatch. It was 5 minutes to 3 p.m. He called Sara and Shapor in English, asking them to stop playing because they had to go pick up Sheila from their school. This way, he also indicated to Allen that he had to go.

But Allen, not wasting the chance, quickly said, "Ok, my friend, please accept my condolences for the loss of your daughter-in-law—and please be strong because, unfortunately, whatever has happened cannot be reversed."

Hekmat also hastily replied with increased seriousness.

"Yes, no one can give life back to the dead. But more innocent lives can be saved. Guns can be eliminated, the Constitution can be changed No one can deny the fact that more than 300 million guns in the hands of American civilians will continue to take more and more innocent lives—they will destroy more and more families, sooner or later!"

After ending the conversation with Allen, he quickly picked up Sara by his right arm and walked faster toward the school, holding Shapor's hand with his left hand. Sheila was already out waiting to be picked up.

"Where is your car grandpa?" she asked sounding tired under the weight of her heavy backpack.

"We just came from the park, honey," Hekmat replied kindly as he realized that she was tired.

Other kids were also tired and hungry. It was rush hour, crossing the road in the heavy traffic caused them all to be impatient and in a hurry to get home.

A heart-grinding noise from tires and brakes screeching caused them to stop and look back as they were about to turn into their street; two sports cars, a Ford Mustang, and a Chevy Camaro were racing.

"Hurry up, kids, they are crazy," Hekmat shouted.

The cars disappeared in a blink of an eye, but they reappeared in just a few seconds, one chasing the other at a frighteningly high speed. This time the Mustang drove in the same direction that Hekmat and the kids were heading but the second car couldn't make it to turn into the street due to its high speed. The sounds of its tires and brakes as well as that of gunfire were followed by a heartbreaking scream that came out of little Sheila's mouth.

Hekmat put Sara down on the sidewalk and grabbed Sheila who was lying flat on the ground but not screaming anymore. She passed out. Both of her legs were flooded with her blood.

"I am going to call 911," shouted an old lady from the neighborhood who happened to be working in the front yard of her house nearby.

She will be okay, please don't cry kids, Hekmat wanted to tell Shapor and Sara who were sobbing aloud and shivering. He couldn't because he was in shock and shivering too.

The ambulance took Sheila to the county hospital. Hekmat took the other two children home as they were not allowed to accompany their wounded sister to the hospital.

Despite witnessing the horrible scene of their sister being shot at, Shapor and Sara couldn't resist hunger and sleeplessness longer than a few minutes, during which time they cried aloud, and then ate lunch, and fell asleep.

During the almost two-hour time that the kids were asleep, Hekmat was constantly on the phone trying to find out about Sheila's condition from the emergency room, while silently blaming himself for not driving his car to pick up Sheila as he would usually do. *Her father is going to blame me for that,* he said to himself.

He impatiently waited for the kids to wake up. He prayed that Zahir didn't arrive before they leave for the hospital. He prayed that Sheila was not injured badly and that he could bring her home before Zahir came.

"Ok, kids, let's go to see Sheila," He told Shapor and Sara who were still in their beds. The kids obeyed him and ran to their car.

At the hospital emergency department, they advised him that "no visit was allowed until the doctor is done examining her." He kept the kids in the waiting area and wouldn't leave until after little Sara cried. He took her and Shapor back to the car to wait for as long as it took to find out about Sheila.

After sitting in his vehicle for thirty minutes, he called the security desk, asking if they would now be allowed to see the wounded. The answer was, "Not yet, call later."

A little while later, both Sara and Shapor started complaining about being cold and hungry. In the meantime, he was more concerned about Zahir, who had called him several times, but he didn't answer because he didn't know what to tell him.

It got dark and cold. When he called the security desk again, he was told that no visitation will be allowed until tomorrow morning because the patient was admitted to the ICU.

It means that she is all injured—seriously injured, but not dead yet, he concluded and it put his mind at ease a little bit. He had no choice but to go home.

He arrived home at the same time as Zahir. As he had

anticipated, Zahir was really mad at him. He screamed as soon as he pulled his car into the driveway.

"Uncle, what happened to my daughter? Why didn't you answer the phone? I called you ten times!"

Hekmat got out of the car and approached Zahir to hug him in empathy, but Zahir backed off violently.

"Sorry, son, my phone battery died. Let's take the kids inside, they are hungry and sleepy," Hekmat said as his voice cracked, echoing the extreme anxiety of the situation.

He let Zahir grab Sara from the back seat of the car. He held Shapor's hand and walked him to the living room.

"Calm down, son, hopefully, Sheila will be ok, God willing," he spoke, trying to console Zahir. However, he was unsuccessful in helping himself to absorb the bitterness of the lie he just told his "nephew" for the first time since they met.

"But what exactly happened? I didn't listen to the news while I was driving, but someone told me at the company when I returned the cab."

"We were walking home from Sheila's school, two crazy kids were chasing each other and then one of them opened fire on the other and hit my daughter," he said.

"Why didn't you drive your car like every other day?" Zahir asked angrily.

"I had taken Shapor and Sara to the park and from there we just walked home."

Zahir frowned and sighed heavily, signaling his disappointment with what he heard from Hekmat.

They fed Sara and Shapor and took them to their bedroom. None of the men ate anything, though. Zahir switched on the TV and moved from channel to channel, searching for details of his daughter's condition. Both were daydreaming about hearing news such as, "the little girl is doing well, she will be discharged soon. The shooter was apprehended by police."

They stayed together in the living room until 2 a.m. Both were silent for most of the time. Hekmat thought several times to call Allen to tell him what happened to his granddaughter but felt too exhausted and disappointed to do so.

"Sheila was shot in the legs and her condition is not critical. The doctors are suggesting that she will be fine."

Hekmat received this information at 6 a.m. from the emergency room. He got up and changed quickly to let Zahir know about it and to prepare to go to the hospital. Zahir was already standing by the door of his bedroom, trying to listen to Hekmat's phone conversation with the ER.

"The hospital says Sheila's condition is not critical, she is going to be ok."

He came out of his bedroom and shared this news with Zahir.

Zahir's eyes were red and half-open. His voice cracked and his mouth was dry.

"Can we go to the hospital now?" he asked Hekmat.

"Sure, I was also planning that. Let me wake Sara and Shapor to eat something."

Hekmat did what he said and readied the kids to be put in the car.

Around 7 a.m., they all left for the hospital.

Their group was the first people who appeared by the hospital security desk that day. They got permission to see Sheila.

Both of her legs were in plaster. Seeing her family, she sobbed and extended her open arms toward her father. Her father and "grandfather" kissed her on the forehead. Sara and Shapor touched and rubbed her hands repeatedly.

They stayed by the little girl's bed, she was in pain. She wanted to go home. Little Sara became uncomfortable standing up for that long. Hekmat and Zahir were sleep-deprived and distressed.

"She may not be able to walk on her own but other than that she will be fine," Sheila's doctor said to her family in a comforting voice.

"Do you mean, never?" Zahir asked anxiously.

"I am afraid, yes." The doctor replied.

Zahir put Sara down on the floor and circled his arms around his "uncle's" waist to prevent him from falling. He walked Hekmat slowly to the waiting room and seated him in a chair. Zahir, Shapor, and Sara sat by his side silently. When Hekmat opened his eyes a few seconds later, he pulled his hands over Sara and Shapor's heads and then turned to Zahir, "May God give you strength and peace, I know you are going through a lot. I am, too."

"I wish we hadn't come to America," Zahir murmured when crying.

Hekmat, unable to find words to console Zahir, placed his forearm on his shoulder and kissed him on the forehead. He whispered in his ear, "Son, this is a test, please stay strong for your children!"

"I am lost, uncle. I brought my family to America hoping for safety. But here I lost my wife and my daughter has become permanently disabled. I wish I hadn't come here!" Zahir couldn't control his anger. He continued to throw it out in such a loud voice that everyone in the waiting room could hear him.

His forearm still over Zahir's shoulder, Hekmat put his head down as if he had committed an unforgivable crime against Zahir. He thought to himself, *it was also my fault, it was me who brought them to my house. I am responsible for the destruction of Majid's son's family.* He felt a sharp pain in his skull and quickly rubbed that spot.

"I am lost, too, son," he groaned.

Zahir didn't go to work for three weeks. Fever, headache, body ache, and depression consumed his energy. His beard grew, which now had plenty of gray hair in it. He moved Shapor and Sara's beds into his bedroom and never allowed them to be away from him—day and night. Sheila remained in the hospital for two weeks. The rest of the family visited her every single day. Both of her legs were hit by bullets in the knee area, and she was going to be crippled for the rest of her life. The day she was released from the hospital, Zahir still couldn't or didn't want to believe that his daughter would never be able to walk again on her own. He didn't allow the hospital staff to carry her in a wheelchair to the car. He carried her in his arms instead. In a little while, however, he accepted the reality that his daughter was to be handicapped for life. He, himself, would push her wheelchair back and forth in the family room, pretending that he was the only one in the whole world who was aware of that bitter reality.

From that point on, Zahir forbade his children to go out to the park even in the company of Hekmat. He also categorically rejected Hekmat's idea to enroll Sheila in a *special needs* school.

"I am afraid that, someday, another stray bullet or a bullet from racing cars might come out of the blue and kill another one or more of my children," Zahir said resolutely.

"I understand, son. I do realize that you fear for your children. Believe me, I am afraid, too. But how can we keep them home all the time?"

"Maybe you are right but, for the time being, I have no control over my feelings."

"Ok, son. I hope that your fear will go away soon and that you will go back to normal as time passes. For now, I am going to talk to the school and will tell them that I am homeschooling Sheila."

"Thank you, uncle, now I feel better. I'm going to go back to work tomorrow. I have one more thing to tell you," Zahir paused briefly as if he was not sure whether or not to share his determination with Hekmat. "I have to buy a pistol and carry it with me all the time," Zahir stressed on the phrase "all the time."

"What for, dear son? Why would you want to buy a

gun and carry it with you?" Hekmat asked in a sharp tone, reflecting his strong disagreement.

"Because I'm scared. If someone kills me, then my children will be alone. You will be the only one left to take care of them, which I don't want to happen to you either."

"Look, son," Hekmat tried to argue with Zahir mildly. "First, why would anybody want to kill you? Second, God forbid, if someone is after you to kill you, the gun you would carry cannot save your life because that person would follow you and hit you from behind—so, don't worry, let's live freely without a gun!"

"That's not what I mean. My point is that, in the business of taxi driving, it's dangerous to go to some areas. Cab drivers get robbed inside the city and in bright daylight. You know, all kinds of people ride with me, there have been numerous incidences where taxi drivers were robbed and killed by their passengers."

"Right, there have been many such incidences. But still, I don't think that the drivers could save their lives by carrying guns because, as I said, the criminals attack from behind. There are other measures and cautions that you could adopt for self-safety.

Zahir wasn't fully convinced but stopped arguing with his "uncle" out of respect for him. Instead, he stressed his other request.

"Ok, uncle, I'm not going to buy a gun right now but I would like to ask you—please don't take my children out to the park or shopping with you. I don't feel good about it. Like in the past, do the shopping on Mondays, which is my day off, and I will be home with them."

Hekmat remained silent.

Zahir added, "I know uncle that you like walking in the park, but you know, in this country, bullets are flying everywhere and anyone can be hit at one time or another as my Sheila is the living example of it."

He spoke from the bottom of his heart. Therefore, Hekmat didn't pick an argument with him, preferring to stay silent instead.

After noticing Hekmat was in deep thought and seemed to disagree with him, Zahir added, "The other day, one of my fellow taxi drivers—who is from Mexico—told me a story that he was going home from the park one day and a stray bullet hit his three-year-old son in the head…while he carried him in his arms! The child died on the spot."

"That's possible, I understand your feelings. I will do whatever you wish," Hekmat said submissively. "Even though, to me, taking a daily walk is like medication. I've been doing this for as long as I can remember. I will fulfill your wish as far as the children and will limit my walking to Mondays only for the time being."

"Thank you, uncle."

Zahir resumed his taxi-driving job. He would leave home for work at 6 a.m. and would return home at 6 p.m. Every day after returning from work, instead of getting some rest, he would push Sheila's wheelchair around inside the home until Hekmat served dinner. He quit attending adult school. He was, however, working the maximum number of hours allowed by the taxi company. He was quieter than before. His answers were short. He would avoid having discussions with Hekmat and sometimes he did not even join the family for dinner.

Hekmat taught Sheila at home in accordance with the rules set by the school district. He became both a teacher and a playmate to the girl. In order to make up for his daily walk and also to ward off the stress of the recent tragic events, he tried to keep moving inside the house.

The sorrow that was vivid on the faces of Sheila and the other little children as a result of having lost their mother was contagious; it affected him deeply. In addition to it all, his inner self was gravely disturbed by self-blame. He couldn't avoid telling himself that he was the one who destroyed the life of this family. He gradually lost interest in taking notes of every gun–related crime whenever there were reports on TV or the Internet. Sometimes, he didn't even want to watch the news and let the children watch their cartons instead.

A few months went by. Apparently, Zahir had come to terms with his daughter's inability to walk on her own. Hekmat had taken not of his (nephew's) calmness and felt delighted. One day Hekmat prepared breakfast and woke up the kids so they could eat together. Sheila turned on the TV and, while switching channels, she accidentally tuned into ABC. The 8 a.m. newscast had no story that interested the little girl. Still, the news of a shooting on Highway 80 pulled Hekmat out of his deep reverie as he drank his green tea.

"A commuter opened fire on a taxi cab, injuring the driver and a passenger. Both injured were taken to the Alta Bates Summit Hospital in Berkeley and their condition is reported to be critical."

"Oh God, Zahir is working on this route, please save him!" he prayed as loud as he could. The kids looked at him.

"What's going on, grandpa?" Sheila asked.

He didn't answer. He quickly dialed Zahir's number.

"*Salaam*, son, how you are doing, is everything ok?"

"Uncle, my heart is trembling. Someone fired the gun on a taxi that was just a few feet ahead of me. Thank God the bullet didn't hit me!"

"Yes, thank God. Just heard the news on TV and was worried about you. I'm so glad that you are ok."

"Your dad is fine." He assured the kids.

Zahir didn't continue working that day. He returned his cab to the company and went home, where Hekmat was expecting him. His face was pale. Of course, he didn't make enough money to even pay the taxi lease dues. He wasn't able to talk. Hekmat gave him time to relax until lunch was eaten.

"It was just a matter of seconds," Zahir started telling the story. "I was behind that taxi, we were driving 75 miles per hour. I heard gunshots...tak, tak, tak." Zahir sighed heavily. "That cab slipped to the right side of the road and I changed the lane at the speed of light. Thank God my car didn't slip or roll because the road was wet... changing the like that lane at that speed is extremely dangerous."

Zahir paused. He wasn't able to continue talking for a few seconds.

"Had the shooting occurred one second later or had I not changed the lane so quickly, I would be dead now," Zahir flicked his tongue over his dry lips. "When I went to my company to return the car, they told me that that taxi driver belonged to our company. His name was Manan and I knew him."

"How did you know him?" Hekmat asked.

Zahir remained silent for a second in sadness.

"Whenever we waited in line at the airport or in front of a hotel, we would chat with one another. He was a good man. They said he was hit in the head and died at the hospital."

"Another victim of gun freedom," Hekmat said.

Zahir nodded in agreement and added, "This poor Afghan had four children, and he came to America 15 years ago. He lived in a rental apartment in San Leandro."

Zahir paused and Hekmat took the opportunity to speak.

"This situation confirms what I have said to you time and again—even if he had a gun, he still couldn't protect himself from this shooting, which means that there is no point for one to have a gun in his pocket."

"Yes, uncle, but the thing is—if it were me, my children would all be orphans now, without parents, and it's very possible that, sooner or later, I might be a victim of a gunshot as well."

Hekmat had no convincing words to debate with Zahir. All he could do was try to console him.

"God forbid son, I pray day and night for your safety."

"The prayers are not working uncle," Zahir became apprehensive in an unusual way. "He was also a Muslim, he and his family must have prayed many times in the past—but a gun can kill anyone regardless of prayer. He was also an Afghan immigrant and a taxi driver, exactly like me. Is there any guarantee that it will never happen to me? I think that the shooter was after him for one reason only—I think it was a hate crime!"

Hekmat listened to him carefully. Both remained silent for a few seconds. Zahir repeatedly wiped his hand over his chest.

"If it was a hate crime, why would the shooter also hit the passenger?" Hekmat asked.

"The shooter just wanted to kill the driver, he didn't care about the passenger."

"It's strange. Let me do some research about the shooter, as well as about the lady passenger, to see whether it was a hate crime or not," Hekmat said, hoping to calm Zahir's anxiety.

The next day was Monday. Zahir was off and stayed home with his children. Hekmat went to the Oakland Police Department and asked an officer if he could get the report related to that shooting incident on Highway 80.

"What makes you interested in the report?" the officer asked him.

"I want to know who the intended target was—the taxi driver or the passenger."

"Why do you want to know that?"

"The taxi driver killed in the shooting was my

nephew's friend. He was a Muslim and our countryman—an Afghan. My nephew is suspecting it was a hate crime."

"So?" the officer shrugged.

"It's scary. My nephew is also a taxi driver. He thinks that certain cab drivers are being targeted by certain groups of people."

"Interesting, we have no indication of such a thing. If your nephew wants to talk to us, he is welcome to come and talk to us."

"I will let him know—but what about the report, can I have it?"

"Actually," the police officer said. "We don't cover highways, the CHP does."

"Can you please give me the CHP number?"

"Yes."

He spoke with the CHP over the phone and was told that all he could get was whatever information the media had. They don't publicize all parts of the report.

The public portion of the report was broadcasted on most TV channels during their evening news.

"The shooter was driving a Cady. He fired at a taxi vehicle on Highway 80 on Sunday morning. The taxi driver was hit in the head and died at the hospital. The female passenger is hospitalized and is in critical condition. No arrest has been made yet."

One week later, the wounded lady was released from the hospital. She told the media that she had no idea why she was a target of the shooting. She said she had no problems with anyone.

The police concluded that "Probably, she was mistaken for someone else. No evidence was found indicating that the cab driver was a target either."

"There was no indication that it was a hate crime," Hekmat told Zahir.

"If it wasn't, then I think that the only other possible motive for this incident would be that the shooter must have wanted to kill the cab driver for some reason—which means that I am in the same boat as him."

Zahir's mental condition gradually deteriorated. He would cut his workdays short now and then. He tried to stay away from everyone, avoiding getting together with the family even at mealtime. He especially avoided Hekmat.

The fear of losing Zahir as a young family member scared Hekmat. In addition to all other responsibilities, he mandated himself to help Zahir cope with his emotional trauma.

"Dear son, I know you are stressed," said Hekmat in a soft fatherly tone when he went to Zahir's bedroom one evening before dinner. "These things are not new in America. They happen all the time here and everywhere in the country. You should not lose your hope for the future. Try to look after yourself and make sure you are safe. Your children need your love and attention. I need your company and your friendship. You should care about us, too. Please come and join us for dinner!"

Zahir listened to his "uncle" while lying down on his

bed and replied only after Hekmat was about to leave him alone, walking away in disappointment.

"Sorry, uncle! I can't help it. I hate to be away from you and my children, but sometimes I have no patience for sitting and chatting with you."

"What's bothering you the most? Tell me, we can talk it over. You know very well that I am also saddened by the deaths of Fahima and by what happened to Sheila. Still, we cannot forget our responsibilities and we can't forget to take care of our children."

Still lying on his back, Zahir put his hands on his chest, closed his eyes, and murmured, "Everyone out there carries a gun; the men and even women that get in my taxi all have a gun on them—someone will someday shot and kill me. Then my children will be alone and you will be alone, too."

"Son, you are spending a lot of time thinking about this, I can see that you have become overly anxious. Let's go and see a therapist, I'm sure that your condition will improve."

Zahir's eyes were still closed.

Hekmat continued, "We will, in the meantime, look for another job for you. I'm sure that your English is a lot better now. You can work in a store, you can get a job at a prestigious store where you can feel safer."

Zahir looked up, nodded in agreement, and said, "There is no need to see a therapist, I like the idea of working in a store."

That night for the first time in a few days, Zahir joined the family for dinner and had extensive discussions with his "uncle" regarding his future job prospects and the future of his children.

The next morning Zahir tried to apply online for a job with several different stores, such as Target, JC Penney, and Macy's. He found the long questionnaires that all job seekers must answer very hard. He told Hekmat that his English was not advanced enough to do a good job of answering all the questions. After reviewing the questions, Hekmat said to himself, *it's not about English, it's about his mental weakness.*

Zahir red his "uncle's" mind and asked, "What do you think, uncle? My brain doesn't work properly, right?"

"No, son, that's not the case. I know you are so sensitive to this issue, no doubt you have been gravely affected by the recent events. Still, I am sure that, after a while, you will regain your normal mental strength and will be able to answer all these questions."

"But you know uncle," Zahir said, shaking his head negatively, "working in stores, under other people, brings its own problems. Tomorrow, I will be going back to the taxi job." Zahir was determined.

"Like what, what kind of problems?"

"I like to be my own boss. I don't feel comfortable working for a supervisor."

"But you worked in a more challenging and disciplined environment before, with the Americans, didn't you?"

"I did. But I'm no longer that strong man, I know myself."

"Ok, son, whatever you like. But don't hurry, wait a few more days and give yourself time!"

"My mind is made up, uncle. I'm going back to the taxi business and when I save some money, I will buy a gun."

Hekmat didn't show any reaction. He put his head down. Zahir realized that his "uncle" was disappointed by his determination but had no patience for reasoning. Therefore, he also put his head down.

"What would be the benefit of having a gun?" Hekmat asked while his head was still down and he sipped his tea.

"The benefit of having a gun is that my mind will be at ease. I know you don't agree with me, but please allow me to buy a gun so that I will feel safer and have a little bit of peace of mind!"

Hekmat emptied his cup of tea in silence and then looked up and addressed Zahir while staring at the opposite wall in the living room.

"Son, there are other ways to make your mind peaceful and to relax. Owning a gun may not actually give you peace of mind—it might cause you more trouble."

Hekmat got up and pushed Sheila's wheelchair to the corner of the family room, where he taught her lessons for the day.

Zahir resumed his job at the same taxi company as before. He worked full time, six days a week. After three weeks, he looked better and was making over $100 per day. He would give this information voluntarily to Hekmat every day as soon as he came home from work.

"I'm glad to see that you are feeling well and doing a good job," Hekmat said one day after Zahir counted his pocket money in front of him, which amounted to $120.

"Yes, uncle, now I can save some money to buy anything I want."

"You mean a pistol?" Hekmat asked.

"No, a pistol is cheap, it costs just $50 or so. I am thinking about buying an electric wheelchair for Sheila, so then she would be able to move around on her own."

"That's a great idea, thank you."

Suddenly, things changed once again. One day, Zahir stopped working in the middle of the day, returned the cab to the company, and went home.

"*Salaam*, uncle," he sounded miserable. "Did you hear the news?"

Hekmat looked at his pale and nervous face in astonishment.

"No, what happened, why did you come home so early?"

Zahir sighed heavily. He shook his head in despair.

"I gave a ride to a passenger somewhere in Union City. At the very moment that my passenger got out of the car, another car stopped right behind me—a man got out and shot my passenger right before my eyes, then took off." Zahir sat on the sofa, leaned back, and closed his eyes. "He was a young guy."

"Who, the killer, or the passenger?"

"The killer. My passenger was a middle-aged man."

"What happened then?"

Zahir was silent. He opened his eyes a few seconds later, placed his hand over his chest, and answered, "My heart is still pounding. I was terrified. I stayed in my car until the police arrived," Zahir sighed heavily. "The police asked me some questions and then let me go. I couldn't work anymore. I went straight to the company, and returned the cab."

"You did the right thing, son. I'm glad that nothing happened to you. Now, try to get some rest and to relax!"

"I can't drive a taxi anymore," Zahir stated with a firm resolution.

"That's okay son, we'll talk about it later."

Zahir was down again and was depressed even more severely than before. He stopped working. He stayed in his bedroom again and avoided coming out to the living room. He refused Hekmat's numerous requests to come to the living room and to talk to him. He would leave his bedroom to get some food and drinks from the kitchen only when Hekmat was out shopping or in his bedroom. His only communication with Hekmat was when he watched the news on TV in the living room—he would shout from his bedroom.

"Turn it off uncle, it's all about shootings and killings!"

Hekmat would obediently turn the TV volume down.

He must see a therapist, Hekmat thought.

From that point on, Hekmat approached him more aggressively. He would go to his bedroom more often and advise him to go see a psychologist. This went on for a week and a half until Zahir became sick and tired of being pushed by his "uncle" to go to a therapist.

What would my children think of me? Everyone will consider me mentally sick, Zahir thought to himself.

He finally decided to go back to work instead. This time he worked more steadily and more hours than before. Some days, he even worked the night shift, which, in the past, he had refused to do despite repeatedly being requested by the taxi company. When Hekmat asked him about the schedule change from the day shift to the night shift, he responded, "The night shift is good, I want to make more money."

"I don't feel good about it, because now you sleep in the day and go to work at night, the children can't see you. They miss you and sometimes they cry for you when you are not home at night."

"It will only be a few nights," Zahir answered indignantly.

"What about your safety—in the past you mentioned that the night shift was dangerous?"

"Well," Zahir stretched his arms as if feeling sleepy. "To tell you the truth, uncle—if I don't have a gun, I don't see any difference between a dayshift and a nightshift."

"No son, come to your senses, in the night, if you drive to a bad area, it's easy to get robbed," Hekmat said, a bit irritated by Zahir's naivety.

"Just pray for me, uncle, I am kind of bored with my life," Zahir said and walked away from the conversation.

He worked the night shift for four weeks in a row, seven days a week. During this period, he maintained minimal contact with his children. He would start working at 6 p.m. and would come home around 6:30 a.m. while everyone was still in their beds and slept until 4:30 p.m. Hekmat used the 30 minutes to one hour that Zahir spent with the children before going to work to do some shopping. It was stressful.

It was Monday again. Hekmat didn't hear Zahir coming home in the usual morning time. He waited until 10 a.m. but there was still no sign of Zahir. He snuck into his bedroom; he wasn't there. Hekmat closed the door slowly and then knocked on it, in case Zahir was in the bathroom. He wasn't there either. Then, he ran to the living room, grabbed his cell phone to call him to make sure he was ok.

"*Salaam*, uncle," Zahir entered home at the same moment that Hekmat was calling him.

He was in an unusually cheerful mood. Hekmat stopped dialing his number and stared at him, expecting him to deliver bad news or to look sick or something. But he waved to his "uncle" while smiling instead.

"*Salaam*, son. You are late, I was concerned about you."

"Look, uncle, what I bought!" he went near Hekmat and showed him a pistol secretly, trying to hide it from the children, who ran toward their father.

Hekmat stared at the gun dejectedly. He pushed Zahir's hand away and tried to say something but Zahir was quick to present his reason for purchasing the gun while putting it back in his coat's inner pocket.

"I have no other way, uncle, but to get one. My life is full of fear without it."

"May God save us all," Hekmat said disappointedly. "Now that you bought it, make sure that you store it in a safe place, where the children can't see and won't have access to it!"

"What's the point of keeping it at home? I have the permit to carry it with me, that's what I bought it for," Zahir said indecently.

"I don't agree with you, son," Hekmat uttered in a serious tone. "As I said before, a gun can't save your life. I'm afraid it may even cause you some more trouble. God forbid."

"Nothing bad is going to happen to me, uncle. Don't worry."

"I hope so. But please go back to the day shift, so we will not be worried about you at night. I never have peace of mind and never sleep without being worried about you—not for a single night since you started working the night shift!"

"Ok, uncle, I will do that starting tomorrow."

Having a gun in his pocket heightened Zahir's morale. He now left for work early in the morning, without the usual feelings of anxiety. He would examine and revolve the gun magazine in his hands every night before going to bed, placing it under his pillow. Before leaving home, he would stick it in the back of his pants, cover it with his coat—the way the movie stars do. Touching his gun with his hand would give him a sincere feeling of pride and security. He would do that at least five to ten times during his ten-hour shift every day.

I am no longer afraid of anyone, he told himself every time he touched his revolver.

This provided him with the audacity to travel and take fares to any dangerous part of the city. He was also speaking in a different tone and conversed with passengers more boldly in case of a dispute, whatever the reason. Unlike in the past, he was in a better mood at home as well. He ate with his family and told stories about his daily work.

"Don't look back—take out all your money!"

During the second week of being a gun owner, a heavy young guy pressed the muzzle of a larger revolver to the back of his neck from the back seat of his cab.

"Quickly, you punk!" the guy shouted before getting out of the taxi.

It was five in the evening. Not dark yet. He was told to stop in the middle of a street from where he could see other cars driving by less than 200 feet away. He slowly extended his hand under his coat toward his back, but immediately heard another gruff roaring voice from the back seat.

"Don't try it, you jerk, hand me all your money, quickly!"

He moved his hand away from his back and pulled out all the money he had made during the day, plus a few hundred dollars of his savings from the inside pocket of his jacket, and handed it over to the man.

"Don't look behind, run straight!"

The man grabbed the money from his hand and ran away down the back of the street. Zahir, too, took off hurriedly and without glancing at the thief, left the scene, and went straight to the taxi company.

"I got robbed, have no money today," he told the person behind the cashier window.

"You still have to pay your dues!"

"I have nothing today, I will pay you tomorrow."

He was let go without paying the daily rental fee. He borrowed a couple of dollars from another fellow driver and took a bus home. While walking home from the bus stop, he looked around, still afraid of the man, and he couldn't even touch his own gun until he got home.

"What was the use of my gun? Had I taken it out, he would have killed me right away."

While he was telling Hekmat the story, he inadvertently admitted this.

Hekmat praised him for not pulling his gun out and reminded him.

"I told you that having a gun would not save your life always—and that sometimes it might even cost your life." Hekmat said compassionately and added. Thank god he didn't kill you because, as you said, the guy kind of sensed that you have a gun on you, I am surprised he even didn't try to take it from you."

Zahir lost his recent euphoric feeling of being safe and sound. His fear returned, now intensified by the bad experience; he became disappointed with gun ownership forever. He worked for one more week. This time, he developed a complete hatred for his job and never demonstrated an interest in doing anything else either. Hekmat also refrained from making any suggestion to him about looking for another job. He preferred to have his "nephew" safe at home rather than him making money but being exposed to danger.

Zahir locked himself in his bedroom. He even ignored his children's knocks on his door.

"It's Shapor's birthday tomorrow," Sheila shouted at his bedroom door but he disregarded her.

He skipped eating for three days in a row. After

knocking and pounding on the door, Hekmat finally thought of breaking his bedroom lock to do a welfare check on him—or, if needed, to call the police to do just that.

"Leave me alone," Zahir screamed when Hekmat used a screwdriver and hammer to break his bedroom lock.

"Come out, son, it's not right that you've locked yourself in your room, your children need you," Hekmat said authoritatively.

"What do you want me to do?" Zahir said, squeaking.

"You should see a therapist or your life will be wasted!"

"What can a therapist do for me? Can they give me my Fahima back, can they restore my little girl's healthy legs?" he grumbled while wiping a dry drop of blood that was stuck on his lower lip by the corner of his mouth.

"No son, they can't do any of these things. What they can do is to help you diminish your pain, they can help empower you to cope with your sorrow efficiently so that you are capable of going on with your life. Therapy can assist you to take care of your three children," Hekmat lectured him while standing by his bedroom door.

"Go ahead, make me a quick appointment, I'm dying," Zahir shouted.

On the day of the appointment, which was a week later, Zahir's body was shaking, his eyes were red, and snoozing. Hekmat held his hand, walked him to his car, and drove him to the doctor's office.

At the psychologist's place, Hekmat was seated between Zahir and the three children, holding Zahir's shoulders to keep him from falling. When it was Zahir's turn, the female therapist called his name in the waiting room. She looked at him with astonishment and directed him to her office. After both were seated face-to-face, she extended her hand toward him.

"My name is Elizabeth, what's your name?"

"Zahir."

The psychologist gazed at her patient, attentively. Even though he didn't shave for two weeks and his face was pale and his lips dry and cracked, she thought he looked familiar.

"I think I have seen you somewhere, but I can't remember where," the doctor said.

Zahir pressed his eyes, briefly glanced at the therapist, but said nothing.

"What do you do for a living?"

"Nothing."

"You've never worked before?"

"Before, I drove a taxi," Zahir said with a minor accent.

"Aha," she exclaimed. "Now I remember you, don't you remember me?"

He immediately and without looking at her, shook his head negatively.

"I'm the passenger that you took me to the SFO, who left my wallet in your cab. I had hoped that you would call me someday so that I could thank you again."

Zahir glanced at her and then put his head back down without showing any reaction.

"By the way, do you understand me well or do you need an interpreter?"

"I understand you," Zahir answered in a low whimper of a voice.

"Good. Please let me know if you don't understand anything, I can repeat until you do."

Zahir nodded in agreement.

"Ok, tell me what brings you here today?" she asked him in a tender, soft voice.

Zahir didn't answer and she observed tears in his eyes. She didn't ask another question for a while. He blinked a few times so that he could make tears in his eyes disappear. He continued to remain silent.

"Please tell me what bothers you, I hope I can help you," she spoke again in a kind and compassionate tone.

"I lost my wife," Zahir cried.

"I am so sorry to hear that. How? What happened to them?"

"In mass shootings. My wife was on a bus when she was shot by a gunman."

The lady expressed empathy for Zahir's agony as he repeatedly wiped the tears running down his cheeks. He pulled out a tissue from the tissue box that she held out to him.

"Unfortunately, this is the bare reality of our society, some sick people take the lives of others." The therapist wondered whether Zahir was with her because he seemed distracted. "Do you have other children too?" she asked.

"Yes."

"How old are they?"

"My eight-year-old daughter was permanently disabled by gunshots another day, and I have two other small children."

"It's regrettable that your children lost their mother."

Zahir remained silent.

"I know it's hard to cope with this kind of tragedy. Still, you need to look into the future and try to be strong for your children," the therapist said.

"How can I be strong when my daughter is crippled for the rest of her life? Her entire life will be miserable, she will never be able to make a family, and she will be ashamed before her friends. I will suffer because of her for the rest of my life," Zahir said as he reached for the paper tissue box again and pulled another one.

The therapist let him go on talking. After a few moments, he added, "My other daughter is only three years old and my son is five years old, they will grow up without a mother. I became a widower at this age—this is the gift that America gave me!"

"I know it's sad," the doctor said. After a brief pause, she asked, "Do you have parents?"

"My mother is alive, but my father was killed in a suicide explosion in Afghanistan."

"Sorry to hear that. I know, a lot is going on in Afghanistan."

The doctor noticed that her patient was gradually opening up. Therefore, she tried to go deeper into his childhood background.

"If you don't mind, tell me something about your childhood—your parents and anything else that is important to you that you want to talk about."

"My parents were very good people, they loved me and they loved each other too."

"Very good," the psychologist said appreciating the fact. "Besides the agony of losing your wife and your daughter becoming disable, is there anything else that bothers you?"

"Sheila's future and the safety of my other children bother me a lot. I'm afraid that the same thing will happen to them or to myself one day."

"I understand your concern. I sympathize with you. This is a source of anxiety for some people, unfortunately."

"So, what is the solution?" Zahir asked bluntly.

"Well, unfortunately, one thing is obvious—there is nothing that can give you your wife back or return your daughter's health. But what you need to do is try to overcome your fear. In the meantime, in the future, try harder to look after yourself and your children!"

"What do you mean by looking after myself and my children? When people can be killed on a bus or children can be shot on the streets—how can I save them from being killed?" Zahir got heated and went on. "Do you mean that I should carry a gun myself? And I did that too. It didn't save me from being robbed. Actually, I would even have been killed had I pulled my gun out of my pocket while the criminal was pointing his gun at me."

"Honestly, I don't know much about gun politics. As far as your depression and anxiety, I will have some more professional advice for you next week, as our time is almost up."

When the therapist walked Zahir to the exit door of the building, Hekmat was there, waiting for him with the children.

"Is this your uncle?" she asked Zahir.

"Yes."

The therapist shook hands with Hekmat and gave him her business card.

"Please feel free to call me whenever you have a question or if you want to tell me something about your nephew's condition!"

"Thank you. I do want to talk to you about him, is it ok to call you on the phone?"

"Certainly."

On the way home, Zahir was quiet. When Hekmat asked him about his session with the therapist, he murmured disappointedly, "It was nothing. She did not offer me any solution to my problem. But she did say that she will give me some more professional advice next week." He paused a moment and then expressed his dissatisfaction. "Why next week, I am crazy now? Why is she making me wait until next week?"

"Let's be patient, she is an experienced professional. She knows how to treat you step–by–step. Next week she might have something more positive that will help you!" Hekmat said while silently feeling for him.

It was the middle of the night when Hekmat heard sobbing. He stopped reading the book titled *Inside the Criminal Mind* by Stanton Samenow and sharpened his ears. This time he was able to identify the direction from where the cry had come. He rushed to Zahir's bedroom, sat down by his bed, and held his head in his arms.

"What's going on, son, why are you crying?" Hekmat asked his "nephew" in a soft, empathetic tone. Zahir wiped his tears with his hand and remained silent.

"What is that makes you cry, son, please tell me!"

"Nothing," Zahir replied and pulled his blanket over his head.

This situation repeated a few more nights before Zahir's second session with his therapist.

"How are you feeling, how was your week?" asked the psychologist.

"Not good," Zahir answered.

"I know, what happened to your family is nothing that can be forgotten that soon. As I mentioned at the end of our last meeting, I have prepared some advice for you, which is based on scientific research and with which many mental health professionals agreed."

As she spoke, she took a one-page paper out from inside one of the books that sat on her desk.

"Luckily, I found a very recent New York Times article—dated August 6, 2019—which contains an abundance of good advice for parents like you."

Zahir looked up at her mouth with the utmost interest, hoping to hear important words that would benefit his and his children's lives.

"Managing Fear after Mass Violence," the psychologist started reading the paper. "This is the title of an article authored by Jessica Grose. This article was inspired by recent mass shootings in several American schools. It quotes the professional advice rendered by some known mental health professionals."

Zahir tried to focus on what his therapist was going to quote.

She went on to read, "Parenting is an ongoing process of learning to tolerate the idea 'That you cannot entirely keep your children safe,' said Dr. Alexandra Sacks, M.D."

The therapist put down the paper onto her desk and went on to provide her own interpretation of the paragraph.

"That's one idea, which means that we should acknowledge the harsh reality of our society in which these crimes might happen again and again."

Zahir blinked in astonishment as Dr. Elizabeth concluded.

"It's even worse than I thought," Zahir said. "I never imagined that there will be no ending to the killings in America—is it what you mean?" he asked sounding genuinely shocked.

"Unfortunately, that's what it is," the therapist said and went on to continue reading the article. "Understand that a few days of increased anxiety is normal. 'It's an appropriate response to a really traumatic event,' said Dr. Pooja Lakshmin, M.D."

After finishing the quotation, she commented on the author's qualifications.

"Dr. Lakshmin is an expert on healing techniques for those affected by gun violence."

She skipped a portion of the article because it didn't relate to her patient's condition. She then read the following paragraph, which caused Zahir's eyes to open widely.

"Try to stick to your routine. 'Every time a shooting happens, our sense of reality falls apart,' Dr. Lakshmin said. 'The world you thought you were living in is not the world you're actually in. So trying to maintain your routine keeps you tethered to your day-to-day life. Overcoming your fears by taking your kids to the park, to the store, or to camp as planned can help to keep the anxiety from overwhelming you.'"

After finishing reading the article, she left the room and returned a few moments later with a copy of the article. She handed it to Zahir.

He extended his hand to take the paper from her very reluctantly and, while looking in her eyes for the first time, said, "I think that last time when I explained my condition to you, I said that I haven't been feeling good, that I haven't been sleeping well for weeks now, and that I don't let my children go to school—I don't even let them go out to the park in the company of my uncle. Now, can you imagine better how I am doing? And what will your advice to me be?"

The therapist looked impatiently at the clock on the opposite wall, indicating that their time was almost up. She rose, opened the door for Zahir.

"I will talk to you next week and I promise to find you more resources that will be conducive to your condition." She walked Zahir out to the lobby.

"How was it this time, was it helpful?" Hekmat asked Zahir about the session when he started driving them back home.

Zahir put his hand up, holding the article paper high.

"Yes, she told me that the complete solution to my problem was in this paper," he said cynically.

"What is it?" Hekmat asked, sensing Zahir's disappointment.

"I don't know, uncle. You can look at it at home, but I think that I should not be wasting your time anymore. The doctor doesn't understand at all what I am going through."

Once home, Hekmat went through the article from A to Z.

"This article contains good guidelines for those Americans who have experienced the loss of their children to school shootings. However, I do agree with your concern because some of these guidelines don't speak to your unique situation. I will talk to the psychologist on the phone tomorrow and explain to her what you are going through—and we'll see if she could address the root causes of your trauma and come up with a clinical remedy."

"Uncle, she can't help me. I think my brain is being squeezed, tortured, and hammered by so many things. I can't get any sleep at night and don't feel like I have a life. I am especially troubled by Sheila's anguish," Zahir said while sitting across from his "uncle" on the sofa and holding his head in both his hands.

"I know, son, but Sheila's morale is high. She is studying with enthusiasm—she never shows any sign of desperation," Hekmat said.

"She is still little, she doesn't realize the implication of her disability. When she grows up and starts dreaming about her future life, then she will realize her agony. When she compares herself to her peers, when she experiences being bullied by them—from that point on, she will live in great sadness for the rest of her life."

"That's what you think. You should understand that human beings get used to their condition. There are a lot of girls and boys, as well as adults, who are crippled—there are so many individuals who have other disabilities. Yet, they still live happy lives or, at least, they don't agonize as much as you think they do."

Zahir removed his hands from his head. He pulled himself closer to Hekmat and said, "Uncle, I'm finally going to tell you what's really going on in my head," Zahir looked around. The children were busy playing. "I have thought several times of shooting one bullet in Sheila's head and then one in my own—this way, she will be relieved from lifelong suffering and I will be done with the heartache forever as well."

Oh God, a strange motive for such a kind and caring father like him—to kill his lovely daughter to stop her anguish, he thought quickly and then leaned back on the couch and gazed at his "nephew."

"Hmm," he paused for a moment. "What about your little Sara, little Shapor, and myself? Don't you have any mercy toward us? Do you have the right to take your innocent daughter's—lovely Sheila's—life?"

Zahir remained silent for a second, then put his head back into his hands and started crying.

"Son, you need to be strong, you still have a long life ahead. You have a responsibility to your little three children!" Hekmat addressed his" nephew" in an influential fatherly manner.

Zahir kept his head down in his hands and stayed silent.

Hekmat realized the gravity of the situation. He was prepared for a more serious conversation. He even thought about calling the county hotline or 911, asking them to take Zahir to a psychiatric facility. The young man abruptly got up and ran to his bedroom. He grabbed his handgun from under his pillow and then ran to the garage, after which he rushed to the backyard of the house.

"What are you doing, Zahir? For God's sake, don't multiply our tragedy!" Hekmat shouted in a very loud voice and then ran after Zahir to the backyard.

"Don't worry, uncle," Zahir said unequivocally. "I am not doing anything stupid, I am going to destroy this gun!"

He emptied the gun magazine first, then put the gun on the concrete and started hammering it until it was sandwiched under the heavy strikes and completely unusable.

"This gun and these bullets are not going to kill my little Sheila! I was so close to committing this crime!" he said loudly and then ran to the children's bedroom, where all three of them were playing. He hugged Sheila and kissed her, then kissed the other two children on their foreheads, too.

Hekmat went back to the living room, where he met Zahir whose tears were running down his cheeks. He kneeled right in front of his "uncle" trying to kiss his feet.

"No, son, no!" Hekmat grabbed Zahir's arms and lifted him up. "I am proud of you son, you are a great man—you are my only companion and the only hope of our beautiful kids."

"Uncle, you are my angel. You are my rescuer, you saved me from committing a grave sin. I was on the verge of falling into hell—thank you for saving me!"

Hekmat cuddled Zahir firmly and kissed him on the cheek.

"Uncle, I want to go back and make an appointment with Dr. Elizabeth."

"That's a good idea son. Also, ask her to send a referral to a psychiatrist who can prescribe you medication, I am sure it will help you to get better."

That night, for the first time after a long while, Hekmat was able to get a relatively good night's sleep. In the morning, unlike in the past, he didn't feel his head and body ache. He taught Sheila her daily lessons and had a long chat with Zahir, who was also in an unusually cheerful mood. Then he made his usual announcement, which the kids loved

"I am going to bring ice cream!"

"Yes, grandpa. Yes, grandpa, thank you, grandpa!"

All the children raised their voices in cheers. He was quick. Instead of walking to the market, he used his car. Around 4 p.m., he proposed to Zahir that the weather was great and that taking a walk in the park would feel good for everyone.

"Yes, uncle, it's a good idea. But believe me, I still feel fragile and feeble. I don't think I can walk much. I can stay home with the kids, you please go and have a good walk as you haven't for a long time. I'm sorry, it was all my fault, but today you can go to the park and walk, I wish you enjoy it!"

"Ok, son, whatever you like," Hekmat said and prepared to go out for a walk alone.

It was a nice sunny, mild day. The air on that last Sunday afternoon in October spread the aroma of night jasmine all around the park. A group of children played on the swings under the watchful eyes of their parents. People—men and women—walked along the long walk trail inside and around the park. Hekmat, too, took a walk on the long road, enjoying the fresh air after quite a while. He inhaled and exhaled several times, trying to satisfy his longtime thirst for breathing fresh air.

After briskly walking for a full hour, he sat down on a cement bench. The sun rays had climbed up to the crowns of the trees and, from there, they were gradually disappearing.

Children played and made noises in the park and their cheerful clamor drew his attention—some chased others, some played on the spiral slide, some on the slipper, and two girls helped push one another on a swing set.

My Sheilas are playing and swinging each other on a swing set.

He blinked. When back to the real world, he remembered that one Sheila was home in her wheelchair and the other Sheila was resting in her grave.

His imagination made him emotional. His eyes became teary. His hot tears rekindled his burning desire to write a novel that would condemn the criminal murders of his loved ones. After taking a deep breath, he told himself, *Night is approaching. I will again seclude myself with my thoughts. Zahir is getting better, he will help me care for the kids and I will have the opportunity to restart my writing and to empty my heart of this burning fire.*

As usual, at the time of such emotions, he desired to listen to music. He took out his cell phone and a headset from the pocket of his jacket and, via YouTube, first listened to Beethoven's Moonlight Sonata, then to the Raag Bhairavi violin piece by Kala Ramnath, and, in the end, he listened to Dr. Fetrat Nashnas singing "Sweet life is going faster, like the stream of running water." He repeated this song. Inadvertently, he apprehended the reality that 65 years of his life had gone by already. He immediately remembered a quote that he had memorized years ago: "Don't die before showing your skill to the world."

With this in mind, he murmured, "Don't let yourself die before you achieve the dream of your life!"

This fantasy kept him in the park until it was dark. Everyone left. He became excited by his determination. He jumped up from the bench and strode home. He looked up toward the sky—it was clear and some stars were already blinking. The last breeze of the day pumped oxygen into his brain and now spread the aroma of night jasmine more intensely. At that moment of joy, he heard a voice from behind.

"Stop! Give me your wallet! Quickly!"

He looked back and saw, under the light of a street light, the face of a 14- or 15-year-old boy who had a gun in his hand and was pointing it at him. Another young boy had extended his hand toward him to take his wallet.

"Ok, here is my wallet," Hekmat said while trying to take his wallet out of his pants back pocket.

"Shoot him, he's got a gun!" shouted the other young boy.

"No, I don't have a gun," said Hekmat loudly. While still trying to pull out his wallet, he added, "I wouldn't shoot you even if I did!"

"Liar! You would if you did!" yelled the boy with the gun and, with that, Hekmat's wallet fell to the ground, followed by his bloody body.

The boys fled with Hekmat's wallet and the 25 dollars in it.

Chapter VII

Filling in for his "uncle" seemed to him to be harder than any other job in the world. In his lifetime, Zahir never did house chores, especially cooking, dishwashing, and cleaning the house. In his parental home, it was his mother who cooked delicious ethnic food and did all the housework. After marrying Fahima, he enjoyed the same luxurious lifestyle as in the past. His wife was as skilled a cook as other Afghan ladies and was a dedicated housewife, taking care of all affairs inside the house. Now that he was alone with his three kids, he had no idea what is where. On the first day after Hekmat was shot, he repeatedly asked himself, how the old man had done all these things on his own. He especially found himself weak and unqualified for homeschooling Sheila and for caring for his little children who had become extremely problematic after their mother died.

"I wish he was here. I could go and drive a taxi despite the fear of being robbed," he said to himself.

The children gradually became uncomfortable with their dad. He lacked the patience to endure their noisiness, to play with them, to tell them kid's stories, and to answer their endless childish questions. He would get depressed and annoyed whenever one of the kids mentioned their mother. He depleted his few hundred dollar savings and had no way to go back to work to make more money.

His therapist was the only human connection he had left that he could talk to and share his misery with. He missed the appointment that was scheduled for a week after Hekmat was shot, but he was glad when, a couple of weeks later, she called him on the phone to see whether he wanted to schedule another appointment.

"I'm not sure, but the reason I didn't keep my last session was that my uncle was shot on the day before the appointment," he replied

"Oh, I'm sorry to hear that! What happened?"

"He was walking in the park and somebody shot him."

"Oh, God! It's so unfortunate. What happened then? I mean, did he die?"

"Thank God, no. We just came from the hospital. He is going to be discharged tomorrow."

"Oh, I am glad he will be ok. He is very important to you and your children."

"Absolutely. He is more than important to us."

"Ok, take care. If you can't come tomorrow, that's fine; call me after your uncle is back home and we will schedule you for next week," the therapist said, emphasizing that he should continue to attend his sessions with her.

The kids were jumping spiritedly, making voices, and playing cheerfully in the living room because their grandpa was coming back home after two weeks of hospitalization. Hekmat's wound was healing fast. The bullet had missed his heart by a couple of centimeters. Therefore, while being extraordinarily delighted that he had escaped the "decree of death" for the third time, he was feeling kinder and more devoted to his "nephew" and "grandchildren." Thus, despite having pain and complications in his wounded chest, he resumed his fatherly role as far as making a trip to the nearby market and bringing ice cream and other goodies for the kids.

From the day Hekmat returned home from the hospital, Zahir became absorbed by deep thoughts for his own and his children's futures. He wanted to make a change in his life and to raise his children the way he desired. It took him quite a few days to make up his mind. When he made his "life-changing decision" as he would later call it, he thought of making a surprise announcement to Hekmat. However, seeing his "uncle's" well-founded jubilance and increased warmth towards the family made him put off revealing his decision for the time being. Instead, he asked Hekmat a question.

"Uncle, what do you think, had you been carrying a gun that day—could you have shot the assailants or, at least, scare them off before they shot you?"

Hekmat smiled slightly. He rubbed his chest's wounded area slowly, then replied coolly.

"I don't blame you for thinking like that. But here is the truth, son—the real world is a lot different from the world of movies. Suppose that I did have a gun on me, I am sure that the boy would still have shot me because he was already prepared and set to shoot me—unless I acted as fast as James Bond and shot him at the speed of light before he had a chance to touch the trigger of his pistol. Right?"

Zahir put his head down. After a little delay, he raised his hand, signaling that he had a better suggestion.

"If you have a gun and are walking in such places like a park or a secluded street, especially in the dark, you should have your hand on your gun and ready to use it at any moment."

"Huh," Hekmat giggled loudly. "You would be right if we lived in a war zone, where everyone had to carry a gun and had it ready to use for protection anytime they walked out of their homes. Son, this is America, this is an advanced country, and it's the land of law and order. It has powerful security forces to safeguard the citizens. Still, restricting the ability to carry guns to members of the military and other armed forces only is necessary. I am one hundred percent certain that the government is capable of doing this and is also capable of winning the support of the people to achieve this goal."

Zahir's facial expression signified he was in deep thought. Hekmat believed that he would agree with him.

"I think that I made a mistake when I destroyed my gun," Zahir said to the contrary.

Hekmat leaned back in his seat, pinning his gaze at the ceiling as if preparing for a lengthy argument. He stayed silent for quite a while because he didn't feel like having such a discussion again.

"Why do you think so?" he finally asked.

Zahir pointed his hand to the TV that sat in the corner of the living room.

"Because when you were in the hospital, I was sometimes watching the news. There have been numerous cases of burglary in so many areas, ours included. Just two streets from here, they looted one home that belonged to an old lady. In another instance, they killed a father and a twelve-year-old son."

Zahir paused and tried to remember other such incidents. His memory didn't help and he concluded, "That's why I think we should have a gun at home."

"Did they say anything about the exact circumstances of the incident in which a father and a son were killed?" Hekmat asked.

"Yes, they said they were awake. The father went out to the back yard and the thieves ran away. Still, when the father tried to call the police, the burglar returned and shot him fatally. One bullet went through the kitchen sliding door and hit his son."

"Didn't they say whether the father was armed, too?"

"No, that's why they got killed. Otherwise, the man could have eliminated the intruder or scared him away by firing his gun in the air," Zahir said loudly, justifying the need for owning a gun. He quickly added, "The man's wife told the police that she was on her phone calling 911 at the same time that her husband ran to the backyard."

"You see, there was a deadly mistake made on the part of the father in dealing with the situation. He shouldn't have gone out to the backyard because he gave the burglar the chance to shoot him. Anyway, it's hard to make the right decision in this kind of situation," Hekmat said. "One more thing," he added, "due to the Californian law that pertains to self-defense, one cannot use deadly force to shoot a person who is illegally on your property unless you prove that you defended yourself against the threat of death or great bodily injury."

"So, one cannot shoot a burglar until he fires his gun—is that what you are saying?"

"Sort of," Hekmat said feebly. "I mean some people

would just shoot anyone that intrudes on their property, regardless of whether that person is armed or not. If you kill an unarmed person who broke into your home, this would be considered to be an overreaction to the violation of your property."

Zahir impatiently waited for his turn to speak.

"Still, when there is a home invasion, you don't know whether your life will be threatened or not, but it's certainly a possibility. So, having a gun is better than not having it," he said.

Hekmat stayed silent for a few moments. After sighing heavily, he responded.

"To be honest with you, I've never touched a gun in my entire life and might not use it even if my life is in danger. I will never want to have a gun on me because I might end up taking someone's life if that happens—then I will suffer for the rest of my life. Even if an armed person invades my home, I cannot shoot him because I wouldn't be sure whether that person is determined to kill me or not. Therefore, I prefer to stay away from possessing a gun at all. Instead, I would like to look after myself. Next time, I will try to leave the park earlier rather than staying there until after dark," he became emotional. "I am glad that I did not have a gun when I got robbed by the two youths because taking the life of one or both of them would have caused me eternal pain and suffering."

"But they almost killed you," Zahir argued.

"Right. But next time, besides trying to leave before it gets dark, I will raise both my hands up in the air and ask them to search me first—this way they will be sure that I don't have a gun and then they will take the 25 dollars and leave me alone."

Zahir became weary of his "uncle's" reasoning. He twisted his body, signaling his uneasiness.

"I don't know, uncle, what you are talking about. You don't care about my children's safety. I am determined to buy another gun because I love my children. I have to protect them whenever there is a threat to their lives. If you don't like the gun in the home, then I will have to move out and rent my own apartment. I can drive a taxi in the night shift with a gun in my pocket." Zahir got up to leave the discussion.

"No, son, you don't need to move out. If you want to buy a gun, you can do that but you need to agree on one thing with me—you have to lock it in a suitcase so that the kids would not have access to it."

Zahir walked towards his bedroom, not bothering to reply to the condition Hekmat put forward.

"Listen, son," Hekmat said before Zahir disappeared from the living room entirely. "What do you say?"

Zahir nodded, implying "It's ok."

"Tomorrow is your appointment with the therapist. We should go because this time is more important. Remember, she mentioned last time that she will give us a referral to see a psychiatrist who can give you medication that will help you with your anxiety and sleeping disorder.

Zahir entered his bedroom, showing no reaction.

The young man went back to his previous behavior—staying in bed most of the time. His depression and anxiety resurfaced. He tried to avoid Hekmat and to make trips to the kitchen to get some food or drink only when Hekmat was in his own bedroom or out of the house shopping or something similar. On the day of his appointment, which was a week after Hekmat returned home from the hospital, Zahir excused himself from coming out of his room the whole day. It was 15 minutes before the appointment that Hekmat knocked on his door.

"Son, let's go to your appointment, the children and I are ready!"

"I'm not going," Zahir murmured.

Hekmat was not sure if he really meant it; he knocked on the door again.

"Sorry, son, I didn't hear you; it's time to leave for your appointment!"

"I told you, I'm not going!" Zahir shouted loud enough to astonish Hekmat for the rude manner in which Zahir addressed him.

"Why not, why aren't you going, are you ok?"

"No, I am not ok. Don't bother me anymore!"

Hekmat couldn't believe what Zahir was saying to him. He stayed by Zahir's bedroom door for quite a while, thinking.

"Can you please open the door, so we can talk?" Hekmat said in a tender voice.

"No, I don't want to talk to you!"

"I just want to know, what's wrong? Is there anything I can help you with?'

"No. In fact, you are the one who caused all the anguish to my family and me!" Zahir's voice was extremely harsh.

"Oh God, something terrible is wrong with him,"

Hekmat said quietly and left him alone. He noticed a strange smell coming out of the bedroom.

Allen, Hekmat started an imaginary quarrel with his American friend, *you were telling me that mental illness was the reason for gun violence, but I can prove to you that the opposite is also true. My nephew's mental illness is the outcome of gun violence. He and his family fell victim to gun freedom that you and your NRA friends are so proud of.*

Hekmat couldn't figure out what the smell coming from Zahir's bedroom was. He did realize, however, that it wasn't a nice one. *It smells like hashish, how did he get it?* He asked himself. Losing Zahir to drug and mental illness was not only about losing a young friend or a nephew. It was more about losing his moral values, his commitment to his brother Majid's soul. Worst of all, today, his "nephew" personally blamed him for destroying his family. This caused his feelings of guilt to resurface. His conscience suffered a heavy blow and an avalanche of anguish tormented him.

Hekmat was desperate for help. On top of caring for the three children, he had to deal with a mentally sick man as well. He was obligated to protect his grandchildren from their father, who could be a danger to them in so many ways.

He called the therapist on the phone and told her, "My nephew is not feeling well, I want to come over and talk to you about his condition?"

The psychologist agreed to the meeting.

"He is withdrawn, introverted. He is avoiding me, in

particular. Meanwhile, he might have purchased a gun. In the past, he did talk about killing his daughter and himself."

"This sounds alarming. I didn't know," the mental health professional said. "You know, in this kind of situation—besides having a moral responsibility—you also have legal duty to safeguard the kids from his probable harm as well as yourself. You should be careful and watch his movements."

"Right, but what should I do?' Hekmat asked.

"If he is talking about killing himself or if you sense that anything he is doing is harmful to anyone, you need to call the suicide hotline or the police."

"He is pretty much against me. He blames me for his agonies and I am desperately trying to be careful with him. With him, it's like I am walking on eggshells," Hekmat said.

"I know that you are having a hard time dealing with him; still, do try to convince him to come to our sessions every once in a while."

A few days later, Hekmat went to Zahir's bedroom and softly called his name. There was no answer. When he knocked on the door, a harsh voice roared, "What?"

"*Salaam*, son, how are you?"

"What do you want?"

"Dr. Elizabeth said that she wanted to talk to you and give you some good advice."

"You're the one who needs good advice, not me! You're sick, not me!" Zahir shouted angrily.

Once again, Hekmat couldn't sleep at night. His

feelings of love and dedication were rejected. Zahir acted as if Hekmat was going to harm his kids. One day he warned him not to touch his children anymore. Also, he instructed them in front of him.

"Don't go to him. He is not my uncle, not your grandpa—he is nothing to us."

In the meantime, Zahir also started taking the kids to his bedroom and trying to keep them in there for extended hours until they started crying because of hunger or boredom.

Being kept away from Majid's grandchildren, toward whom Hekmat had developed a deep love and affection, made him feel he was being emotionally blackmailed. One day, the kids called him while their father was pushing them into his bedroom.

"Grandpa, we want ice cream and cookies!"

This was followed by a harsh roar from Zahir, "Shut up! Or I will smash your teeth!"

Hekmat dreadfully needed a way to force Zahir to seek professional help, but there was none. Both the therapist and the city police department told him that they couldn't do any such thing because he was an adult. Without his consent, neither the health organizations nor the governmental authorities could force him to see a doctor, except in a situation in which he tries to hurt himself or someone else—only then could he be taken to a psychiatric hospital by force.

"Son, let's talk man-to-man, like family members or friends. Even suppose I am not your uncle or your late father's best friend; still, I can help you and your children because I love all of you to the bottom of my heart. Please just tell me what made you hate me, what did I do wrong? I will listen to you, I will correct my mistake if there is any!" Hekmat addressed Zahir one day when he appeared in the living room.

Before replying, Zahir first repeated his orders to his kids not to call Hekmat their grandpa and not to get closer to him. Then he turned to Hekmat.

"My father died because of you—he went to Kabul just to visit you," Zahir started crying. "You knew what America was like, you've lived here for thirty years and were aware of the killings and shootings—why didn't you tell me not to come to this country?"

Hekmat closed his eyes and got lost in his thoughts. When he opened his eyes a few moments later, ready to answer Zahir's questions, the angry man had already gone to his bedroom.

I must find out whether he is doing drugs and has bought another gun, Hekmat thought.

A few days later, it was 10 p.m. when Zahir left home as secretly as he could. But Hekmat noticed his unusual move. He was out for approximately 25 minutes before he returned home. He went to his bedroom in the same covert manner.

Three days later, he again left home around 10 p.m. Hekmat locked the house door and waited in the living room. Zahir was mad when he returned home and found that the door was locked. He pounded on the door with a closed fist. When Hekmat opened the door and asked him where he went, he shrugged, "It's none of your business."

"I need to know because you had left the door unlocked, I am responsible for the kid's safety."

"They are my kids, not yours. Next time don't lock the door for me or you will regret it!"

Hekmat observed that Zahir kept his right hand in the pocket of his shabby casual jacket all the time when talking to him and until entering his bedroom.

Hekmat was aware that next to the 7-Eleven, which was located about a 10-minute walk from his home, there was a methamphetamine laboratory and guys would be gathering there in the nights. He suspected that Zahir was visiting that place and probably purchasing the drug there.

By now, Hekmat was seriously suspecting that Zahir was using drugs. He also had doubts that he might have tried to or even succeeded at acquiring a gun. He feared that Zahir and, consequently, his kids were facing grave danger. This situation prompted him to immediately think of something. The first step he thought of was to talk to Zahir once again and to try to find out what he was thinking about. For this purpose, Hekmat looked for an appropriate moment to have a conversation with him. He watched and waited for the day when he would see Zahir out in the kitchen or in the living room.

When Zahir did came to the kitchen to get a bottle of water from the fridge, Hekmat approached him and addressed him in his usual nice and friendly manner.

"*Salaam*, son, how are you feeling?"

"Not good!" Zahir mumbled.

"Is there anything I can help you with?"

"No."

"By the way, are you upset with me, did I do anything wrong?" Hekmat asked humbly.

Zahir grabbed a bottle of water from the fridge and took a step back toward his bedroom.

"Please son, I'm going through a lot, I'm suffering because of your condition. Tell me what's going on?" Hekmat took Zahir's hand before he left the kitchen.

Zahir removed his hand from Hekmat's belligerently and replied while looking down at the bottle of water he was holding.

"All I know is this," Zahir sniffled. "Had you not been in our lives, my family would not have been destroyed."

Hekmat suffered pangs of guilt inside and replied sounding shameful. "You were already planning to come to America, even if I had not come to Kabul and had never met you."

"What about my father's death? He wouldn't have died if it weren't for you." Zahir said triumphantly confident of winning the argument.

"Son," Hekmat murmured. "You know very well that I loved your father, we were like brothers for over fifty-five years. Whatever happened was beyond our control. Now you and I should sympathize with each other and support each other to provide normal living conditions to the rest of our family."

Zahir left for his bedroom, feeling mad and shaking his head negatively.

Hekmat was aware that besides the methamphetamine

laboratory nearby, there were also pot dealers a few blocks down from his house. Zahir's nightly trips outside the home were nothing more than visits to the drug dealers. Above all, how Zahir was starting to treat his handicapped daughter was of utmost concern to Hekmat. Sometimes, after leaving her father's bedroom, she seemed extremely depressed—her eyes were red and her facial expression severely sorrowful. Hekmat profoundly loved Sheila. He cared about her no less than he did for his own Sheila —his own granddaughter. He felt sick whenever Zahir shouted at her, forbidding her to call him grandpa.

The day Sheila turned nine, Hekmat bought a cake with her name on it and a HAPPY BIRTHDAY balloon. He and the kids sang the Happy Birthday song.

"Stop it! There is no reason for celebration," Zahir shouted at the kids when he snuck out of his bedroom. "You know that I don't feel good about it and you shouldn't be pouring salt on my wounds," he addressed Hekmat.

Like a fish thrown out of the water, this was how Hekmat thought of himself because he couldn't see his "grandkids" for days. Zahir would purposely keep them inside his bedroom from morning until their bedtime. Hekmat would still bring home ice cream and cookies for the kids and leave them in the kitchen in the hope that Zahir would take them to the kids, but he never did.

This compulsory and painful isolation resurrected Hekmat's old pain of losing his own Sheila. As the sole remedy for escaping the agony of the situation, he took refuge in resuming his search for the motive of the man who had killed his granddaughter. To achieve this, he decided to interview school officials as well as the shooter's wife.

One day, he prepared breakfast for everyone, as usual. The children were still in their room, scared to come out. He drank a cup of plain green tea and left home so that the kids and their father would feel free to come out and eat their breakfast.

He used this opportunity and walked to the elementary school where he met with the headteacher. He introduced himself as one of the neighbors whose grandchild fell victim to the gun shootings at the school. He was well received by the school authorities. They offered their condolences to him and vowed to assist him with whatever information he was looking for.

"In that sad event, the perpetrator was the father of one of the victims, right?"

"Yes," the school headteacher confirmed.

"I've been asking myself ever since how a normal person could kill his only little daughter. I followed the police reports on this case, but never got any indication about the killer's possible motive. Do you perhaps know anything about it?"

"Hmm," the head of the school said. "It's hard to tell. You might have also heard that the shooter was a nice and normal human being and that he had a good family life."

"Yes, I know that. I also gathered information regarding his educational background and the job he was doing," Hekmat said.

"Yes. As far as the girl, just a month or two before her tragic death, she had fallen ill as a result of bacterial meningitis. Her teacher reported that she had developed some mental deficiencies as a result, such as memory loss, lack of concentration, and certain other neurological problems," the head of the school explained.

"According to her mother, he was crazy about his daughter. I mean he loved her very much," said one of the teachers who was also present at the meeting.

"Thank you for that information," Hekmat said. "Can you please give me any contact information for the girl's mother, so I can talk to her in this regard?" He asked the school headmaster.

"No, unfortunately, I can't. Because it's a matter of privacy.

Hekmat left the school, but not empty-handed. From what he heard at the school, he drew certain similarities between the two situations: 1) The shooter was crazy about his daughter, so was Zahir about his daughter; 2) The shooter couldn't stand seeing his daughter in agony due to her crippling disease and that was how Zahir behaved toward his daughter's agony of being a crippled girl; 3) The shooter couldn't afford to live after taking his daughter's life, so he took his own life too. Reviewing these facts, Hekmat recalled how Zahir had been behaving after Sheila became crippled. Consequently, he concluded that *Zahir is surely thinking about killing both Sheila and himself.*

After this realization, Hekmat had mixed feelings—he

was happy because he thought his efforts led him closer to achieving his goal: finding the motive why the shooter had killed his beautiful little girl. At the same time, his anxiety worsened regarding Zahir's possible motive for taking his and his daughter's lives.

It's a time bomb, he concluded about the situation in his own home.

Walking back home, Hekmat recalled the details of the police reports related to this case and remembered the murderer's last name and the name of the department store at which the girl's mother had worked. While home, he found the store's address on Google. It was located in the city of Fremont. He drove to the store in the afternoon.

"Is Mrs. Angelo working today?" he asked a female employee.

"I don't know, I have just started my shift."

"Who wants to know?" asked a lady who happened to be passing by.

"Hi, my name is Hekmat, I live in the neighborhood in which she lives, and I want to talk to her about a related issue."

The lady pointed to another lady who was professionally dressed in a pink suit, with a slender figure, blond hair, and green eyes in a somewhat larger face, which made her look very pretty. She was speaking to another employee as if she were giving instructions. Hekmat approached her.

"Hi!" he greeted her.

The lady ignored him for a moment until she had

finished talking to another female employee, who nodded obediently and then turned to him.

"May I help you?"

"Yes, Mrs. Angelo, please!" Hekmat said, extending his hand toward her. "My name is Hekmat. I live in the same city in which the elementary school shooting took place last year. I would like to ask you a question."

The lady directed Hekmat to her managerial office, invited him to take a seat across from her, and then asked with a sigh, "What kind of question you have?"

"Please pardon me for taking your time. I am an unlucky grandfather whose granddaughter was killed in the mass shootings at the elementary school, where, unfortunately, your child was also killed by her father in the incident. I am trying to write a book and have been searching for some information to solve this puzzle—to find the motive of a father who took the life of his one and only beautiful child as well as his own."

Mrs. Angelo frowned slightly. After a moment of thinking, she spoke.

"I'm not sure whether I want to talk about this as I suffered enough already having lost my one and only child and my good husband."

"Absolutely. I fully understand how you feel; the only thing I'm interested in knowing is related to the fact that your daughter contracted bacterial meningitis, which presumably led to some brain damage—could you tell me how your husband reacted to her illness?"

"Oh, God," she squealed and suddenly lowered her voice so that no one outside her office could hear. After thinking about whether to answer or not, she finally decided not to.

"I can't discuss this issue with you. I'm trying to go on with my life after a long period of living with the pain of that tragedy."

"I don't blame you. I can't imagine how difficult it was for you to go through such a catastrophe. The reason I came to you is that your information might help prevent other such tragedies in the future," Hekmat said.

"What's your book about?" she asked bluntly, expressing her interest in getting the answer by her facial expression.

"Good question," responded Hekmat enthusiastically. "For you to understand me, I would like to share with you a family secret," Hekmat lowered his voice. "Besides my granddaughter, who was killed during the shooting, my other granddaughter—who just turned nine—lost both her legs as the result of a street shooting?" Hekmat paused for a moment and then added, "Of course every parent loves their children, but my son has gone crazy about her after she became handicapped—he is extremely anxious about her future and thinks that she will have a miserable life ahead. He suffers because of this to the point that he is thinking of freeing her and himself by taking her life and then his own."

Hekmat stopped talking again as he became emotional. Before he could resume, the lady spoke abruptly.

"Very interesting, I have similar feelings about the reaction of my late husband toward our daughter's illness." The lady glanced at her wristwatch, then said, "It's a very interesting subject, but I can't talk much about the matter here. Give me your phone number and I will call you once I get off work at 5 p.m."

"Sure, I very much appreciate your time!"

When he got home, Sara and Shapor were asleep in their bedroom. Sheila was in her wheelchair in the living room, alone, with her head down.

"Sheila Jan," Hekmat called her name, she didn't answer. She looked up only after he touched her head. Her eyes were teary.

"What's going on my dear, why are you crying?"

She carefully turned her head towards her father's bedroom, located in the corner of the lobby adjacent to the children's bedroom, and pointed her finger to it.

"What? Did he hit you?" Hekmat asked in a lower and softer voice while wiping her tears with his palm.

Hekmat pulled Sheila's wheelchair toward the kitchen away from Zahir's bedroom so that she would not be afraid to speak about what happened to her.

"Tell me, why did he hit you?"

She sobbed louder but immediately covered her mouth with her left palm as she noticed that her father opened his bedroom door.

"*Salaam*, Zahir Jan, how are you?" Hekmat greeted him courteously as he entered the kitchen.

"I don't know how I am, I have a severe headache. I feel like my head is exploding."

"Do you want me to take you to a doctor or emergency?"

"No. I just want to be left alone and for you to never ask me about anything!"

"Son, I'm worried about you and your children! Let me help you, let's go to a doctor and get medication for your headache. You know they have good medication for almost everything, including your unhappiness and stress."

"I said, leave me alone!" Zahir said while turning around and walking back to his bedroom. "No one can give me my family back—doctors and medication are all shit!"

He slammed his bedroom door hard.

Sheila looked like she was feeling sleepy or severely depressed. Her head was hanging down. Hekmat rolled her wheelchair to the children's bedroom and put her in the bed.

He received a phone call from Mrs. Angelo around 6 p.m.

"Hello, Mr. Hekmat, this is Mrs. Angelo, where do you want to meet?"

"Anywhere that is convenient for you. If you would like to talk over the phone, that's fine with me," Hekmat responded.

"I don't mind meeting with you because, in my office, you mentioned something that I have been stuck with the whole time after that tragedy."

"Ok, please tell me where you would like to meet."

"There is a coffee shop near my house. If you don't mind, we can meet there," she replied.

"That's fine, please text me the address."

At their meeting, Hekmat repeated his question.

"Once again, how did your husband react to your daughter's illness?"

"After the doctor gave us a long list of the after-effects of the disease, such as memory loss, lack of concentration, clumsiness, headaches, deafness, loss of balance, epilepsy, paralysis, speech problems, and vision problem, my husband started crying. He kept crying all the way from the hospital to our home."

"Did he ever mentioned that he was suffering because of your daughter's condition or that he was worried about her future as a disabled female?"

"Absolutely," Mrs. Angelo replied, stressing the word "absolutely." "That's the point. One time, he even cruelly wished that she would die in a car accident or by some other means before she grows up."

"Were they close to each other?" Hekmat asked curiously.

"Yes, very much. My daughter was an exceptionally sweet, tender, and lovely kid. Her father loved her happy face. He would play with her every day after work and on the weekends."

"I know, it's strange when a father wishes to see his lovely daughter dead," Hekmat said soothingly and continued with his next question. "Did he own that shotgun before that day?"

"No, never. He never even indicated that he bought a gun. He was strongly against the gun lobby and gun violence. I think he acquired that weapon the day before."

Hekmat started thinking. He remained silent longer than Mrs. Angelo could wait.

"What are you thinking about?" she asked.

"Well," Hekmat sighed heavily. "Maybe I got what I've been searching for over a year since that tragic day. My son is behaving similarly. He is crazy about the quality of life of his daughter after she was hit by the bullets and became permanently disabled."

"Oh, God!" Mrs. Angelo exclaimed. "Watch him, I'm afraid that, sooner or later, he will harm her. Especially watch that he doesn't get his hands on a gun."

"Yes, your husband and daughter's story has made me afraid. I should be watching him closely," Hekmat said. "I will even take the kitchen knives away because I'm afraid he will use a kitchen knife to commit the evil act against his daughter."

"I don't think so," Mrs. Angelo said, which surprised Hekmat.

"Why? Don't you think he will use a knife?"

"I don't know your son. But as far as my husband, he had a different mindset about the use of a knife for committing a crime."

"How?" asked Hekmat impatiently?

"Every time we watched a crime movie on TV or when there was news of violence committed with the use of a knife, my husband would always turn away and comment."

Mrs. Angelo paused.

Hekmat looked at her with his eyes wide open. "What would he say?"

"He would say he can't watch it."

"Why?"

"One time, I asked him why he was okay to watch violence with guns but not with knives. And he responded that he couldn't afford to see the horror, the screaming of the victim, and the blood scene involved—but using a gun is easy—just pull the trigger and the job is done."

"Oh, God," Hekmat shouted. "That's how my son is, he hates seeing bloody scenes and that's why he insisted on getting another gun."

"As I said, you need to watch him closely," Mrs. Angelo said sympathetically.

"Ok, Mrs. Angelo, I very much appreciate your time. Do you mind if I call you again in the future in case I have another question?"

"Not at all. But there is one thing that I would ask you if you don't mind," she said and pulled a picture from her purse. "You are writing a book about that incident right?"

"Yes."

"My daughter had a good friend in her class who, I think, was from an immigrant family that had recently come to the United States. My daughter was always talking about her and even when she got sick this girl was still her friend. If possible, I want you to find out who this pretty girl was and if she was also the victim of the shooting or not?"

She showed him the picture.

Hekmat looked at the picture and, in a second, his eyes became full of tears, which he wiped with his left palm.

"What? Why are you crying?" she asked.

"It's my granddaughter," Hekmat said while groaning.

The puzzle was solved. He had finally found out the complicated motive for the school shooting that he had so fervently wanted to find for nearly two years. However, this finding brought a serious warning sign for him. His concern over Sheila's fate became more real. Now he considered Zahir to be a time bomb that could explode any day and take the life of the innocent Sheila and then his own life at the same time.

Sheila began resisting her father's orders to go to his bedroom. She did receive support and camaraderie from her siblings—Shapor and Sara would cry and resist following their father to his room. Sheila wanted to stay in the living room and watch Mr. Roger's videos and cartoons and do her homework. Also, she felt bad for Shapor and Sara and wanted them to be with her and play freely. All three of them loved to listen to the stories that Hekmat would tell them. More importantly, they were desperate to go out of the house to the front yard to get some fresh air, to see the sky, and to play at the playground. But this was precisely what Zahir was against. He even started physically punishing Sheila for her disobedience and for engaging in arguments with him.

Hekmat closely watched the situation. He noticed that the suffocating smell of marijuana was increasingly spreading everywhere in the house. Zahir was now smoking more often and going out of the house more often as well. The children and Hekmat himself started coughing because of that.

"Son, I have noticed that you are smoking marijuana, which is dangerous to both your health and ours. Also, it's a crime to smoke marijuana inside the house and affect the children's health. I am telling you that because

I am not happy about it and I have both a moral and a legal obligation to protect the children from this hazard," Hekmat told him aggressively one day.

Zahir stared at him and, for the first time, Hekmat observed the young man's red eyes and outrageous looks, indicating a deep sorrow as well as dangerous intention.

"What are you going to do? They are my children, not yours!"

"Yes, no doubt about it, they are your children. But I have a responsibility toward them. I feel responsible for you as well but, unfortunately, you are refusing my assistance."

"I don't need your assistance—I have no life, let the pot kill me," Zahir roared and left the kitchen for his bedroom.

One night, around 4 a.m., Hekmat heard a noise in the kitchen as if someone were going through the drawers, shuffling the cutlery. It went on for a while, so he slowly opened his bedroom door and saw Zahir hurriedly searching the drawers one by one. He closed the door without being seen by Zahir and whispered to himself, "I already took the knives away from the kitchen."

Zahir left the kitchen, apparently without finding anything sharp. However, Hekmat still followed Zahir's footsteps carefully to make sure he didn't go into the children's bedroom with something in his hand. The children's room was located between his bedroom and the master bedroom that Zahir was using. He didn't hear anything. He went out to the lobby, pretending to go to the bathroom. Zahir was standing by the children's bedroom and, seeing Hekmat, he quickly moved toward his own room.

As Sheila grew and her breast started showing under her thick Afghan-style shirt, her father tended to aggressively bar her from being with her "grandpa." He was increasingly more verbally abusive toward her while she was in desperate need of fatherly love and care.

"I don't want to see you with him anymore, you either come to my room or stay in yours," he pulled Sheila's wheelchair into his bedroom one day and shouted at her.

"Why? I want to go to the park with my grandpa, you never take me to the park!" she whispered while wiping teardrops from her cheeks.

"No! Don't you know that there are people with guns in the park, they'll kill you? Don't you remember that they shot him a few months ago?" Zahir addressed his daughter dauntingly and then snuck out of his room to make sure Hekmat was not listening.

Hekmat heard the noise but didn't intervene, as "his parrot was deaf lately" (this is an Afghan expression, referring to a person who is unusually and strangely quiet). Hekmat was quiet, notably refraining from intervening between the father and the children.

Hekmat would, from now on, be alone in the living room. He did not feel like watching dramas or his favorite movies nor even like listening to music. All he would do was go out to the backyard, take a short walk, and then go back to the living room. At night, he no longer enjoyed his solitude with his novel file. To avoid the boredom and dullness of life, he tried to kill his time by reviewing books and studying articles online randomly.

Life is getting unbearable, he would think.

One night, he started reading again one of the books he had read a part of before, *Hunting Humans: Inside the Minds of Mass Murderers* by Elliott Leyton. This book took Hekmat inside the minds of some of the deadliest serial killers and mass murderers. Likewise, it gave him insights into the root causes of why they became such "freaks" as Mr. Leyton put it.

On page 1 of the book, the author, a well-known anthropologist, asks an interesting question which was the core of Hekmat's research. The question is: "… Why does modern America produce proportionately so many more of these "freaks" than any other industrial nation?"

Now, the above question is significant because it sounds legitimate when considering the free gun market factor that makes America unique and distinguishes it from other industrial nations. It's a fact that private gun ownership in American society is far larger than that in any other industrial society and, obviously, the reason for that is the gun lobby and the money.

Hekmat was not sure whether Zahir had acquired another gun or not. He was aware that he had no money because he hadn't worked in the last several months and might have exhausted his savings on drugs. Still, as a measure of extra caution, he put the kitchen knives in the drawer of his computer desk in his bedroom, assuming that Zahir wouldn't enter his bedroom even when he was away from home. He also suspected that Zahir might have sold his wife's jewelry and used the money to buy a gun as well as drugs. Therefore, he thought he should consult the city police department. They told him that mentally ill persons who are on drugs will do everything possible to get money to get drugs, including borrowing money from friends and family members, selling their personal stuff, and doing shoplifting. If that doesn't satisfy their needs, then they will commit all kinds of crimes.

Hence, Hekmat determined that it was crucial for his peace of mind and for the safety of the children to find out whether Zahir did something with the jewelry or not. He decided to risk Zahir's probable wrath and to search his bedroom the next time he left the house at night.

One night, Zahir took longer to return home and Hekmat had enough time to search all the suitcases and the drawers of Fahima's dresser. He couldn't see any jewelry nor a gun in. The room was a total miss, however. It smelled like pot. Clothes, dirty dishes, empty bottles of water, cigarette buts and ashes, and match sticks were scattered everywhere. Zahir's pocket wallet was also there, sitting on top of the dresser but without any money in it. His driver's license, a debit card, and a couple of small pictures of Fahima were dispersed on the floor too. Strangely enough, however, under the pillow, Hekmat found a large-sized butcher's blade, wrapped in paper towels. Hekmat examined the knife, it didn't belong to the home. It looked brand new.

A ring on the house doorbell stopped Hekmat from further searching Zahir's bedroom—he turned the light off and ran to the door. A couple of police officers were there, along with Zahir in handcuffs.

"Do you know this gentleman?" one officer asked Hekmat.

"Yes, sir, he is my nephew."

"He was caught shoplifting at Walmart, we are going to take him with us. Here is the phone number for the jail authority in case you want to know what is going on with him."

Zahir was silent, looking down. When Hekmat asked him why he did this, he looked up and replied boldly.

"You take care of my children, never take them outside!"

The police officers wondered what Zahir had said. One of them asked Hekmat to move with him a few feet away from Zahir to talk in private.

"Tell me about him, what's going on with him?"

Hekmat sighed and replied, "He was a nice, intelligent, and hardworking man, but after his wife died in a bus shooting and his daughter lost her legs to a street shooting, he became depressed. He doesn't want to see a therapist, he is not working anymore, and he is smoking marijuana and sometimes talking about killing himself and his young daughter—who is permanently crippled."

"Does he have a gun?"

"I don't know, he used to. But I just searched his bedroom, he concealed a large knife under his pillow."

"What happened to the gun?"

"He broke it one day when he was emotional."

"Can I see the knife?" the officer asked.

"Yes." Hekmat went inside and returned with the knife, still wrapped in paper towels.

The police officer took the knife from Hekmat, unwrapped it, and asked Zahir, "What is this for?"

Instead of answering the officer, Zahir gave an outrageous look to Hekmat and said, "You are my enemy. You've ruined my life and now you want to send me to jail!"

Hekmat interpreted to the officer what Zahir said at the officer's request.

Before the officers took Zahir with them, Hekmat told them that he has a mental condition and should be taken to a mental health facility rather than to jail.

"The jail will provide a mental health worker for him, don't worry," one of the officers said while putting Zahir in the back seat of the police patrol vehicle.

The *back-to-school* day was approaching fast. Little Shapor had just turned six and, according to the State of California Compulsory Education Law, he had to be enrolled in school now. Hekmat had no idea what would happen to Zahir nor how long he would be in jail. Still, as the sole responsible adult person in the house, Hekmat enrolled the boy at the same elementary school that the two Sheilas went to. He bought him new clothes, a backpack, pens, pencils, and crayons. When school started, besides Shapor, he would put all three children in his car and drive to and from the school because he didn't want to leave Sheila and Sara home alone.

Watching Shapor's excitement at going to school and remembering her own time as a student, Sheila wished that she could go to school again. She expressed her wish to her "grandpa."

"Yes, daughter, of course, if you want to," Hekmat said.

Sheila's face changed. Her lips started shivering and her eyes teared up.

"I want, but how can I go in this?" she pointed to her wheelchair.

"Of course you can, let me find you a special needs school. They have special buses that carry students like you."

Sheila's wrinkled lips stretched into a sweet and innocent childish smile.

After a couple of days of calling the county education district office, he delivered good news to his girl, who couldn't wait to hear it. Following the required procedures, Sheila was enrolled in a special education school and her transportation was provided by the school district. Hekmat also bought her new clothes, a backpack, and all the necessary ancillary.

Zahir was transferred to a psychiatric facility after spending four days at the county jail. He had confessed to the jail investigator that the idea behind buying the large blade was to kill himself and his daughter, but that he couldn't do it.

"What made you think of killing yourself and your little daughter?"

Zahir looked down and, within seconds, his eyes became teary.

"I couldn't do it."

The investigator asked him another question, "You couldn't do it because…?"

Still looking down, Zahir remained silent.

"You didn't do it because you were waiting for something to happen or for some particular moment to arrive?" the officer asked.

Zahir shook his head.

"I couldn't tolerate the horror of the scene and the screaming of my child."

"So, you were planning to acquire a firearm and then do it."

Zahir was silent for a moment. When the investigator asked him to answer his question, he started crying, first in a low voice but, gradually, he sobbed as loud as he could.

"No more. I don't want to do it, I love my daughter," he said tumultuously.

"You said no more, does that mean that you were thinking about doing it at some point?"

Zahir nodded his head slowly.

On the last day of his stay at the facility, the treating doctors—one a psychiatrist and one a psychologist—convened a meeting with Zahir to which Hekmat was also invited as the designated authorized representative of the patient. When Hekmat entered the meeting room inside the psychiatric hospital building, Zahir raised and kissed his hands with the same passion as he had shown on the day that Hekmat accepted his request to convey his father's corpse to Kandahar. Zahir then grabbed the four-year-old Sara from Hekmat's arms, squeezed her in his arms, and kissed her warmly on the forehead.

"Uncle, I am sorry for what happened, please help me out of this place, it's killing me!" Zahir said while hugging Sara to his chest repeatedly.

"Let's see what your doctors are going to say, "Hekmat placed his hand on his "nephew's" shoulder and took a seat next to him.

"Where are Sheila and Shapor?" Zahir asked, wondering why they were not with Hekmat.

"They are at school."

Zahir's face turned pale but he didn't say anything as the psychologist addressed Hekmat.

"Your nephew is doing well now. He received proper treatment here as far talk therapy and medication."

"Thank you, sir, I'm so glad to hear that. I've missed him very much and I know how much my grandchildren have missed him too," Hekmat said while tapping Zahir on the shoulder. "I know he was going through a lot due to the loss of his wife. I am wondering if there is anything else needed for him, like medication or seeing a therapist, in the future?"

"Oh yes," the psychologist replied quickly. "Unfortunately, besides depression, he showed signs of anxiety and paranoia as well. Also, he has suffered from severe emotional trauma due to the loss of his wife and the disability of his daughter. Hence, he will need to continue therapy and taking medication."

After the therapist was done with his instruction, the psychiatrist handed a prescription to Hekmat and said, "Take this prescription downstairs to the pharmacy and get this medication." He then looked at Zahir and continued, "Make sure you take the medication regularly or there might be severe side effects. Also, you must refrain from doing crystal because Zyprexa, Celexa, and Clonazepam that I have prescribed are going to have a severe interaction with it."

Hekmat looked at Zahir in bewilderment, then asked the doctor, "what's crystal?'

"It's the street name for a strong stimulating drug called methamphetamine, which is dangerous stuff."

Hekmat gazed at Zahir anxiously.

So my guess was true, he thought. "Is he free to go home?" he asked the doctors out loud.

"Yes, the gentleman is eligible for release from here because, except for the first few days during which he still had some unacceptable thoughts, his condition significantly improved as time went on and he is now ok to go home."

The psychiatrist handed his business card to Hekmat.

"Here is my card, you can call me anytime you feel you need to talk to me about him—or if there is any change in his behavior. Just give us a call."

"I'm glad to hear that he is fine to go home and be with his children again," Hekmat said but still wished that they had kept him at the facility long enough for him to fully recover from his drug addiction. Therefore, despite being mindful of the fact that if he openly put forward his request, Zahir would be irritated, he went ahead and mentioned it to the doctors.

"Just thinking whether it would be better if he stayed here for a few more days—I'm sure he would further benefit from your professional attention and care."

Zahir made a movement that signaled his discontent with the proposal.

"Unfortunately, fourteen days is the maximum time that a patient can stay here unless he still has harmful thoughts or demonstrates dangerous behavior; in such a case, they qualify for long-term psychiatric treatment."

On the way home, Zahir was quiet. However, when Hekmat mentioned that Sara's fourth birthday was going to be tomorrow, he broke his silence.

"Why did you enroll my children in school without my permission? You know I don't want that!"

"Because," Hekmat cleared his throat, "when Shapor started going to school, Sheila felt down and wished to go to school too."

"So you enrolled Shapor in school too? You want my children to die in school shootings as your granddaughter did?"

"No, son, I don't want your children to die. You know, I love them very much. But it's the law that, when a child turns six, they must be enrolled in school."

Zahir sighed heavily but didn't say anything for a few moments. He then sighed heavily again and said unemotionally, "I know, uncle, you are a good man and have been trying to help us, but I think that I don't have any good luck in America, so I have made a life-changing decision which is to take my children back to Afghanistan." This was what he called "lifetime decision" that he had made earlier.

Hekmat looked at him in surprise and started thinking about his own reaction to Zahir's intention.

I don't blame you, but it's going to kill me, he thought.

"Well," he ambiguously said aloud.

"I am wondering why you would want to take your kids back to a country in which there is no security, there are suicide attacks everywhere, there is no electricity, the air is polluted, and so many other negatives exist."

"Despite all those negatives, it's better than living under the shadow of guns and the constant fear of gun violence," Zahir paused briefly and then looked back at Sara who was sitting in her car seat. "Can I use your phone, mine has no battery?"

"Sure."

Hekmat handed him his cell phone. Zahir called his mother in Kandahar. He informed her of his decision to return with his children.

"Really? Why, son? Why are you leaving America?" his mother said, surprised by what she just heard from her son.

"You don't know mother, I will tell you everything once I am there."

"What does your uncle have to say about this?" his mother asked.

"I don't care what he says," Zahir said loudly. "As soon as I get some money to buy tickets, I will leave this country before I lose my own life or my children's lives."

"I want to talk to him, is he there?"

"Not now, mother, maybe some other time," Zahir said without looking at Hekmat.

"Listen, son, I am very sick with a heart problem. I want to speak with him to know what is going on between the two of you," his mother demanded as her voice started shaking.

"Mother, I will call you later, goodbye now," Zahir hung up.

"How is your mom doing?" Asked Hekmat.

"She is fine."

"Why didn't you let her talk to me? She is sick, she shouldn't be bothered with bad news."

"Because I knew what you were going to say to her— but my mind is made up," Zahir said firmly.

"That's fine, son. If you truly feel to go back to Afghanistan, it is ok—but I still want to know what your reason for making such an important decision is?"

"Because my life is important and my children's lives are important."

"Of course they are. But think about this, when your children grow up, they will ask you about your decision and they may not be happy with you."

Zahir gave him a greedy look, catching his eyes.

"Don't worry, that's not your problem. I can explain to them what you have done to my family."

"You are cruel, son," Hekmat addressed Zahir silently as he stopped the car by a grocery store.

"Let's go buy a balloon and a cake for my little Sara's birthday!"

Zahir picked Sara up in his arms and unwillingly followed Hekmat into the store. He sat down on a long bench by the wall near the restrooms, instead of accompanying Hekmat shopping.

"I want cookies!" Sara said loud enough that Hekmat could hear her before he walked too far away.

"Of course, honey," Hekmat looked back and acknowledged Sara by raising his hand.

"I want to go with you!" she begged Hekmat.

Hekmat turned back and held little Sara's hand in his own and let her walk with him toward the bakery section of the store. Zahir frowned heavily and remained sitting on the bench. Hekmat first picked the cookies that Sara pointed to, then selected a vanilla cake, and then walked to the balloon section. He held the shopping cart in one hand and Sara's hand in the other. While viewing colorful birthday balloons, he suddenly heard a violent voice ordering him and all the customers.

"Get down, no one move, get down everyone!"

Sara, terrified by the screaming of the customers, which was followed by the sound of a gunshot, put herself into Hekmat's arms. He picked her up and ran to hide behind a Gondola shelf. Another gunshot in the cashier register area made Hekmat think of Zahir, who stayed there. He tried to sneak through the shelf row behind which he and Sara were hiding. He saw a masked gunman emptying one of the registers and blocking his view of Zahir.

"Shhhhh," he whispered to Sara, who started sobbing. At that moment, a second masked gunman pointed his gun at him.

"Don't move, old man, or you are dead!" the gunman ordered him.

He raised his right hand while holding Sara with his

left hand close to his heart and stayed that way until the gunmen had run away and left the store.

The customers, some of whom had been lying down on the floor and some of whom had been sitting behind the merchandise shelves with their heads down, all rose one after another as the shooting stopped and silence prevailed in the store. Hekmat hurriedly took Sara in his arms and ran toward the area in which he had left Zahir sitting on the bench. He didn't see him there.

He might have left the store at the time of the robbery, he thought.

He wanted to pay for the stuff that he was buying but all three cashiers were in shock, standing by their registers with their arms folded over their chests. The store manager appeared by the exit door and directed the customers out of the store. He repeatedly announced, "Dear customers, please leave the store as the police are arriving soon and we will be closed for business until later."

"They shot two people," a female employee said crying.

Hekmat put the stuff back on one of the cashier counters and while leaving the store he looked around, he noticed one man lying motionless in the corner of the store near the manager's office, the other victim who was lying between the two registers, he didn't see.

An ambulance and three police vehicles arrived within minutes of the store manager's phone call. They entered the store. No one else was allowed to go inside. Hekmat, holding Sara in his arms, ran through each and every row of the parking lot calling Zahir's name as loudly as he could. He went to every corner of the parking lot and passed by his car several times, hoping for Zahir to be standing somewhere nearby. Disappointed with his search, he approached a police officer who was standing inside the yellow taped-off area by the store entrance and asked him whether he could have the names of today's fatalities.

"Why do you want to know?" the officer asked him.

"My nephew," Hekmat couldn't complete his sentence. He then looked at Sara and continued. "This is my granddaughter, her father was with us in the store, but he is nowhere now."

"What does he look like?"

"A tall, young man, 32 years old, he hasn't shaved for a couple of weeks."

"What was he wearing?" the officer asked.

"Blue pants and a gray shirt."

The police officer consulted with a fellow officer who had just come out of the store. When the second officer nodded positively, Hekmat pulled Sara toward the wall and stood there with his back leaning on it. The first police officer approached him.

"Unfortunately, the other officer said that one of the victims matches the description you gave me. But the good news is, he is still alive."

"Oh God, thank you, can I go see him?"

"No, please move to the side, so that the child can't see her father!" the officer instructed Hekmat to move aside as the medical emergency personnel pulled both bodies—one on a stretcher and the other one on a longboard, both covered with white sheets. The bodies were loaded on the ambulance that stood in front of the store. Hekmat quickly blocked Sara's view by standing in front of her until the ambulance took off.

"Where are they going to take him?" Hekmat asked one of the police officers who was talking to the store manager.

"To the county hospital."

It was about time to pick up Shapor from school and Sheila was also going to be home soon. He put Sara in her car seat and drove to the elementary school. Little Sara was hungry and crying. He was crying too, silently. He was crying not only because of the fear of losing Zahir forever but because of the disgrace that he was going to earn for what had happened to his "brother" Majid's son and his family.

Again, it was you who stopped by this store and caused Zahir to be shot, he told himself.

After picking up Shapor, he drove home. Sheila's school bus had just arrived. He fed the children with the rice and chicken meal left from last night. He didn't feel like eating. He drank water and continued thinking until the kids were done eating. Then, he boarded the children into the car and drove quickly to the county hospital, which was located almost twenty miles from his home.

Hekmat and the kids waited for over two hours in the emergency room until a hospital staff member came out.

"Who is here for Zahir?" asked an old but seasoned-looking male doctor.

Hekmat raised his hand.

"Let's go to this room, please!"

The doctor pointed to a small-sized meeting room located in the lobby. Hekmat told Sheila and Shapor to stay in the waiting area. Sara was asleep and he carried her in his arms with him into the room.

"Zahir is your nephew, right?" the doctor asked.

"Yes, doctor. How is he doing?"

"Well, his injuries are quite severe. We just extracted the bullet from the right part of his brain. He has lost a lot of blood. Hopefully, we get him his blood type from our blood bank."

"Can I see him?"

"No, you can't," the doctor replied decisively. "He is in the operating room and will be taken to the ICU afterward. You may not be able to see him for a while."

"How many bullets did he get?" he asked the doctor.

"Just the one."

Back home, Hekmat left the children in the living room, gave them some cookies, and then rushed to his bedroom. He laid down on the bed with his coat and shoes still on. The storm of bitter events made his brain ache merely from thinking about them.

"You are the reason for my family's destruction," he recalled Zahir telling him.

Despite his mental and physical exhaustion and despite knowing that he could call the emergency department to inquire about Zahir's condition, he would make trips to the hospital daily. This was a way of killing his time. He was told he wouldn't be allowed to see his nephew, but he couldn't stay home. He was desperate. He was unsure what to wish for—wishing for Zahir's health and having him stay in America? *What if another family member gets victimized by gun violence, how can I bear the agony?* Or should he wish that Zahir gets better and takes his children back to Afghanistan? *In this case, how can I afford to separate from the kids that I am profoundly and emotionally bonded to?*

His non-stop moral debate went on until the fourth day of Zahir's hospitalization. On that day, after dropping Shapor off at his school, he combed little Sara's hair, dressed her nicely, and took her to the hospital. At the front desk, he was told that his nephew was in the ICU and on a breathing respirator."

"Do you know how long he will stay in the ICU?" he asked.

"We don't know. You don't need to come every day. Just call us on the phone," the person at the front desk told him.

"I know," he whispered.

That day, he kept himself moving around inside his house the whole day. Shapor and Sheila returned from their schools. Little Sara played with her siblings. Near early evening he picked the phone and called the hospital emergency department.

"How is my nephew doing? Is he still in the ICU?"

"Hold on, please, I am going to ask," the lady who answered the phone said.

A couple of minutes later, the lady on the phone had news for him. "Sorry to inform you, your nephew has passed away."

He wasn't sure whether to relay the news to Zahir's mother or not. He knew that she was a heart patient and that she could die of a heart attack if she heard the news. *You don't want to be the cause of the death of another family member—you are already being blamed for the deaths of Majid, Zahir, and Fahima.* He put off that decision for the time being as he found himself emotionally too weak to do so. The day after Zahir's funeral, he called his health care provider and requested a referral to see a psychologist instead. In the two weeks, before he could see his therapist, Hekmat functioned as a perfect mother, father, and grandfather to the kids.

You've got to accept the harsh reality of your life, he said to himself.

His coping mechanism in the face of his emotional trauma and inner uneasiness confined him to the task. Even though he did succeed in solving the hard puzzle of the school shooting motive, he couldn't, however, even think about working on his book. It was another source of distress for him. Still, what was hurting him the most, had no prospect of any remedy—his feelings of guilt.

During his first session with his therapist, Hekmat had the chance to provide a long list of the tragedies that happened to him in the last three years—the death of his granddaughter, the criminal murders of Majid, Jaafar, Sultan, Farooq, Fahima, and Zahir, the disability of Sheila as well as his own stories of being hurt during the explosion at Majid's funeral, being taken prisoner by the Taliban and being robbed and shot at by a teenager.

He also mentioned the incident in which his neighbor was accidentally killed by another neighbor—and the one in which he himself was nearly killed.

"Hmm," said the mental health professional, who was a clinical psychologist with a Ph.D., after listening to Hekmat's terrifying stories. "It's incomprehensible; how come you didn't seek professional help earlier?"

"Good question, doctor." He looked down for a moment. "The reason I didn't see a therapist all that time might be even more incomprehensible."

"I see. Do you want to tell me about it?"

"I will try. I hope I can explain."

He moved in his seat and pointed to little Sara who was seated on a sofa next to him.

"This little girl and her siblings, a six-year-old brother and a nine-year-old sister are the grandchildren of my best friend who was like a brother to me. I am responsible for raising these kids, which is not an issue, of course. But the issue is that I feel accountable for the deaths of their grandfather, and their parents," he said, sounding as if was pleading guilty in a court of law.

"Why? Why do think you are accountable? Please tell me the whole story," the psychologist said in a genuinely empathetic and caring tone, which made Hekmat feel comfortable to articulate everything—from the day he lost his granddaughter until the day Zahir got shot and died. During his recounting, he stressed, "I think that I am the reason for the deaths of some of my loved ones. I didn't do what I could to prevent what happened to them and, besides, some of them died following my advice."

By the time he finished telling the story, the one-hour

session time was up. However, the doctor seemed very interested in continuing to listen to him. He picked the phone and asked the front desk whether the next patient was there. It was not. Hekmat talked for another 20 minutes, explaining his feelings in the face of the deaths of his friend and family members. However, in the end, he stressed the issue of being afraid for the safety of his "grandkids."

The mental health professional took a deep breath, looked at his patient, and said, "Mr. Hekmat, you need help, a lot of it. You are overwhelmed by cumulative grief. You are affected by a combination of grief, regret, and guilt. Furthermore, you need social support, as you just told me that you have none. That's what makes me worry about you. I know that you are a strong person but human capacities have limits too. How is your sleep, by the way?" the doctor asked.

"Terrible," he said.

"I can imagine," the therapist said and invited him to continue talking.

"I live in constant fear, I can't get more than two to three hours sleep," he said looking at and pointing to little Sara. "I have nightmares almost every night. Last night, for example, there were guys with shotguns drawn trying to break into my house and to kidnap her from me."

The psychologist, with much experience in the profession, thought about his situation—probably searching for a proper solution to these difficult issues.

"You have a legitimate concern," the psychologist said after a long silence. "I think that what you urgently need is, first of all, to see a psychiatrist to prescribe you some medication. Second, you need some kind of social support, that's very important. There are support groups; I will give you some phone numbers to call. I think the largest one is called NAMI—the National Alliance for Mental Illness. They have offices all over the country. Last but not least, your feelings of guilt are something that we have to work on it together."

The doctor paused again and then asked his patient, "I said 'we' because you need to follow what the science says and, for your part, you must try to take care of your stress management. What do you usually do to cope with your stress?"

"Well," Hekmat said fervently. "I've had no chance to use any stress management mechanisms. In the past, I walked for at least one hour a day, seven days a week. I am a music lover and enjoy listening to smooth Jazz music Indian Ghazals and instrumental music, such as sitar, sarod, violin, and guitar as well as some country music. In addition, I am a fiction writer and have published a collection of short stories and a couple of novels."

"Ah, that's wonderful," the therapist, who looked in his mid–fifties said passionately. "I love all these activities that you named. These are the best things one can do to cope with stress. So why do you think that you have no chance to continue doing them?" the doctor asked.

"Because," Hekmat said sounding extremely desperate, "I can't take my daily walk because of the kids. I don't want to leave them home alone. I have no opportunity to listen to music either because I am with the kids all day. As for writing, for the last three years I have been dreaming of writing a book based on the true events I told you about, but disturbing things have been happening one after another, holding me off until today."

"Well," the therapist said looking Hekmat in the eyes. "Life is like a stormy river, we've got to be swimming non-stop until we reach the shore." The doctor gestured with his hand indicating the significance of what he was going to say next "You are already sailing toward your shore. It's great to have a dream that makes one's life meaningful. But may I ask what your book is specifically about?"

"Good question doctor," Hekmat said enthusiastically. "Actually, in the beginning, I was going to write about the tragic story of my granddaughter's death. But later on, as I lost more of my loved ones to gun violence, I realized that the gun lobby is a dangerous public enemy that has taken the peace of mind of millions and millions of Americans hostage and must be fought."

"I agree," the doctor said hearteningly. "But it's a huge fight, you need to take care of yourself first. I mean, you should take medication that is going to alleviate your fear and sleeping disorder."

"Will do," Hekmat agreed and left the doctor's office.

He saw a psychiatrist as recommended by his therapist. She was a kindhearted lady. Like the psychologist, she also stressed, "You certainly need to take care of yourself in order to be able to protect the kids."

She prescribed medication for his depression and sleeping disorder and cautioned him that,

"These tablets are going to put you on a good night's sleep. But, if they make you too sleepy or drowsy during the day, then let me know and I will reduce the dosage."

That afternoon, after he picked up Shapor from his school and Sheila also came back home, he found himself to be in a good mood. He was pleased to have gotten professional assistance and that he was going to have a restful night. Therefore, he felt a deep craving to get to his novel file as soon as possible. Now that the puzzle of motive was solved, he would time to time gave thoughts to the beginning, to the plot, to the characters, and other aspects of his book.

He loaded the kids into his car, drove to the supermarket, and bought them ice cream and cookies. While the kids were busy with their goodies in the living room, he opened his laptop and reviewed the few paragraphs he had written and the many notes that he had taken since the day that his granddaughter was killed. Now that he had a clear idea of the motive of the shooter and plenty of information regarding the various aspects of the gun lobby as well as enough facts and figures about gun violence, he decided to use the weapon of his pen against the empire of the gun lobby.

That night, he took his medication and then served dinner earlier than usual.

"Kids, I'm going to sleep earlier tonight, see you tomorrow," he told his "grandkids," kissing them one after another.

"Good night, grandpa," shouted all three of them.

"Make sure you guys go to bed at 9, ok?" he told the children.

"Ok, grandpa."

Going to bed at 8 p.m. was something he couldn't remember doing in years. Likewise, falling asleep before the children have gone to their beds was something more unusual and even bothersome. So, he tried hard to keep his eyes open in the bed despite feeling very sleepy under the influence of the medication. Close to 9, he heard Sheila calling on her siblings to follow her to the bedroom as she moved in her electric wheelchair first.

For a few more minutes, he periodically sharpened his ears to make sure the kids were quiet and asleep so that he could go to sleep as well.

"Duzzz!"

The heavy sound of a gunshot made him jump up and sit upon his bed, wondering if it was a bad dream or reality. He was confused. The gunshot was so close that he suspected that it came either from the living room or the bedroom next to his. He rubbed his eyes and swayed his head a few times to awaken the still sleepy cells of his brain. Then, he struggled to get up and sneak out of his bedroom. No sign of kids in the living room. He went to their bedroom and carefully opened the door not to disturb their sleep. Instead of being in their beds, all three of them were sitting in the middle of the room. Their faces seemed pale and frozen and their mouths and eyes were wide open.

"What's going on kids?" he asked with panic.

Everyone burst into tears one after another—first little

Sara then Shapor, and then Sheila. Sheila extended her hand and took a small-sized pistol from Shapor's behind who was sitting next to her.

"He fired this," she said pointing to Shapor.

"I was playing with it," Shapor said, now crying loudly.

"Where was it?" he asked Shapor.

"It was there," Sheila answered, pointing to the carpet underneath Shapor and Sara's bunk bed. Little Sara raised her hands toward her "grandpa" and started crying aloud. He picked her up into his arms and kissed her on the cheek. He also grabbed the gun from the floor and asked Shapor, "Where did you get it from?"

"I was looking for my eraser, which had rolled down beneath my bed, and I saw that there was something under the carpet."

"Where? Show me,"

Shapor pulled the edge of the carpet by the wall under his and Sara's bunker bed.

He certainly feared that I was going to inspect his room someday, so he hide it here, he thought of Zahir. And while still holding Sara in his arms, he walked to the front door to answer the doorbell.

"Hello, this is the police department, please open the door."

When he did, he saw two uniformed police officers with their guns drawn. One of them said: "One of your neighbors called that there was a gunshot in your house.

He recognized the officers. They were the same individuals who once took Zahir to jail for shoplifting.

"What happened?" asked one of the officers.

"My grandson was playing with this," he said handing the gun over to the officer.

"Can I see where it was fired?"

"Yes, sir."

The police went to the room and extracted the bullet from the wall.

While explaining the situation to the police officers, Hekmat mentioned the incident when they had arrested Zahir for shoplifting and that how and where he had concealed the weapon.

The police told him that they did remember the story and that they were aware of Zahir's death which had happened in a grocery store and how he had been killed. But still, they took Hekmat into custody. They also took the children to the county child protective services.

However, he was not charged for negligence or any other illegal activity because the police department had a record of Zahir's situation during which Hekmat had cooperated with them. They released him the next day but told him that they had to confiscate the gun because it was a stolen one, and probably Zahir had purchased it from someone on the street.

"That's fine, I don't need it," Hekmat said humbly.

Alone and lonely again, he told himself, when sitting in his living room and looking at his front yard, where his granddaughter Sheila used to play with her friend Kathy. This time, this memory was accompanied by deep emotional wounds, grief, guilt, and regret. He tried to follow his mental health professionals' recommendations to take his medication regularly. Nonetheless, in two weeks, his blood pressure increased. He felt both mentally and physically anesthetized and fatigue. His weakness and inability to pursue his long-overdue dream and to deliver his promise to his loved ones caused him more discomfort than anything else. Still, a blurry light of hope that he might be reunited with the kids sometime in the future, encouraged him to keep his optimism alive and think about doing anything in his power to serve their needs.

Since the day Zahir died, Hekmat thought about taking the kids back to their grandma in Afghanistan. He was extremely anxious about their safety. He couldn't afford to even imagine the endangerment of the children's lives while living with him. He was facing a moral dilemma—his love for the children and his commitment to their grandfather, Majid, on one hand, and his concern for their future in that war-torn country, on the other. He couldn't decide whether the kids would be safer here in America or Afghanistan. He recalled the events that had happened in the last three years alone since the kids had been in the US. He was stunned by the numbers—nearly 110,000 human beings were killed by gun-related crimes, including school shootings, home invasions, and other gun-related incidents during which thousands of children also fell victim. Likewise, the situation in Afghanistan, the terrorism, the suicidal attacks, and the bombings by the government and NATO forces, as well as the hunger, pollution, and lack of a good education system in the country, were also hindering him from determining the right place for his "grandchildren's" wellbeing.

Anyway, he obligated himself to stay strong and do things that were good for the kids for the time being. In the nights, he tried to suppress the fear of his home being burglarized, and in the days, he walked with his head up pretending as if nothing was going to happen to him or the children. However, one night, he couldn't fall asleep until past midnight due to hearing quite a few gunshots fired in the neighborhood. That night, he gave thoughts to an idea which he never had previously imagined. *You should get a gun, you might feel at peace as Allen has been saying.*

But keeping a firearm in his home was running against his values, let alone shooting another human- a thief, even when inside his house. But despite pushing this idea to the back of his head, the endless incidents of gun violence that continued to happen now and then in his immediate neighborhood, made him ask himself this question over and over: *So, what's the solution, life can't go on like this?*

It took him weeks to decide whether to bring another gun to his home or just forget about it and tolerate life as it is. One day, he drove to a Big 5 store in his city, parked his car in the parking lot, and walked by the store's entrance back and forth, but didn't have the nerves to go inside.

A phone call from his friend, Allen, woke him up around 9 a.m. one of those days that he was overwhelmed by his inner struggle. His brain was still lethargic because the three hours of sleep couldn't satisfy his daily need for rest. Seeing Allen's name on the screen, he jumped and sat up on his bed and answered.

"Hello, Mr. Allen!"

"Hey buddy, how are you doing?"

"I'm doing fine. Where are you?"

"I'm in my hometown for a couple of weeks."

"That's good."

"Listen, Hekmat," Allen said in a friendly tone. "Tomorrow there is going to be a gun show near your city. I would like you to go with me, I think you are going to like it."

"Why do you think I might like a gun show?" Hekmat asked.

"Because you can see for yourself how it operates. On the airplane, you talked about the so-called gun show loophole—it's not like what you thought about it."

Hekmat was silent for a moment and then said, "Is it possible that you come to my home before going there, I want to talk to you about something?"

"Not sure, I will try. But what do you want to talk to me about?"

"I can't discuss it over the phone, I would like to talk to you in private."

Allen was silent and amazed by his friend's request. He reviewed his schedule for the day, then agreed to visit Hekmat at his home.

"Ok, text me your address, I will see you tomorrow at 9 a.m., and then we can go to the gun show together."

When Allen was seated on the sofa across from his host and listened to his request, he blinked in astonishment.

"Do you really want to own a gun?" he asked.

"Yes, I do," Hekmat replied decisively.

"Of course, I can help you get a good handgun. I told you before that you can't have peace of mind without having a firearm in your home," Allen said sympathetically.

"But I can't wait for the results of my fingerprints, I just want it today."

"Well," Allen hesitated. "It's kind of hard to get a gun without doing fingerprints and a background check. But why do you need it right away?" Allen asked curiously.

"Well," Hekmat said, reluctant to reveal the reason why he needed a gun today. "Ok then, if I can't get it without going through a background check, I can't get it."

"Fine, I will get you one without being fingerprinted," Allen said arrogantly.

Hekmat gave Allen a skeptical look and said, "So, there is a way to buy a weapon without following the law!"

Allen felt irritated and asked Hekmat in a harsh tone, "Do you want one or not?"

"I do. I also need you to train me on how to use it."

Allen looked around the room and asked. "Where are your grandkids?"

"They are with the Child Protective Services."

Allen wide opened his eyes as a sign of amazement. "Ha, why?"

He told Allen the story.

"I am glad none of them was hurt. But why do you need a gun now, do you have any plan or something?"

"No, I have no plans to kill anyone. I am scared," Hekmat said nervously. "I can't sleep at night. I fear being robbed and shot during the day. And I am particularly worried about my grandchildren's safety when they come back home."

"That's what I've been trying to tell you. You do need a weapon for your peace of mind."

"Allen," Hekmat said firmly. "I still believe that weapon is not the answer to my concern over my safety or the safety of my grandkids. I am not sure if will be ever able to use it, but I need one for a different reason; I want to see how it feel to own a weapon, I want to see if possessing a gun really makes me feel arrogant and see myself as a potentially harmful person if so, this experiment will give me a stronger reason for fighting the gun freedom. And, if need be, I would like to use it for scaring bad guys away whenever they threaten my life and my property instead of hitting them with bullets.

"Huh," Allen laughed. I don't blame you Mr. Hekmat, even if you don't want to shoot an assailant who threatens your life, still, owning a firearm is the right thing,"

"That's what I thought."

"But it's strange, why do you want me to train you on how to use it because you will never dare to use it against a human target, right?" Allen asked with a sneer.

"Right. But I want to learn how to hold the gun in my hands properly and fire it in the air instead of striking a human."

"Huh, you are funny Hekmat," Allen chuckled.

"No, I am not. I am serious," Hekmat said. He quickly straightened himself up in his armchair, and added, "I believe that the mother of all problems is the misinterpretation of the Second Amendment. I would, however, like to take a different course of action to get to my destination.

Allen was looking at his host in bewilderment, expecting him to spill out his new idea.

Hekmat picked up a one-page paper from his coffee table and said, "This is going to be the manifesto of my fight for the rest of my life. I will not rest until I get this to the ears of everyone in America."

Hekmat held the paper in front of him.

"May I read it to you?" he asked his guest.

Allen looked at his wristwatch and said: "It's getting late, let's go, you can read that to me in the car."

Hekmat jumped up from his armchair to follow his guest toward the exit door, but a call to his cell phone stopped him.

"Wonderful, thank you very much!" he exclaimed. "When can I come?" He asked the caller enthusiastically.

The answer from the other side made him scream even louder: "Ok, great!"

"Not today Mr. Allen, I am going to pick up my kids, they said I can get them back now," he shouted cheerfully as soon as he hanged up.

"Good for you," said Allen who was already out of Hekmat's house. "Can you pick them up later in the afternoon after the trip to the gun show?"

"No, my friend, I have to get my lovely grandchildren first. Maybe I will talk to you about that thing some other day." He sounded pretty determined and therefore, Allen did not insist on taking him to a gun show that day. He said goodbye to him. "I will be here around ten more days, you better call me before I leave for Afghanistan."

"Sure, goodbye now," Hekmat said raising his hand. He ran to his vehicle and took off for the CPS office, not even waiting until Allen to start the ignition of his car.

The return of the children to him came with strict guidelines concerning the safety and wellbeing of the kids.

"Do you still have the gun in your home?" an official from Child Protective Services asked him.

"No. The police got it because originally it was a stolen gun,"

"Do you have any other firearm in your house?"

"No, not yet."

"Well," the official said. "Because of the incident that happened to your children and nearly killed at least one of them while you were at home with them, and also our investigation revealed that you have had some mental issues, you can't own a gun or keep one in your home until you are certified by your mental health provider."

"Sure," he said with mixed feelings; he was disappointed for not being able to own a gun for his intended purposes, and was happy at the same time because this restriction eliminated the burden of his moral dilemma.

"I love my grandkids and even though I don't see myself as a harmful person, but I accept whatever you say." He told the officer while receiving the kids.

"I know," the CPS official said. "You are a good person, the police told us about you. But it's the law."

Barred from acquiring a gun, he felt relieved. The law resolved his inner conflict. He started accepting the inescapable reality of living under the shadow of gun violence. Fighting the culture, however, was the inseparable ingredient of acceptance. He became determined more than ever to face the challenge head-on by seeking more practical ways and methods to deliver his promise to his loved ones whose lives were taken by the gun barbarism: He decided to get involved in the gun control advocacy movement and to play an active role in the collective efforts in combating the gun lobby.

"Hey buddy, how are you?" Allen called one day as Hekmat was saying to himself: *They consider me mentally ill, right, I am mentally ill like millions of people who are affected by gun violence.*

"I am good. How are you doing?" he answered gleefully.

"You sound like you got the thing you were looking for?"

"No, I can't have one."

"Why?" Allen asked.

"Because they at the Child Protective Services told me that I didn't look brave enough to handle a gun and therefore, was disqualified to own one," he said sounding serious.

"No, kidding," Allen said.

Hekmat then told Allen what the CPS had said to him.

"No good. What are you going to do now?"

"I don't know," Hekmat answered regretfully.

One year passed. He didn't have luck with getting a certification from his doctor to be qualified for owning a gun. But he didn't care much about it as his mind was engulfed in attending gun control advocacy meetings, making speeches as well as staying up until midnight arguing with opponents via emails and text messages. Based on his manifesto, he preached for the repealing of the Second Amendment because he thought the root cause of gun violence lies in the misinterpretation of the Second Amendment. But despite his hard work, his quest for gathering support to promote his cause didn't appeal to some of his audience. He would sometimes get scoffed at when speaking of that. He even started receiving death threats through emails and phone calls. *Now what?* He murmured to himself. *Having enemies is the last thing I can wish for.* He whispered to himself in a lower voice. *I will not quit fighting for what I believe in.* He thought quietly but suddenly came to his senses: *What about the kids, what's going to happen to them if I die?*

When he shared his concerns with his friend, who just called him after a year, the reaction from the other side was disappointing:

"Don't be silly," Allen said bitterly. "Get a gun and get it sooner rather than later. I suspect that now you will need to own a firearm more than ever before, do you know why?" Allen raised his voice.

"No. Why?" Hekmat was then listening with his mouth wide open to what his friend was saying.

"Because there have been are numerous attempts by the congress to pass laws limiting the rights of citizens to own guns."

"Are they going to close gun shops?" Hekmat asked teasingly.

"They are not. They cannot do that because gun busyness is considered an essential busyness. The gun freedom advocates will not allow your government to close those shops." Allen responded triumphantly.

"Wow," Hekmat exclaimed sardonically. "Do they have more power than the government does?"

"You don't understand my friend." Allen asserted with utmost seriousness. "This is the land of freedom, free people always have far more power than the government."

"Well," Hekmat mumbled in a low voice as if talking to himself rather than to Allen on the other end of the phone. "To be honest with you, I am thinking about taking the kids back to Afghanistan, to their grandmother."

"Oh no Hekmat! You don't want to do that," Allan was furious. You have no idea what's going on in your country. I just returned from there. You know you and your grandchildren will be soft targets for the Taliban, ISIS, Al Qaeda, let alone countless thieves and burglars."

"I know," Hekmat said feebly. "Still, there we may not get shot inside our home or on the streets."

"Well," Allen said. "You never know. But good luck my friend. Do whatever you think is best for you and your kids."

The sixty-six-year-old man feels stranded over

a crossroad. He couldn't decide as to where Majid's grandkids should spend the rest of their lives; should he keep them here- in the land of freedom where they already lost their parents, or take them to their native country where the suicidal barbarism took the lives of their uncle and grandfather.

While still undecided about the two options, he was now and then thinking about hiring a company to install a security camera outside his house, an alarm system inside, and a Doorbell Camera on the front door. He took it upon himself to homeschool all three kids and instead of taking his daily walk in the park, he decided to purchase a treadmill wishing to enjoy staying in his gun-free home rather than walking out in the land of gun- tyranny.

With all the safety measures taken, he felt a bet safe and secured. He decided in the meantime, to pursue his fight against gun violence by writing about it, by exposing the ugly face of it, and thus, keeping his word to his Sheila. *It feels like the best medication for my heartache.* He thought to himself elatedly. One more year passed, however, he wasn't able to make progress. His depression and anxiety deteriorated, he lost his night sleep and the kids also became depressed.

It was the Christmas Eve of 2019. Like in the past few years, there was a knock on the door; Kathy's mother had her hands full of gifts for the kids. A Barbie Doll for little Sara, a sports car for Shapor, and a personalized nail art caddy for Sheila.

"Again? You guys are so kind, thank you very

much." Hekmat said as soon as he opened the door for his neighbor.

"Not a problem. How are your kids doing, we haven't seen them outside your house for a while?"

"You are right, they are staying home all the time."

Hekmat invited his neighbor to his living room where all the children were present.

"Hi kids. How are you?" She asked the kids before she sat down on the couch closer to Sheila.

Sheila didn't answer. They were quiet and looked pale and blue.

"What about their school?" Kathy's mother asked Hekmat.

"I am homeschooling them, I don't think schools are safe."

"I don't blame you," the lady echoed Hekmat's concern. "Did you hear about the school shooting where a sixth-grader girl shot three students in her school?"

"I did, but that's nothing comparing to what's going on in the country."

"What do you mean?"

"Huh," Hekmat sighed heavily. "You know, this year there have been over four hundred mass shootings in the country, more than the number of days in the year."

"Really?" The lady said. "I do watch the news and hear about mass shootings but never thought they were that many."

"Yes. This year there were 25 school shootings alone."

"Oh, God. It's scary. Since the day my Kathy died, I have been worry about my two little nieces and all the school children."

"That's why I am thinking about taking them to their grandmother in Afghanistan." Hekmat pointed to the kids who are listening to the two adults discussing their fate.

"Poor kids," Kathy's mother said as she rose and walked toward the door. "They looked so depressed you should do something about them sooner," Kathy's mother whispered to Hekmat before saying goodbye to him.

The next day he called Majid's wife on the phone telling her that he planned to bring the kids over to her.

"Thank you brother, God bless you. But you know, life is very tough here. My brothers lost their businesses and are hardly able to support me."

"Don't worry sister, that will be my responsibility, I will support you and my brother's grandchildren for as long as I live."

"But how can I care for them, I am old and sick with a heart problem?" The lady started moaning. "You promised me and Majid to care for them like your own grandkids, but now you want to get rid of them."

"Oh, no sister, don't say that," Hekmat cried out loud. "That's not the reason I want to bring them to you, but I want them to be safe."

"How can they be safe here if they cannot be safe in America." Majid's widow raised her voice in anger.

"But sister, you don't know how many kids die here by gunshots every day,"

"What about their parents, they were not children." The lady further raised her voice and added: "You destroyed my son's family."

"Adults get killed too," Hekmat shouted. "For God's

sake, sister, It's was not my fault. Almost 40,000 people lose their lives to gun violence every year here."

"I can't believe it," Zahir's mother said crying. "How can they live here? There are killings, kidnapping, and suicidal explosions every day. They kill everyone, they even kill school kids!"

"Sister, please, believe me, I am trying to save our kids' lives," Hekmat uttered innocuously. "Bullets are flying everywhere in this country too; in schools, in markets, in parks, in buses, and the streets. We don't feel safe even inside our own home," Hekmat said and then listened to the heartbreaking weeping coming from the other end of the phone call.

Printed in the United States
by Baker & Taylor Publisher Services